Ghost Stories and Folk Tales of New Orleans

Copyright © 2021 by Jannette Quackenbush

Ghost Stories and Folk Tales of
New Orleans

I0654102

ISBN: 978-1-940087-46-7
21 Crows Dusk to Dawn Publishing, 21 Crows, LLC

All rights reserved. No part of this book may be reproduced or transmitted in any form or by any means, electronic or mechanical, including photocopying, recording, or by any information storage and retrieval system, without permission in writing from the copyright owner. This is a work of fiction. Names, characters, places and incidents either are the product of the author's imagination or are used fictitiously, and any resemblance to any actual persons, living or dead, events, or locales is entirely coincidental. This book was printed in the United States of America.

The stories and legends in this book are for enjoyment purposes and taken from many different resources. Many have been passed down and have been altered along the way. I attempt to sort through the many different variations found on a story and find the most popular and the most supported by historical evidence/verbal interviews. Not all sources and legends can be substantiated. Public properties may become private after the printing of the book or they may simply be listed with the address so you know the historical area where the story originated. Listing the GPS and address does not mean you can visit. Regardless if the area is listed as private or not, please respect the landowner and do not disturb their privacy, nor trespass. Readers assume full responsibility for use of information in this book. Please use common sense.

Jannette Quackenbush

Table of Contents

Prelude   10

French Quarter

Jackson Square   15
Rebel Ghosts of the German Coast Uprising

Café du Monde in the French Market   18
Beignets, Café au lait , and a Ghostly Server

The Old Chandlery -Café Sbisa   19
The Never-ending Debt

St Louis Cathedral and Pirate Alley   21
The Legends of Pirate Alley -Storm and the Singing Monk

Pirate Alley and Cabildo Alley   29
The Legends of Pirate Alley—Jean Lafitte

Pirate Alley and the Wrought Iron Gate   33
The Legends of Pirate Alley—Reginald Hicks

The Cabildo and the Old Jail   35
A Hanging at the Cabildo

Faulkner House Books   37
Haunted Bookshop

Père Antoine Alley   39
Black-Robed Ghost

The Old Site of Crescent City Books   41
In the Presence of Ghostly Children

Napoléon House   42
The Elaborate Plan

New Orleans Pharmacy Museum   46
Phantoms of the Pharmacy

Old Ursuline Convent Museum   48
Casket Girls

Beauregard-Keyes House   53
Went to the Grave With His Boots Off

Beauregard-Keyes House   54
The Day the Black Hands Got What Was Due

Louisiana Supreme Court Building   57
The One Thing in Common

Brennan's Restaurant-Patio Royal   59
A Ghost Once Haunted Patio Royal

The Court of Two Sisters   60
The Many Legends of The Court of Two Sisters

734 Royal Street   62
Dancing Octoroon Mistress

Cornstalk Fence Hotel   65
A Haunting at the Cornstalk Fence Hotel

Andrew Jackson Hotel   66
Up in Smoke

LaLaurie Mansion   68
The Old Haunted House of New Orleans

Jean Lafitte's Old Absinthe House   73
Laughter

The Site of the Old French Opera House   77
Witch of the French Opera—'Tis Not Just the Eye That Wanders

Bourbon Heat—The Old Tricou House   83
The Fallen

Café Lafitte in Exile   85
Sipping Cocktails

Lafitte's Blacksmith Shop Bar   86
Dark Chill

Corner of Orleans and Dauphine   88
The Date Palm—Mysterious Tale of the Sultan's Disappearance

Corner of Orleans and Dauphine   91
The Date Palm—Père Antoine's Date Palm—From the Heart

Sausage Factory   97
The Ghost Who Walked the Sausage Factory

Place d' Armes Hotel   99
Old School

Inn on St Ann   100
Knobby

Marie Laveau and the Site of her Old Home   101
Vodou Queen of New Orleans

Bourbon Orleans Hotel   106
The Phantom Dancer

Bourbon Orleans Hotel   109
Dueling Twins

Bourbon Orleans Hotel   110
Soldier in the Hall

Bourbon Orleans Hotel   111
The Orphanage

Le Petit Theatre du Vieux Carré   114
Primping Ghost

Café Beignet-Former Old Coffeepot Restaurant   115
The Sordid Tale of Etienne Deschamps

Pat O'Briens   118
Spirits of a Building's Past

New Orleans Creole Cookery 119
Fountain of Youth

Olivier House Hotel 122
Woman in Black

Antoine's Restaurant 124
Watchful Eye

Bienville street Shell Road-Basin Street 125
Ghost of Shell Road

Old Parish Prison 133
Red-Headed Ghost of Parish Prison

The Old Tremé Street Bridge Over the Canal 137
A Ghost at the Old Basin Canal

Congo Square 142
Congo Square and the Tale of the Haunted Tree

Marigny/Bywater

House of Sirens 146
Madame Mineurecanal and Her Little Terrier

Mid-City

The Old Mortuary and Gates of Prayer 150
Dead Man in a Top Hat

Lower Garden

Griffin House 153
Yankee Soldiers Who Just Won't Rest

Saint Vincent's Guest House (Old Orphan Asylum) 158
Giggles

Josephine and Rousseau Streets 160
Headless Woman in a Drab Gingham Dress

Irish Channel

Seaman's Bethel on St Thomas 166
Lost Boys

Central City

100 Block of Chartres Street 171
Misfortune in a Keg of Rum

Fourth Street 173
Fourth Street Ghost

The Devil's Mansion 174
The Devil's Mistress

Uptown/Carrollton

Cherokee Street   181
Flying Bricks of Cherokee Street

Site of The Old Carrollton Jail   184
Ghosts of Old Carrollton Jail

Near the Old Dairy Farms on S Carrollton   187
Milk Stable Ghost

City Park

City Park —Lover's Lane- Mona Lisa Drive   189
The Legend of Wandering Moaning Mona Lisa

City Park—Dueling Oaks   191
Deadly Clashes at the Dueling Oaks

City Park—Suicide Oak   195
Suicide Oak

Third District

A Stately Mansion in the Third District   197
The Witch of Casa Rosa and the Gay Caballeros

Around New Orleans

The Italian Neighborhoods of New Orleans   204
The Axeman

S.S. Watertown   208
Ghost in the Photo

A House near Eighth and Chippewa Streets and Other   210
Notable Short and Long Tales Around New Orleans—
Delightful Short Tales of the Dead

Plantations Nearby

Myrtles Plantation   212
Faces in the Mirror

Destréhan Plantation   219
Wandering Stephen

Bayous Nearby

A Bayou near New Orleans   222
Singing Bones

Frenier —Manchac Swamp   226
The Warning

Barataria Region   231
The Phantom Canoe

Vodou

New Orleans Vodou   237
A Brief Background of Vodou In New Orleans

Mardi Gras

Mardi Gras   241
Of Celebration

The Cemeteries

A Little About the Tombs   247

St Peter Street Cemetery

St Peter Street Cemetery   249
Underfoot

St Louis No 1

St Louis No 1   252
Background

St Louis No 1   255
Marie Laveau Tomb

St Louis No 1   258
Hex Tomb

St Louis No 1   260
Henry Vignes

St Louis No 1   262
The Widow

St Louis No 2

St Louis No 2   263
Ghastly Moans

St Louis No 2   264
Wishing Vault

St Louis No 3

St Louis No 3   266
Disappearing Trick

Lafayette No 1

Lafayette No 1   267
Just Passersby

Cyprus Grove

Cyprus Grove   268
Up In Smoke

Greenwood

Greenwood   269
Ambling Writer

Charity Hospital Cemetery

Charity Hospital Cemetery   270
Buried Alive

St Patrick No 1,2,3

St Patrick No 1,2,3   275
Photobombers

St Joseph

St Joseph   278
A Sure Shot

Odd Fellows

Odd Fellows   279
Spectral Lights

Holt Cemetery

Holt Cemetery   280
Heavenly Singer

The Mortuary

The Mortuary   281
Haunted House

Chev A Thilim Cemetery – Gates of Prayer

Chev A Thilim Cemetery–Gates of Prayer   282
Top Hat

Masonic

Masonic   283
Little Girl in the Tomb

Metairie Cemetery

Metairie Cemetery—Charles Howard Tomb   285
Background and The Loudest Tomb

Metairie Cemetery—Francis Masich Tomb   287
Weeping Dog

Metairie Cemetery—Army of Tennessee Monument   288
Shadows in the Tomb

Metairie Cemetery—Grave of David Hennessey   289
Still On the Beat

Metairie Cemetery—Tomb of Josie Arlington   290
The Wandering Statue

St Roch Cemetery

St Roch   293
Background

St Roch   295
Petrified Child

St Roch   296
Saint of Lovers . . .?

Gates of Mercy Cemetery

Gates of Mercy Cemetery   299
Lost Golden Children

More Notable Boneyard Haunts   303

And . . . Other Things That Go Bump in the Night

Rougarou   307
13 Pennies

Vampire of New Orleans   310
The Strange Tale of Jacques d'Saint Germain

Mississippi Riverfront at the Old New Orleans Wharf   314
A Little Hoodoo on the Wharf

Walking Tour/Map   319

Citations   324

A taste of New Orleans' past to get you familiar to the ghosts you will meet—

Jean Baptiste Le Moyne de Bienville founded La Nouvelle-Orléans in 1718 as little more than an outpost with a couple of cabins randomly settled in the woodland along a bend of the Mississippi River. French cartographer Adrien de Pauger visited the area in 1721 and mapped out a 6-block by an 11-block grid of streets named after French royals. Pauger centered the grid along the riverfront around an open square (now Jackson Square) with a church and where St Louis Cathedral is today. Although France slated the colony seat as Biloxi, Nouvelle-Orléans was established as the capital of the French Colony of Louisiana after Bienville sent a copy of the street design vision to French government leaders, influencing them to change their minds. When a hurricane destroyed the erratically placed buildings of the settlement, it was rebuilt in Pauger's grid pattern. In 1723, Nouvelle-Orléans became the capital of the French Colony of Louisiana.

Almost forty years later, in 1762, France relinquished Louisiana to Spain to keep the land from becoming Britain's possession after the French and Indian War. Along with Louisiana, the tiny village of La Nouvelle-Orléans, little more than wooden homes, would grow extensively as a Spanish colony. It would become a city with brick Spanish Colonial-style buildings and an impressive trading hub.

Even in its earliest times, French colonists had introduced slavery to Louisiana. Pierre Le Moyne d'Iberville, Bienville's brother, petitioned the king for slave expeditions to Africa's west coast to gain laborers. In 1719, the enslaved Africans would begin arriving. Up until then, slave labor was mostly Native Indians.

After the abdication to Spain, the practice continued.

However, new laws were put into place permitting slaves to buy their freedom and the freedom of other slaves, and rules allowing for a class of free people of color. Throughout the 1700s, Nouvelle-Orléans would prosper—even after devastating fires, one on Good Friday in 1788 caused by the lighting of a votive candle at the religious alter in a home catching fire and the second in December of 1794 that burned many homes and businesses. Throughout those days, when so many ships would dock along the wharves importing and exporting, smugglers and pirates combed the waterways looking for easy prey. Among them were Jean Lafitte and his brother Pierre known for their ruthless hijacking of enslaved Africans on slave ships for resale.

It would be during the 1800s that Spain returned Nouvelle-Orléans to French hands. Then around 1803, Napoléon sold the colony to the U.S. as part of the Louisiana Purchase. Sugar and cotton came by steamboat down the river and by wagons to the markets in the city. Dockworkers transferred it to ocean-going ships. The Irish came to build new roads, and others like the Latinos, Asians, and Sicilians also came to build new lives. Even though it was no longer a French colony and the name would grow into New Orleans, its locally born descendants' ways and traditions and customs would not change even as they have not today. Through significant battles in the War of 1812 and the Civil War, the French-descended Creoles and the African successors maintain their identity. You can see it today at Mardi Gras, first celebrated by French colonists in 1718 in New Orleans. You can find it in the mixture of Vodou and Catholicism still practiced by some today. And you can taste it in the Creole restaurants on nearly every corner and listen to Jazz slipping out of the bars into the crowded streets.

But for our intentions, you may also come upon it along a dark, lonely stretch of road walking from Bourbon Street when a ghostly voice whispers a good evening in your ear, "Bonswa!"

Or you might find it with the sound of a trumpet blasting a fine jazz tune behind the high stone wall of St Louis Cemetery long after dark when no living person is within. It could be the feeling of something cool snatching at your ankle near the corner of Burgundy and St Peter where the Old Cemetery once held the dead at rest but is no more—even though there are bodies still beneath the sidewalk.

You will not leave New Orleans without feeling something from its rich past. It might be the melt-in-your-mouth, deep-fried beignets generously sprinkled with confectioners' sugar. Or when you least expect it, a shadowy form, lurking, with less-than-respectable intentions as you walk past St Patrick Cemetery.

French Quarter

The Creating of Ghosts in the French Quarter

Legends, folklore, and ghost stories have become sewn into the fabric of life in New Orleans. Not just now, but many, many years ago and before the streets were bricked, bars lined Bourbon Street, and tour guides escorted people through the cemeteries. It is long ago when the stories began to rise from the dead and sometimes the not-so-dead. And those ghosts and their tales are still here, lingering, lurking, and haunting the dark streets and waiting to catch the attention of those who cross their path. And perhaps, drag them down with them.

In 1718, Jean-Baptiste Le Moyne de Bienville founded New Orleans on a bend of the Mississippi, carefully searching out an area far enough away from the Gulf of Mexico that the settlement would be protected from coastal flooding and hurricanes. He built his home on what is now the location of the Custom House, and named this city "La Nouvelle-Orléans" in honor of Philippe II, Duke of Orléans. The streets running from the river would eventually take the names of Catholic saints and the streets crossing them from the Royal House of France— Dumaine and Toulouse streets were named for sons of Louis the Great, King of France. Bourbon Street was Named for France's House of Bourbon. The oldest part of the city, the French Quarter, was thus created. Regardless of Bienville's good intentions, he misjudged the safety of the city's placement. It is hot, frequently bombarded with storms and hurricanes, and it floods. The dampness, standing water, and the still air made it the perfect habitat for mosquitos and bacteria, the breeding ground for yellow fever and cholera. But it still did not stop people from living, dying, hating, loving, and battling on and for the land for centuries. And such, you have the ideal conditions for creating ghosts—

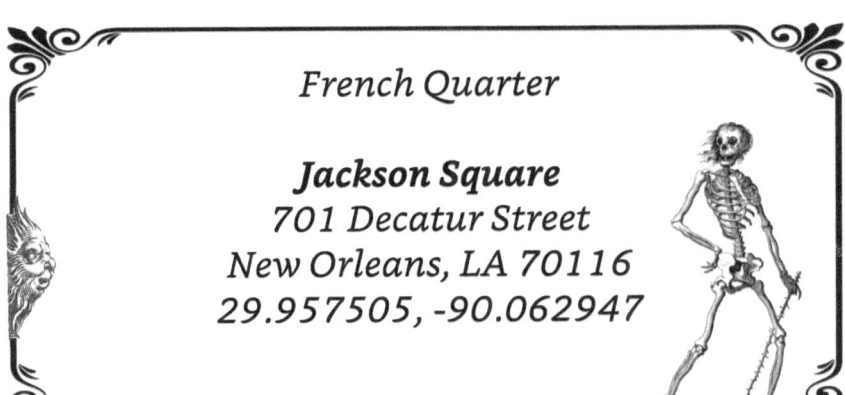

French Quarter

Jackson Square
701 Decatur Street
New Orleans, LA 70116
29.957505, -90.062947

Rebel Ghosts of the German Coast Uprising

The Haitian revolutionaries fighting for independence from 1791 to 1804 gave hope for a slave rebellion near New Orleans on January 8-10 of 1811—and ensuing ghosts. *Image by Auguste Raffet.*

Those walking around Jackson Square after dusk have heard soft wails, mewling, and whispers. Most presume it is the quiet chatter of pedestrians on the street, making their way towards a restful night of sleep. Yet when walkways are empty of the living deep in the early hours before dawn, those long dead offer their own peculiar sounds.

In its early days, the area known as Jackson Square was a trading camp where French voyageurs met to exchange goods. Later, it would be called Place d'Armes and was used as a town square for parades and ceremonies and as an execution ground. Some still plead for their lives here, and those would be the wails riding the wind. But among the unsettling sounds, you may also hear the ghostly outbursts of men and women from the 1811 Louisiana slave revolt.

The rebellion began almost 30 miles upriver from New Orleans by a laborer on a sugar plantation owned by the Deslondes family. The plantation owners fled the Haitian Revolution that played out around 1791 to 1804. The Deslondes brought their property with them, including their slaves. One of these slaves went by the name of Charles, who grew up hearing stories of the Haitian Revolution and the idea of equality and freedom. The idea that someone else could achieve these powers that certainly seemed out of his control sparked something within him. Spurred on by the Haitians' defeat of Napoléon and his allies and their subsequent freedom, Charles hatched a well-laid plan for a two-pronged military assault.

The goal was to capture the city of New Orleans, the capital of the Orleans Territory, and create an independent, Black republic. On January 8, men and women armed with hand tools began a two-day, 20-mile march from plantation to plantation, burning buildings and gaining in their numbers. By the end of the day, over 500 Africans from different nations would battle U.S. troops and local militias.

They did not succeed, yet the courageous rebel men and women proved to all they were a formidable enemy and one to be reckoned with in the future. They left fear in the hearts of slave owners. And among those who were still in bondage, it left a sense that they were not alone and of hope that another day, they might join again and triumph.

Standing on the levee and looking toward Jackson Square.

After the attack, slave owners and troops murdered many leaders and those who followed them into battle. White planters and local officials cut off the heads of forty-five rebels and placed them on spikes on the Mississippi River levee following the river's path as a warning to other slaves—this stretched sixty miles. They also hanged three of the rebels on Jackson Square. Their corpses were left to rot in the weather, and their heads impaled on the city's gates. According to stories told, their bodies may be nothing but dust, but their spirits are still ready to rise against injustice. Bystanders have heard wrathful murmurs, the gnashing of teeth, and the angry growls of those old rebels. For those who disagree, beware. They are a daunting enemy. The darkness from their rage may consume you, and we will find your corpse floating in the Mississippi River, and your head skewered on a gate.

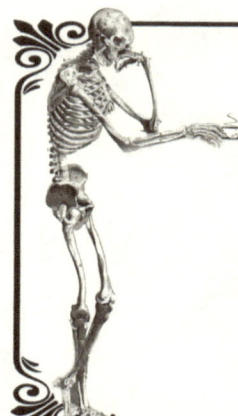

Café du Monde
In the French Market
French Quarter

800 Decatur Street
New Orleans, LA 70116
29.957474, -90.061934

Beignets, Café au lait , and a Ghostly Server

Café du Monde where a ghostly server may take your order!

Since 1791, there has been a French Market along the riverbanks. And Café du Monde is the oldest occupier of the market, here since 1862—serving both café au lait and beignets. It has become one of my favorite morning stops along with many others who chat it up while they eagerly await their morning brew. There is talk on the street that a ghostly server stops in occasionally waiting on customers before disappearing. I have yet to have the spirited waiter offer me another cup, but perhaps one day I will!

The Old Chandlery
French Quarter

Café Sbisa
1011 Decatur Street
New Orleans, LA 70116
29.959481, -90.060630

The Never-ending Debt

Café Sbisa, center.

Established in 1899, Café Sbisa offers fine Creole cuisine and has a wonderful reputation. However, once in a while, someone walking toward the entranceway door gets a gentle push away. There is a good reason—before it became the third oldest fine dining restaurant in New Orleans, it had quite a different reputation.

When sailing ships lined the riverfront, there was a ship chandlery along Decatur Street where boatsmen could find such things as sail-cloth, tar, pitch, and whale oil. It was a popular place across from the French Market and in one of the busiest town areas. In the early years, the lower floor was the warehouse and shop, while the family resided on the upper floors.

As time passed, though, the business continued to offer services for seamen, as a bank where they could deposit their earnings, then a bar with a brothel on the upper floors. When seamen used the building as a brothel, a young girl was sold to the bordello owners by her father to pay his debts. After a little time, she became pregnant but continued working even after her baby daughter was born. Eventually, she paid off her father's debt but found she had accrued expenses for her bed, food, and clothing and realized her debts would be never-ending. Distraught, the girl drowned her baby in the fountain in the courtyard and then hanged herself. Most believe that the young girl's ghost is gently prodding visitors away from what she still believes is a brothel.

St Louis Cathedral (The Cathedral-Basilica of Saint Louis, King of France)
French Quarter

St Louis Cathedral and Pirate Alley
601-649 Pirate Alley
New Orleans, LA 70116
29.957902, -90.063912

The Legends of Pirate Alley—Storm and the Singing Monk

In the alleyway of the cathedral, you may catch the faint singing voice of long-dead Père Dagobert on foggy mornings. He walks along the cobbled path in sandaled feet and robe, in a ghostly procession performing what some believed was a miracle.

On a Tuesday, a woman was walking with her boyfriend along Chartres Street. The rain had begun as a misty drizzle only forty minutes earlier before escalating to a shower with a single flash of lightning in the sky.

They had been shopping for souvenirs in the evening before finding themselves hopping from bar to bar and losing track of time until the wee hours of the night. The bags they had collected their treasures in became makeshift umbrellas as they ducked from beneath one awning to cross a puddled street and head back to their hotel. The couple stopped momentarily to catch their breath in the darkness, noticing fog had begun to creep along the sidewalk and a nearby alley. It parted enough to expose the shadow of something walking along the street ahead of them and perhaps a block away.

Pirate Alley.

Along with the mist, they heard the most pleasant sound—the rich and haunting tone of a man chanting a song. Believing that they must be near St Louis Cathedral and perhaps an early morning mass, moved by the singing, the two decided to seek shelter inside the church until the storm had passed.

But as they came to the steps of the church, the gates were closed. No one was around. Baffled, the two listened to the singing as it faded away to one side of the church, following it until they stopped just short of an alley. There, they once again saw a figure before it suddenly vanished along with the song.

In the mid-1700s, Père Dagobert was a Capuchin monk at the St Louis Cathedral. People throughout the city knew him as being jolly, kind, and delighting in a good joke. He was a fan of wine and food and both in large quantities, sometimes forgetting to fast on Fridays when he would take off to visit the rich plantations in the countryside, all of which made him quite plump. His deep baritone singing voice was a joy to anyone's ears, and when he belted out the sacred musical song-prayer, the Kyrie eléison, people all around stopped to listen to its haunting, beautiful sound. When he finished, many would take a scarf and gently wipe the tears from their eyes. The young women would look at him with wide, adoring eyes that, at times, would lead their young husbands to wrestle with a pinch of jealousy. Yet they knew this man belonged to something much greater.

At times, church officials worried the lighthearted man was a bit too lenient with his wards—he attended many events and parties and rubbed elbows with both the rich and poor, for he cared no less or more for those who had money in their purses or those who did not. He loved them both the same. It only made the Creoles love their happy-go-lucky priest in return. He loved them too. His saintly concern for his fellow man was enough to make many believe he could outwit the wicked in the name of those of faith, even as far as performing a miracle.

In a few aspects, Père Dagobert was like other priests. But mostly, he was not. He was not one to don the typical priestly garb and instead wore such things as a tricorn hat.

He also dressed in clothing made of brightly colored velvets and trimmed with frilly lace, all of these disapproved by his superiors. He had a certain swagger to him that, in his first years as a Capuchin monk, caused more than one eyebrow to rise upward both from young parishioners and old. And there was a twinkle in his eyes rare in somber priests they knew in the past. It was almost as if he was dying to tell them a joke, but it might have a naughty ending better left whispered beyond the walls of the church. Soon on, members of his flock made no feast without inviting him first. The church coffers grew greatly with his presence there. No girl would be married without him sanctioning the marriage and performing the ceremony.

Many girls would confide in him. A year after the monk came to his position, one slipped slowly into the confessional and with a trembling voice told the monk she was to be married to a clever man of money and eloquent tongue. Her father was making arrangements for the couple to wed, and her mother had ordered an exquisite dress of silk and satin and enough lace to cross the city and back. Père Dagobert nodded in approval. He told the young woman that the union would be suitable without question, "And you are happy with the match?" he asked.

She had sobbed deeply, "That is the problem. I have only one man in my heart, and it is not my betrothed." She paused, the silence seeming to consume them both. "It is you." There was no hesitation as Père Dagobert answered in his husky voice, "Ah, you must understand that my eyes can see beauty just like any man. But I cannot love a woman, nor keep her from marrying. I have already given myself to another, and I have nothing to bestow." He smiled softly before sending her away. "Marry this man chosen for you. He will be true to you where I cannot. Go, child, and be happy."

The young woman married only months later, and the priest was true to his words; she was happy. Time would pass, and to the couple, children were born. After the French and Indian Wars, France lost all of its territories in North America, including Louisiana. They also gave Spain control of New Orleans. Some citizens, many of them rich French merchants and government leaders, were quite upset with this change of hands; they had become used to doing as they pleased when it came to trading. Now they could only trade with merchants of Spain. The young woman's husband was one of these French men. He met with others, devising a scheme to oust Antonio de Ulloa sent by Spain to govern them. With fewer soldiers than the angry insurgents had gathered up from around the countryside, the Spanish were outnumbered by the French rebels of New Orleans. The governor was escorted out of the city and sent away.

The Levee about 1902- New Orleans. *Image: Library of Congress*

The Levee as seen today standing not far from Jackson Square.

Spain would return with a new governor—and an army. This new leader was Alejandro O'Reilly, who ordered five of the accused rebels to be sentenced to death. As there was no hangman, on October 25, 1769, O'Reilly's soldiers marched the condemned men through the streets and to the Spanish Barracks to be shot. While the men's families waited in agony behind closed doors for the sound of gunfire, after a delay, a volley of musket balls rang out. One of the men executed was the husband of the young woman who had confessed her love to Père Dagobert.

O'Reilly left the men's corpses to rot along the levee to demonstrate what would happen to others defying Spain again. The brutal act left Alejandro O'Reilly nicknamed "Bloody" O'Reilly. He denied the rebels a traditional Catholic burial, and no one dared to retrieve the corpses, knowing they, too, would be killed. Families of the dead men begged to be allowed to inter their kin. Bloody O'Reilly refused.

Orleans Alley (now called Pirate Alley)—Circa 1920s. The old Creoles would once tell the young to listen with faith in their hearts and wait at this very alley before dawn and when it rained for the monk would surely come and sing— "Kyrie eleison, kyrie eleison—" (Lord, have mercy —) *Image Genthe photograph collection, Library of Congress.*

Several of the congregation came to Père Dagobert, begging him to do something about the men. Among them was the young woman. "Please help us! I am a widow now with no one to come to my aid. You are a priest, and they will listen to you. My husband is lying there, dead in the mud and rain. He must have a proper burial." Father Dagobert was aware of the circumstances playing out with his parishioners. He consoled them, told them to be patient. God would not let them down, nor would he. He told them he had something to do and to pray hard and try to sleep. And they trusted this priest with all their heart and soul, so they did as Père Dagobert directed them to do. "Wait here with the rest," he said softly to those who came to him, "Pray and sleep. I will leave. But I will return. Do not venture out for any reason beyond these walls." It was not long after he left, a horrible storm swept through the city. The rain came in torrents, and water flooded the streets sending soldiers guarding the dead men running for shelter. While it raged, the Father quietly went out into the streets and brought the dead men's widows and children to the church, one by one.

They stood within the church, silent and without lit candles, unsure what was happening. After he left one last time, Père Dagobert returned with a lit candle and let them go to a room. Within, the bodies of the dead men lay covered in a black cloth. Father Dagobert had walked right through the streets with several assistants in tow, eluding the guards under cover of the storm. The families gathered the dead. While softly singing the Kyrie eléison, Père Dagobert led a procession turning into a funeral mass for the men to the St Louis Cemetery No 1 to a grave freshly dug. And all the while, not a single guard let loose an alarm. The dead were laid and covered with brush. Later the guards would not find even a single footprint to disclose the truth.

The rear of St Louis Cathedral. Père Dagobert's ghost makes his way from the front of the St Louis Cathedral, along what was once Orleans Alley and is now known as Pirate Alley, and through the gates of St Anthony's Garden at the rear of St Louis Cathedral.

The couple walking in the rain that Tuesday related their story of the shadowy singer to an artist selling paintings along the street near the church the next day. She laughed softly and told them the story of Père Dagobert and his incredible feat outwitting "Bloody" O'Reilly. "You are really lucky to hear it. Not everyone does," she told them. "But since I've been here, people will say to me they stopped to listen to singing in the early hours of the morning—from the front of the church, along Pirate Alley, and then to St Anthony's Garden in the back. They think it is someone from the theatre practicing for a performance and wonder when his next show will happen. They've got no clue it's a ghost!"

Orleans Alley
French Quarter

Pirate Alley and Cabildo Alley
Alley between Royal & Chartres Streets
New Orleans, LA 70116
29.957863, -90.064179

The Legends of Pirate Alley—Jean Lafitte

Cabildo Alley—area of old prison at rear of Cabildo.

Pirate Alley. The Cabildo (the Spanish municipal government building) is to the left. To the right is St Louis Cathedral. Halfway through Pirate Alley is a small passage called Cabildo Alley. The buildings surrounding the rear of the Cabildo and the alley, including Faulkner House Books, were built in the 1840s. But once, this alley where they stand was the Spanish guardhouse location and the prison called the Calabozo.

There is a quiet cobbled path tucked between St Louis Cathedral and a building called the *Cabildo* which was the center of government during the Spanish colonial period.

Once called Orleans Alley and now called Pirate Alley, this path started as nothing more than a dirt passageway between Chartres and Royal Streets, a shortcut for pedestrians avoiding the longcuts of St Ann and St Peter streets. Halfway through Pirate Alley, another lane meets with it—Cabildo Alley. Along Cabildo Alley are 1840s 3-story mansions with wrought-iron balconies where once, the French Guard House and the Spanish prison, the Calabozo, stood. Those strolling these cobbled alleys have long seen a ghost here. And many believe it to be a pirate.

Cabildo Alley where the old prison once stood.

Pierre Lafitte was a local New Orleans merchant in the early 19th century. He was 5 feet 10 inches, stout, light-complected, and somewhat cross-eyed. He was also a pirate with a respectable amount of wit and charm and enough to handle the sales and marketing aspect of a smuggling operation he held with his brother, Jean. The men, privateers who resided on the island Barataria and located in Barataria Bay south of New Orleans, were notorious bandits, selling and smuggling slaves seized from ships in the Gulf of Mexico and the Caribbean.

Jean Lafitte at Dominique You's Bar. From left to right, the men are Renato Beluche, Jean Lafitte, Pierre Lafitte, and Dominique You. *Image: Louisiana State Museum*

But the brothers also inadvertently became American heroes in the course of their pirate reign. During the Battle of New Orleans and around 1814, US authorities caught Pierre smuggling. They placed him in the Calabozo with a looming execution. Around this time, British officials approached Jean Lafitte with a bribe—they told him that they were sending a fleet to destroy the Baratarias and their refuge due to their pirating of Spanish and British ships. However, if Lafitte and his Baratarian allies would act as guides so the British could gain a waterway advantage, they would abstain from attack, and give them both lands and pardons. Now of the two brothers, Jean was the handsome one at six feet and two inches, powerfully built, with hazel eyes and a stylish mustache. He also favored being well-presented as he donned a green uniform otter skin cap, akilter over one eye. And he certainly proved to be quite the negotiator; he turned the tables on the British to his benefit.

Jean Lafitte gathered evidence of the British offer and secretly contacted the Americans. He offered his own bribe to the US. Lafitte asked for the release of his brother and a promise of amnesty for past offenses for himself and his comrades for aiding the Americans during battle. His offer was refused, and within a couple of weeks, the Americans attacked his island headquarters and confiscated ships and cannons. But not before, curiously, Pierre "escaped" from jail. As Lafitte prepared to resist during the attack, a flag rose from the American ship allowing pardon for any deserters. They did not apprehend either Jean or Pierre.

The Americans won the battle. Pierre and Jean Lafitte received an official pardon for aiding the Americans in the war. Pierre died in 1821, and Jean was wounded in a battle, dying in 1823. It would be many years later when a ghostly, well-groomed man began to show up along the cobbled path of Pirate Alley. Most speculated that Jean Lafitte met in the dark alley negotiating and aiding in Pierre's curious escape. And he still returns today.

Pirate Alley, *left.* Cabildo Alley, *right.* The place where the ghost of Jean Lafitte roams.

Orleans Alley
French Quarter

Pirate Alley and the Wrought-Iron Gate
Alley between Royal & Chartres Streets
New Orleans, LA 70116
29.958191, -90.064337

The Legends of Pirate Alley—Reginald Hicks

More than one pirate shows his ghostly countenance in Pirate Alley. In the early morning hours, pirate Reginald Hicks hovers near the old prison where many choose to carry on his tradition of marrying here today.

In the late 1700s, a young boy was crossing the Atlantic on a ship with his family and was ambushed by pirates none other than Jean Lafitte's clan. He was kidnapped and taken in by the foul lot and raised to be one of their own. As he grew, he took the name of Reginald Hicks, learned the trade of the desperados, and moved up as the first mate.

Handsome and strapping, he had no problem turning the heads of the women along the Gulf.

But there was one, a beautiful French Creole girl named Marie Angel Beauchamp, who caught his eye. Madly, deeply the two fell recklessly in love. Many a night they spent together until one day, the girl found out she was with child. It was 1812, and right before the war, the two lovers decided they would marry. However, Mademoiselle Beauchamp was from a prominent Catholic family, and several wealthy suitors had already asked for her hand in marriage. A ne'er-do-well pirate was certainly not a proper match for this well-bred young lady. Both knew her parents would never approve. But they wanted to get married before Reginald had to return to his ship in a few days.

Reginald Hicks thought about finding a priest who would wed them. However, he was sure any local pastor would divulge the elopement to her parents, who would put an end to their wedding plans. From a fellow thief recently released from jail, Reginald learned of a German-born baker who was also an ordained protestant minister imprisoned in the Calabozo. He bribed the guard to allow the clergyman to come as far as the old iron gate facing Orleans Alley, and with the minister on one side and the young couple on the other, the two were officially married.

A little after the baby was born, Marie and the child disappeared. Most believed she drowned when a hurricane struck the city. Reginald Hicks never returned, and as far as anyone knew, he found a watery grave, although more than a few swore they saw the two traveling happily in a pirate ship in the Gulf. Others would tell a different story. That she died and he lived. Every year around the time of the wedding, a ghostly form hovers near the old wrought-iron gate along Orleans Alley, now called Pirate Alley—a lonely Reginald Hicks returning to find his long, lost love.

The Cabildo
French Quarter

The Cabildo and the Old Jail
701 Chartres Street
New Orleans, LA 70130
29.957518, -90.063877

A Hanging at the Cabildo

The Cabildo.

During a business trip to New Orleans, a salesman had some extra time one evening after meetings. He decided to visit the Cabildo Museum before closing, taking in the picture displays on the walls and historical items beneath the plexiglass casing. In suit and tie, he wandered casually into an enclosed courtyard with thick doors and iron shafts bolting them closed. He began to turn to exit but felt a strange sense that his breath was being taken straight from his lungs. Then a man in a raggedy uniform swept past him.

The businessman turned shocked as he had not seen anyone in the room. Then the figure vanished, unnerving the man to the point that his hands would not stop shaking.

The salesman stated that he was still rattled by the incident when he reached his hotel room not much later. He plopped down in front of his computer and anxiously started searching for more information on the ghost he saw and some comfort that, perhaps, others had seen this figure too. He learned that the Cabildo was the location of the colonial officials when the Spanish ruled Louisiana. It served as a city hall, a courthouse, and a prison. When it was a prison during the Battle of New Orleans, authorities housed British spies in the rear of the building. During this time, a man was found guilty of spying, and soldiers executed him. His ghost is known to inhabit the jail cell, and sure enough, others had seen and felt its presence too!

The old jail at the rear of the Cabildo can still be visited at the Cabildo Museum. If you dare, for it has a ghost. *Image: 1920s*

Trepagnier Row House
French Quarter

Faulkner House Books
624 Pirate Alley
Alley between Royal & Chartres Streets
New Orleans, LA 70116
29.958085, -90.064150

Haunted Bookshop

Orleans Alley (Pirate Alley)—1920s. William Faulkner stayed in the 3rd building to the left—now Faulkner House Books. The building is one of eleven row houses called the LeBranche buildings wrapping around Royal to St Peter. *Image: Library of Congress*

In the 1920s, Mississippi-born novelist William Faulkner rented a small apartment in Pirate Alley. He had certain insight into human nature, and it showed in his writing enough that he won a Nobel Prize.

He was also drawn to the haunting stories around New Orleans. Faulkner died in 1962. It does not appear to stop him from hanging around his old abode, now a bookstore. He likes the pretty young ladies who come in to browse the many shelves of books, taking a naughty moment to poke, prod, or even stroke them.

Pirate Alley today with Faulkner House Books.

Père Antoine Alley
French Quarter

Père Antoine Alley
Alley between Royal &
Chartres Streets
New Orleans, LA 70116
29.958072, -90.063571

Black-Robed Ghost

St Anthony's Garden behind St Louis Cathedral is named after the namesake saint of Capuchin monk Père Antoine and dedicated to Antoine's memory. In the earliest years of the city, the garden was maintained by monks as a food source and a place to meditate and pray. It is also where a ghostly figure is seen making its way along the alley and on to Orleans Street.

In 1774, Père Antoine (also known as Antonio de Sedella) was pastor of the Church of St Louis. Traditionally, church bells are silent on Good Friday and will not ring again until the Easter Vigil in solemn honor of Jesus' crucifixion. On March 21, 1788, on a windy day, a fire broke out at the home of Army Treasurer Don Vincente Jose Nunez, 619 Chartres Street at Toulouse Street, after he lit a votive candle in celebration of the holy day. Antoine refused to allow the muffled bells to ring out an alarm. After that, winds carried the flames until 4/5 of the city burned to ashes. Antoine's decision caused the fiery ruin of the church building along with many homes and businesses in the town. In later years, he was celebrated for his kindness and generosity to the poor, sick, and imprisoned.

Just a couple blocks up from the cathedral at 835-837 Orleans Street, Père Antoine had a little hut beneath a date palm. The man was so beloved and charitable that when he lay on his deathbed in January of 1829, followers took pieces of his hut for keepsakes because they believed the church would honor him with sainthood. The shanty is gone and a Victorian cottage took its place in 1898. Once in a while, a passerby will see a monk in a black Capuchin robe walking and praying from church to where the date palm and hut stood. Many believe it is Père Antoine.

Left above, Père Antoine –*image: Louisiana State Museum.*
Right: St Anthony's Garden, and where the ghost of the monk can be seen on his walk along the alley and to where his hut once stood on Orleans Street and across from the Gardette-Le Pretre House.

Old Commercial Building
French Quarter

The Old Site of Crescent City Books
204 Chartres Street
New Orleans, LA 70130
29.953566, -90.067100

In the Presence of Ghostly Children

Old home of the Crescent City Books.

Once the home of Crescent City books, customers and staff alike felt the presence of long-departed children within this circa 1870 commercial/apartment building. Staring up at the building, it is not difficult to imagine children's faces peering from the old windows.

Mayor Nicholas Girod House
French Quarter

Napoléon House
500 Chartres Street
New Orleans, LA 70130
29.955921, -90.065078

The Elaborate Plan

Girod (Napoléon) House in the 1930s—Mayor Nicholas Girod inherited the property. Locals have traditionally passed down that Girod (mayor from 1812 to 1815) offered his residence to Napoléon, whose empire had dwindled to little more than an island exile in St Helena. Napoléon died before an elaborately laid-out plan to bring him here was implemented. *Image: Library of Congress*

In the early nineteenth century, Emperor of France Napoléon Bonaparte had conquered much of Europe.

However, his rule would take an awful turn for the worse when defeated in Waterloo, Belgium. He would be exiled to the island of St Helena on a windswept plain off the west coast of Africa some 1200 miles from land with little hope of escape. Well, perhaps if not for a certain former mayor in New Orleans—

Napoléon à Sainte-Hélène, based on Hippolyte Paul Delaroche's oil study of abdicated emperor Napoléon's exile on the island from 1815 to his death in 1821. *Photo reproduction of a painting by Robert Jefferson Bingham, 1858.*

It was no secret the Creoles were sympathetic to the doomed Napoléon, now appearing a broken old man imprisoned on the bleak rocks of St Helena. Nicholas Girod, former mayor of New Orleans, was no less compassionate, and there were more of his wealthy friends who felt the same and would conspire to free him. He would offer up his residence for the trounced Emperor to live out his final days.

Thus, a few fellow citizens drafted a risky plan to equip a sound and quick ship that could steal into a secreted St Helena cove by the dark of night. A company of hand-picked able men would scale the cliffs, overpower the guards with swords and stealthy silence, and lower the Emperor with a system of pulleys and ropes into the boat. A respected captain looked over the building of a ship that conformed to the conspirators' needs. It had to be one of speed that could outrun the frigates that would surely be on their heels once the island Governor and overseer of Napoléon, British General Sir Hudson Lowe, learned the escape of his captive.

The Seraphine was indeed a capable and swift 200-ton yacht with clipper sails and a long and low hull. Workers hastily painted the boat black, decks and all, and her sails dyed brown to elude sighting. And who did they find to man this craft? It would be Jean Lafitte and his Baratarian mates. But as the plan was about to commence amidst a grand celebration at Nicholas Girod's fine home, word came in that Napoléon Bonaparte had died.

This traditional story has surpassed the test of time, just like the old home has passed through hands. Over the years, the property appeared to become deeply ingrained with the loss of the banished Emperor, who never appeared. Do not speak ill of the dead if you enter the rooms or walk the staircase. A guest taking the long set of steps mumbled something about not believing in

The second floor stairway.

ghosts, and surely, nothing haunted the restaurant's lovely rooms. A hand firmly placed in her back nearly sent her reeling down the staircase.

The Napoléon House today serves Creole food in a historic setting, and is my favorite place to dine!

The second floor elegant reception room. Where a ghostly woman sweeps.

The Impastato family owned the building for nearly a century running the restaurant on the bottom floor. The grandparents resided on the second floor, and the family rented the third floor as apartments. Family members assert an elderly lady sweeps with the *swish-swish* of her broom on the second floor. In earlier times, soldiers stayed on the third floor—a ghostly sailor drinks in the downstairs bar.

Louis Joseph Dufihlo Pharmacy
French Quarter

New Orleans Pharmacy Museum
514 Chartres Street
New Orleans, LA 70130
29.956070, -90.064866

Phantoms of the Pharmacy

A circa-1930 view of the 500-block of Chartres Street and forefront, the Dufihlo Pharmacy. *Image: Library of Congress.*

Passersby are occasionally startled to see a short-statured man in a brown suit and lab coat in the New Orleans Pharmacy Museum hard-staring them before disappearing. A bit hot-headed, he has been known to throw books or gently prod visitors at the museum. A ghostly young boy and girl play in the upstairs rooms.

Joseph Dufihlo Jr built this three and a half story building in 1823 as an apothecary and residence, operating as a pharmacist for nearly 30 years. It is America's first drug store as Dufihlo was the first licensed pharmacist in the United States. Joseph and his wife had nine children; only four made it into adulthood, and many believe that the ghostly children belong to the Dufihlo family.

Dufihlo later sold the building and the business to Doctor James Dupas. Until 1875, Doctor Dupas continued the pharmacy downstairs, with the upstairs used for his medical practice. A strange story comes from the time this pharmacist practiced—that he cruelly experimented on pregnant women. Perhaps that is why women expecting a baby who come to the property feel uncomfortable—almost as if someone is lurking around in some dark corner, accessing them as the next victim!

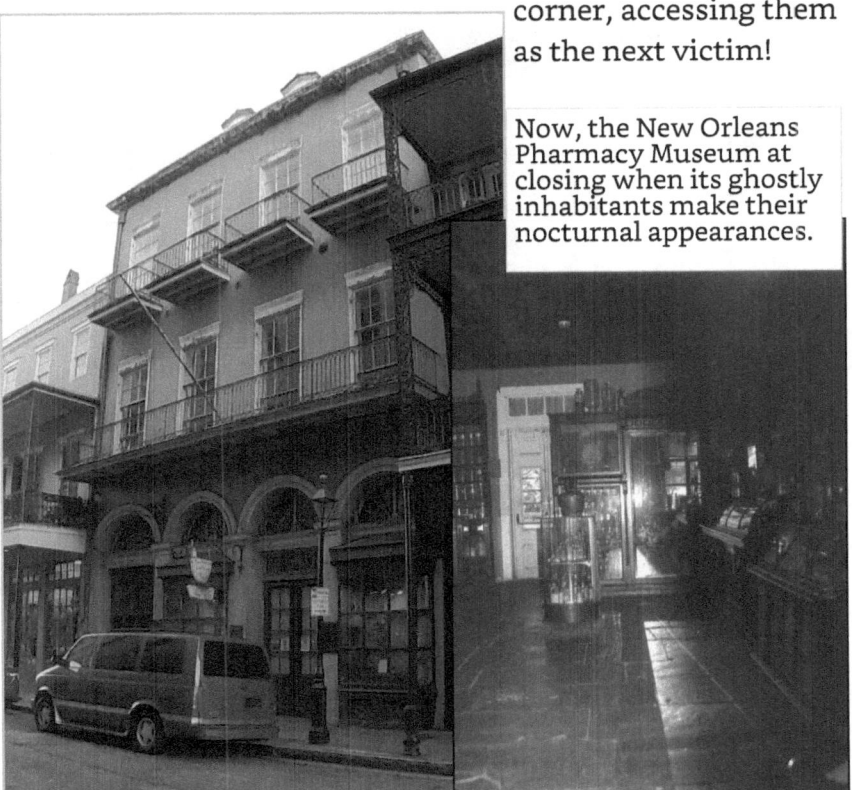

Now, the New Orleans Pharmacy Museum at closing when its ghostly inhabitants make their nocturnal appearances.

Old Ursuline Convent
French Quarter

Old Ursuline Convent Museum
1100 Chartres Street #2505
New Orleans, LA 70116
29.960774, -90.060634

Casket Girls

The Old Ursuline Convent was once an orphanage, school, and home to the Ursuline nuns. It is now a museum.

A story came from behind the thick walls of an old convent veiled on a backstreet in New Orleans and shrouded in mystery. The building has weathered many storms, but none so enormous as one begun nearly 300 years ago. It is about 88 young girls with 88 casket-shaped trousseaus hailing from a French ship and landing on the shores of what is now New Orleans. Bystanders at the docks observed the fair girls in white bonnets and carrying little dowry trunks called *cassettes* enter the city and dubbed them Filles à la Cassettes—*girls with small cases*.

The newcomers were pale creatures with bloodshot eyes and flesh so sensitive that it blistered as soon as the sunlight warmed their cheeks. The French sent them to meet and marry men in this new world. But there was more to their story secreted behind dark walls. For in those cassettes they carried, something dark and evil lay in wait.

"A 'cargo' of young women had been shipped from France, consigned to New Orleans and these girls have gone into history and romance under the name "Filles a La Cassette," on account of the little box or casket of clothes borne by each." From: The story of Louisiana by Maurice Thompson 1888

Upon their arrival, the nuns unexpectedly tightly shuttered every window of the upstairs of the convent. Those who had always noted them open wide began to wonder what grave indiscretion the nuns were hiding within. Onlookers passing on the streets whispered that someone had accidentally discovered the cassettes in a dark, dark attic, unlatched the clasps that held the lids closed and flipped them open wide. There was nothing inside! A night would pass, and church officials opened the windows wide again. When daybreak came, the shutters were closed and latched once more. The nuns pounded nails into the cassette lids and each was blessed by the Pope. And the convent stayed closed.

All knew what transpired. Vampires were running rampant in Europe then. The girls smuggled in vampire bats in those little cassettes, and when they opened the lids, the bats were unleashed, turned to vampires, and let loose in New Orleans. The nuns had opened the windows awaiting their return. Some did. But others never came back. Since, they run rampant in the streets. Some nights, you can see the shutters of the old convent banging open and close all on their own as the undead come and go as they please.

It would be easy to conjure up all sorts of dark and menacing tales passing by the convent years ago . *Image: Library of Congress*

It seems too incredible, but some of the story is based on truth. In the early 1700s, the French colony of Louisiana was inhabited by men—82 actually, along with 13 boys. They were fur traders and mingling mostly with the local Indians, some marrying women of the tribes. Governor Sieur de Bienville found this most inappropriate and possibly dangerous if there was a war. And it was hardly suitable for populating a new world. To solve the issue, the Louisiana governor bade the French government to send young women of marriageable age to wed these settlers and populate the new settlement.

He was, most likely, hoping for virtuous young ladies. However, early on and in the beginnings, these young girls came from dubious backgrounds. Most had been in institutions—prisons for petty crimes, poorhouses, or had grown up in deplorable conditions within the orphanages. It was a forced migration—authorities did not give these young women, from approximately ages 12 to 20, any choice but to travel to this new world and become wives. And the first, most likely, upon arrival, stood there with mouths agape at the wooden hovels with dirt floors where they were supposed to live. The humble homes of the early traders and trappers were nothing they had imagined.

However, a group arriving in 1728 would be different. Eighty-eight girls came on shore with nothing but the clothing they wore and small chests holding attire and linens. These La Fille à la Cassettes were virtuous girls; their supporters wanted their innocence protected so completely that guardians detained them below ship for the entire journey to their new home. The sun had not kissed their skin for many months, and their faces were ghostly pale as each slowly and trembling exited the ship. Some even hissed and winced in pain, holding their hands aloft to shield the sunlight from their eyes, bloodshot, and blinking wildly against the brightness.

Ursuline Sisters were the first Catholic nuns to come to this new land, and in 1727, nuns from France became a part of the French colony in New Orleans. It seemed most appropriate that these nuns were requested to chaperone the young ladies upon walking the wood plank and setting foot on the shoreline. Upon arrival, in a furious swish of black capes, the Sisters enveloped La Fille à la Cassettes protectively in a circle, shielding them from prying eyes. They bustled them to their convent and closed it safely shut.

It was fortified straight to the lower windows locked tightly shut for the girls' safety so no man could sneak inside, opening them in the evening to allow the cool air to sweep within. The Ursulines later developed a school for the girls to attend until they found suitable husbands. And old books pass along that all found husbands within six months.

Well, at least that is what historians have carefully gathered from the event. That the girls harbored vampires has easily been cast aside for a more refined approach. In the 1700s, it is true that doctors compiled research on a mental disorder they believed was running rampant in England—Vampirism with symptoms of bloodshot eyes, shrinking away from light, pale skin, and trembling spasms. Scientists wrote many widely distributed papers with great detail on the undead feasting on the living, of the living digging up graves and thrusting stakes through the hearts of corpses and deep into the casket so the undead could not rise. Some so often scoff and say that it is no wonder that years later, as the story was passed down of the first white women to come to New Orleans, some remembered those pale-faced La Fille à la Cassettes' arrival—they were sickly and trembling and hidden from sight. "Cassettes" would lazily translate to caskets, and the legends originated.

Still, those who dare to embrace the supernatural will always peer with morbid fascination upward to the shutters on the second floor of the Ursuline Convent. They will dare to believe there is more. And perhaps there is.

The Old Ursuline Convent is now a museum.

Beauregard-Keyes House
French Quarter

Beauregard-Keyes House
1113 Chartres Street
New Orleans, LA 70116
29.961024, -90.060887

Went to the Grave With His Boots Off

The Beauregard-Keyes House

Beauregard-
Image: Library of Congress

P.T. Beauregard was a general in the Confederate Army. He and his wife lived in New Orleans before the war in a home owned by her family. However, while Beauregard was away, his wife succumbed to sickness, and her family sold the house. For a short time, he rented the house at 1113 Chartres Street. In later years, novelist Frances Keyes also stayed there and wrote that a houseguest complained that Beauregard's ghost would poke around some nights looking for his boots. The undertaker entombed him in his stocking feet, and as a man who was particular about being well-dressed, the General would not rest until he found them.

Beauregard-Keyes House
French Quarter

Beauregard-Keyes House
*1113 Chartres Street
New Orleans, LA 70116
29.961024, -90.060887*

The Day the Black Hands Got What Was Due

Beauregard-Keyes House circa 1906. *Image: Library of Congress*

Pietro Giacona and his son Corrado opened a wholesale liquor business at 1113 Chartres around 1908 when the neighborhood around the home was becoming rundown. They had been among the first-wave immigrants, leaving Italy after mafia police targeted their successful wine business. Not long after the Giacona family came to the U.S., there was a flood of poor migrants who came to harvest sugarcane, bringing with them the same criminal activities the Giaconas had hoped to leave behind in their old country.

Some were in a mobster gang called the Black Hand. These gangsters would write letters of extortion threatening to kill business owners if they would not give them a percentage of their income. With a bustling business, the Giaconas became one of these thug's targets— a certain gang began to demand money and ordered wine barrels but refused to pay for them.

One day, Pietro had enough. He invited the gangsters to an elaborate dinner on the home's back porch to talk about business dealings. In the middle of a heated conversation where the mobsters demanded a huge sum of money and Corrado's watch, Pietro picked up his rifle and shot the men leaving a gruesome scene of blood and dead bodies.

Above: The back porch of the home where a gruesome scene played out. *Image: Library of Congress*

1920s view of the home. *Images: Library of Congress*

Over a hundred years have passed, but sometimes those passing by hear gunshots and screams when they walk Chartres Street near the home. The only explanation is that it is a ghostly reminder of the day the Black Hands finally got what was due to them.

French Quarter

Louisiana Supreme Court Building
400 Royal Street
New Orleans, LA 70130
29.955746, -90.066028

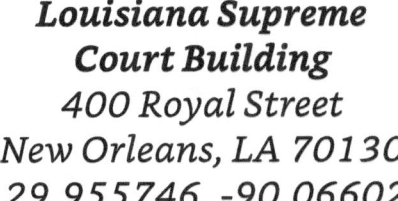

That One Thing In Common

Louisiana Supreme Court building at night from a balcony at the Omni Royal Orleans, a great stay and a place to watch for a ghost and be close to all the French Quarter offers.

It sticks out like a sore thumb plopped on St Louis, Royal, Chartres, and Conti Streets. The structure certainly does not fit in with the rest of the buildings in the French Quarter. It is big and plain, and there was more than a little public outcry when they demolished the old buildings it sits on to build it.

But it does have one thing in common with the many ancient structures around it—The Louisiana Supreme Court Building has ghosts. On the east side of the building, people have witnessed a sharply dressed man staring out a third-floor window. Overnight patrons at the Omni have called guest services to complain about a man standing at the window staring intently into their rooms. They are told not to worry. He is just an attorney at the building across the street, and he is concentrating on a case. He does it all the time. It is all quite true. Except what they do not tell them is that he is a ghost. A good number speculate it is a lawyer who lost a major case in the mid-1900s and shot himself inside the building.

Paul Morphy House
Banque de la Louisiane
French Quarter

Brennan's Restaurant
Patio Royal
417 Royal Street
New Orleans, LA 70130
29.956110, -90.066614

A Ghost Once Haunted Patio Royal

Brennan's Restaurant as it appeared in earlier years was also the home of Paul Morphy, chess champion. *Image: Library of Congress.*

Merchant Don José Faurie had this building constructed in 1795, and it later housed the first bank in Louisiana called Banque de la Louisiane. Later, it was the childhood home of Paul Morphy, a World Chess Champion. It is now Brennan's restaurant. The building has long been known to harbor a ghost—he dresses in 18th-century clothing and peers around doors.

Jean Baptiste Zenon Cavelier House
French Quarter

The Court of Two Sisters
613 Royal Street
New Orleans, LA 70130
29.957579, -90.065280

The Legends of the Court of Two Sisters

A charmed gate, a wishing well, and a deadly duel all have ties to legends at Court of Two Sisters, now a fine dining restaurant.

Bertha Angaud and Emma Camors, two Creole sisters, set up a notion shop in this townhouse. They called it "The Shop of the Two Sisters." It thrived for many years providing elegant gowns, Mardi Gras costumes, and luxurious cloth and fine perfumes imported from Paris.

When purchasing the property, several legends were bestowed upon Bertha and Emma—

At the entrance of the Court of Two Sisters, there are two wrought iron gates from Spain. Locals pass down that Queen Isabella, herself, had them specially blessed so their charm would pass along to anyone who touched them.

Vodou Queen and herbalist Marie Laveau lived nearby and practiced in the vicinity of a well in the courtyard thus dubbed *The Devil's Wishing Well*.

Local lore reveals that pirate Jean Lafitte, in his twenties, held three duels in the course of one night beneath a willow tree once in the courtyard, killing three men!

French Quarter

734 Royal Street
New Orleans, LA 70116
29.958592, -90.064183

Dancing Octoroon Mistress

Stare up at this rooftop, and you may see a young woman dancing without a stitch of clothing—before she vanishes.

There is a three-story brick mansion on the 700-block of Royal Street. It looks like many of the buildings on the street with its ancient arched doorways and old-world intricately detailed iron galleries, except for one thing. Once in a while, people walking the sidewalk see a dead girl on its rooftop, naked and weaving seductively in a dance.

Those passing do not see the ghost just anytime. It is not when the spring rains leave puddles in the streets or during the time the sweet scent of rain on asphalt kissed by the summer sunshine sweeps up to the nose. It is not during the time the trees look cool and gray in autumn. Only in December does the young ghost appear, her long brown arms gracefully sweeping the wind and bare feet pattering on the gritty floor of the rooftop. Her skin glistens nearly golden in the light of the moon from her firm, plump bosoms to the gentle curve of her belly.

She appears inside the home on the dusty mahogany staircase running from attic to roof. Her tiny feet take each step upward, and once upon the rooftop, she paces along the edge, back and forth, back and forth. Her frigid fingers run along her arms as if to warm the dead flesh covered with goosebumps. At some points, she struggles to continue wandering around the roof and almost falls, teeth chattering, body shuddering, marching, dancing. Then her steps become slower and sluggish, and she appears to get smaller and smaller until, like melting grease, she dissolves into the rooftop.

Locals explain her appearance as this—

A rich Frenchman had a residence on Royal Street. He was a widow and cared little for the many slaves he kept. The hard-hearted man treated them as he thought he should, as nothing more than property he paid for like a chair, a horse, or a pair of shoes. Among these slaves, he also had a lover who was an octoroon, 1/8 black, who lived in the upper part of the home, open wide when only he, she, and the slaves were around. But when family or business acquaintances or friends visited, the widowed man locked her in the attic upstairs, keeping his mistress from escaping by a large iron bolt on the door.

Her name was Julie, and although he did not love her, he lavished her with gifts just because he could. Although Julie was in love with him, the man knew they would never wed as his family would not allow him to marry what they believed was beneath his station. And he, of course, thought that too. He never told Julie that and instead blamed their lack of tying the marital knot on the notion that she only stayed with him for his money and the jewels he bestowed upon her.

Julie always denied his accusations and believed that the Frenchman thought it true that she loved him only for his money. She did not know the game he played and that he knew when he tired of her, he could sell her in a blink of an eye and without missing her. One cold, wet evening in December, as the man prepared for a party in the home, before Julie was to go upstairs to her room, the young woman tried to persuade him to ask her hand in marriage. The young woman told him she would do anything to be with him forever, even strip off her clothes and dance on the roof to show her love. In jest, he chuckled and told Julie that certainly, if she did dance naked on the rooftop for him, perhaps he would marry her.

After he left, Julie undressed and stepped out to the roof. She felt the cold rain hit her flesh, and she began to twist and contort in a dance, begging it would keep her warm. Around the roof, the mistress went dancing and swaying and now and then almost slipping to her death. She dreamed of a cozy fire and lying wrapped in warm blankets, of being the man's wife showered with pretty dresses and trinkets and having his babies. She waited there throughout the night, but the Frenchman never showed. When he returned from the party in the early morning and found she was not in her room, he raced to the roof, and there she lay, frozen and dead.

François Xavier Martin Home
French Quarter

Cornstalk Fence Hotel
915 Royal Street
New Orleans, LA 70116
29.960139, -90.063270

A Haunting at the Cornstalk Fence Hotel

In 1840, a husband had a fence built on the lawn to remind his homesick wife of the Iowa cornfields of her hometown.

A ghost haunts a house on Royal Street. The house is the one that has a fence with decorative cornstalks. The spirit that resides there is a woman who walks around the hotel. She also peers out the windows.

1792 Boys Boarding School Via Spanish Colonial Government
French Quarter

Andrew Jackson Hotel
919 Royal Street
New Orleans, LA 70116
29.960064, -90.063058

Up In Smoke

Andrew Jackson Hotel.

More than 230 years ago, when the land was still under Spanish rule, the property where the hotel sits now was once home to a public school with as many as 24 children attending. It withstood a great fire, but afterward, most of its students had moved with their families outside of the city. It left only about 12 schooled there.

The building became a Federal courthouse after the Louisiana Purchase in 1803. At this time, a strange turn of events would occur in the now-defunct building. During the War of 1812 between the U.S. and Britain, General Jackson arrived in New Orleans in December of 1814, ready for a battle. When his troops sighted the British, he declared martial law in the city. Even after defeating the British at the Battle of New Orleans, Jackson feared another attack and continued martial law into March of 1815. A member of the state legislature, Louis Louaillier, openly criticized how the general was handling the situation, and Jackson had him arrested. A release was sought and then granted by Judge Hall, who Jackson also had imprisoned with Louis Louaillier.

Later, Jackson would release and pardon the prisoners. When Judge Hall was back in position, he ordered General Jackson to appear in the courthouse. Jackson was fined $1000.00 for contempt of court and paid the fees. Congress later reimbursed those fees; however, Jackson refused this money and asked to donate it to charity.

The old building remained as the courthouse until 1823. Years would pass, and in 1891, a new property owner tore down the building and replaced it with the 2-story structure seen today. Now, it is a hotel. Over the years, residents and guests awaken to ghostly giggles and soft feet tiptoeing across the floor and credit the sounds to the years it was a school. For as long as people used the property to house a courthouse, it would seem that some naughty ghosts would appear too—and they do. Visitors to the Royal Street hotel, in certain rooms, have felt as if a cold finger runs down their backs. One person even divulged being pushed from her bed!

Pierre E. Trastour House
(Trastour residence was built over the burned remains of Delphine LaLaurie's home)
French Quarter

LaLaurie Mansion
1140 Royal Street
New Orleans, LA 70116
29.961846, -90.061167

The Old Haunted House of New Orleans

LaLaurie Mansion—The Old Haunted House of New Orleans.

Soniat du Fossat began building a beautiful mansion on the corner of Royal and Hospital streets around 1831-32. Even before Soniat du Fossat finished construction, 44-year-old Madame Marie Delphine LaLaurie purchased the property. She lived there with two of her children, and at times, her estranged husband, 28-year-old Doctor Leonard Louis Nicholas LaLaurie. It was a grand home, and being quite a wealthy socialite, Madame LaLaurie held many extravagant balls and cocktail parties. She also had many slaves to do the work she did not want to do, like cooking and cleaning, and driving her carriage.

It was true Madame LaLaurie had accrued much of her money from inheritances and husbands. She had been married three times, the first at the tender age of fourteen to a 35-year-old widow. Five years later, she would become a widow and give birth to her first child only days later. On her twentieth birthday, she married an elderly and incredibly affluent French widower with whom she had four children. After her mother's death, Madame LaLaurie received a healthy inheritance. Unfortunately, her second husband had accrued many debts, and after his death, paying off these arrears greatly depleted her wealth. Not long after, she married her third husband, Doctor LaLaurie, who was much younger.

LaLaurie Mansion—Side view.

From the exterior, it would seem that the family lived a picture-perfect, prosperous life. Of course, there were always the gossips of neighbors who could see into her courtyard and around her home. They were not shy about passing along in palm-cupped whispers that Madame LaLaurie's daughters and her slaves appeared haggard and spiritless. That is, except for one well-treated and loyal servant who drove her carriage to any event her socialite peers would attend. At all times, he was well-dressed in a crisp suit, alert, and immaculate.

One woman living next door to the home had a suspicion something was peculiar about Madame LaLaurie. Indeed, she must be hiding something behind her walls. Then one day, while climbing the steps of her house, she heard terrible, high-pitched shrieks issuing from the adjacent courtyard. Curiously, she peered over to see what all the excitement was about and saw a black child of about eight-years-old, one of the LaLaurie slaves, tearing across the yard. Madame LaLaurie, with tendrils of her dark hair flying in the breeze and her face contorted with determination, was close behind her in pursuit and with a cowhide whip clutched tightly in her hand. The neighbor watched as the poor child ran from story to story until she had no place to run but the roof. Then in utter terror, the girl sprang from the rooftop. In disbelief, the woman quickly covered her eyes yet heard the awful thud of the tiny body hit the ground. The child's corpse was quickly recovered, teeny arms and legs dangling lifelessly. Too horrified to move, the woman stayed at her post until hours later, and under cover of darkness, someone buried the little slave in a shallow hole dug in one corner of the yard.

But then, on April 10, 1834, a fire broke out in the home. Bystanders responded quickly to evacuate anyone inside. They tried to enter the slave quarters; however, the LaLaurie family oddly barred their entrance. Not thwarted, the rescuers pushed past and beheld a horrible sight. Before them, in an outer building, they discovered the home's 70-year-old black cook was shackled and chained near the fireplace where she would prepare their meals. She later admitted to starting the fire as she knew the slaves would be better off dead than living with the brutality of the woman who owned the building and them. She led rescuers to seven male slaves, malnourished and still living, suspended by the necks with spiked collars and chained in painful postures.

Someone had horrifically mutilated their flesh by a whip hanging on a hook in the room still fresh with blood from thrashing the poor men had received that morning. Two more lay nothing but old bones buried in the dirt with them.

When authorities brought the slaves outside, onlookers were stunned, and it was not long before a mob had formed, shouting and waving fists at the family. Madame LaLaurie, her estranged husband, and the two daughters closed the door tightly, warding off the vengeful crowd. The pampered coachman brought a carriage to the back door and set off with Madame LaLaurie, who escaped to a boat. She abandoned her remaining family, and they fled from open windows. She never returned, eventually ending up in Paris.

Children play near the LaLaurie Mansion in 1920, and one little girl peers with frightened eyes up at the building. *Image: Genthe Photograph Collection, Library of Congress.*

The house was torn asunder and burned, only a shell left of its former state.

Madame LaLaurie is long dead, as are those in her immediate family who lived there. Pierre Trastour purchased the property and built a new house over the old one. In this form, it had many faces over time—a school for girls, a boarding house, a conservatory for music and dance, and a private home. No one stayed long. It seemed cursed, plagued with misfortune and strange occurrences. Joseph Edouard Vigne was an eccentric and wealthy tenement of the mansion for a time. He died under strange circumstances with thousands of dollars secreted in nooks and crannies around the rooms.

Many believe that those who resided at the LaLaurie mansion and now long-dead are still around. Caretakers of the building would hear pots and pans banging in the kitchen. A servants' door to the kitchen opens and closes by unseen hands, the knob turning on its own. Most frightening is that passersby have seen a young girl staring down from the roof of the building. And some have even seen Madame LaLaurie peering out the windows.

Francoise Juncadella and Pedro Font Imports of Foodstuff, Wine, Groceries
French Quarter

Jean Lafitte's Old Absinthe House
234 - 242 Bourbon Street
New Orleans, LA 70112
29.955373, -90.068441

Laughter

Old Absinthe House in the early 1900s. *Image: Library of Congress.*

Sometime not long ago, a patron at a bar on the corner of Bourbon and Bienville streets heard deep, hearty laughter issue in the room. He looked around, as people curiously do, to trace the sounds back to its owners, thinking the merriment was either resounding from the street and slipping through the open door or coming from the far side of the room.

Yet it was early morning, and the crowd was still light, and the laughter was strangely boisterous, demanding, and loud, almost as if there was a group of men somewhere in the room and one had just told the punchline of a joke and the patron at the bar was the butt end of it. He could not pinpoint the source even as it occurred three more times. Feeling discomfited, the patron focused on his drink, ignoring the mocking chuckles until he left.

Old Absinthe House —1900. *Image: Library of Congress.*

It was not the first time customers have heard the raucous guffaws and snickers here, coming from corners oozing in shadows or even the ceiling. Many toss it aside as nothing more than street chatter resonating outside the walls. But the Absinthe House is haunted. The laughter comes from a different time and one long ago because it has a storied past since 1806.

Shortly after purchasing the property and erecting a building in 1806, Pedro Front and Francisco Juncadelia had a residence and thriving business here on Bourbon Street, selling groceries and wine imported from their native city Barcelona, Spain. Around 1815, as the French Quarter entered into its golden years, it was a time of prosperity and diversity as new immigrants flooded the city. It was also when the ground floor expanded into a saloon run by nephews of the Juncadelia family.

By 1861, it was Aleix's Coffee House where folks could find more than just the coffee and smokes, but also the high-proof, herbal-tasting absinthe made from anise, fennel, and wormwood. Patrons later dubbed the pub as the Absinthe Room when Cayetano Ferrer took over the lease and, in 1874, created the famous Absinthe House Frappe. The business survived through Prohibition as a speakeasy venture operated out of an abandoned warehouse.

Old Absinthe House today.

As you might imagine, there have been more than a few visitors to this liquor establishment with less than respectable motives. Wicked in life, they do not mean well to those they might run into after death. According to one disputed local legend, a secret chamber on the second floor of the Old Absinthe House was the meeting place for privateer Jean Lafitte with Major General Andrew Jackson and Governor W.C.C. Claiborne before the January 8, 1815 Battle of New Orleans. Many suppose it is the notorious Lafitte bantering with fellow pirates in the Old Absinthe House whose souls are just as tarnished as his.

The patron who heard the ghostly laughter left later that morning sated from the brew he drank in the bar. He thought that he shook off a certain feeling of being ridiculed by someone or something there. But for years after, on many nights, he awakened bathed in sweat to deep, raucous laughter. When he would sit up in bed, no one was there.

Site of Old French Opera House
French Quarter

601 Bourbon Street
Corner of Bourbon & Toulouse
New Orleans, LA 70130
29.957961, -90.066382

Witch of the French Opera—
'Tis Not Just the Eye That Wanders

The Old French Opera House—where a ghostly story begins for Marguerite Sauvé. *Image: The Miriam and Ira D. Wallach Division of Art, Prints and Photographs: Photography Collection, The New York Public Library.*

Marguerite O'Donnell was born of a French maman and an Irish dadaí. All five of her brothers were husky with fiery red hair and a good-humored temperament. Her five sisters were buxom brunettes, perhaps a bit plain, but witty and fine cooks. Maggie, they called her, was the baby of the lot.

Her parents bestowed her the prettiest features of both sides of the family with lush auburn hair and eyes so deep blue that they were the same color as the open ocean water they had sailed to get to New Orleans. Maggie was the last of her brothers and sisters to marry, and maybe she waited so long because she did not want to wed at all. But in 1860, there was not much else any parent expected a good Catholic girl to do. So, when Maggie was eighteen-years-old, she wed Octave Sauvé and became Marguerite Sauvé. As time passed and when she did not bear children, he became bitter and often criticized it. And he had a wandering eye, she knew, for any girl who passed by that was prettier and more youthful. He craned his neck, watching them, a small smile playing on his lips. Out of spite, when Marguerite was about thirty-three years old, the snubbed wife secretly got a job at the French Opera House as a chorus girl when Octave was at work. For a few years, she carried on with her secret life until the yellow fever epidemic of 1878. Then suddenly, she lost her family, and she lost Octave.

But Marguerite Sauvé had her job at the French Opera House, and she loved it so. With just the right amount of makeup, she could look ten years younger, or perhaps more.

Old French Opera House. *Image: Library of Congress.*

She caught the eye of rich Monsieur de Boisblanc, who opened his home and bed to her and even got her a maid. Marguerite was so happy then. She kept waiting for his eyes to wander elsewhere like her husband, to notice what lay beneath the mounds of makeup and discover someone younger and fresher. But a few more months passed, and her lover died suddenly. She would always wonder, though, if he would have strayed away from her too if he had lived.

In the least, Monsieur de Boisblanc left her money, and enough she could open a pastry shop. It was getting too difficult to hide her age beneath the makeup anymore, but she still tried with thick globs on her cheeks, chin, and eyes. She even smeared especially large amounts of pink pearl paint on her wrinkled lips. The chorus girls around her were hardly out of their teens. She hired a baker, and for many years, the shop flourished as it was next to the French Opera House, and those coming and going would stop for treats and tell Madame Marguerite Sauvé how wonderful they tasted. But the time came that the shop needed a new baker and such, Marguerite sent out advertisements for a new one.

Two weeks passed, and she had shuffled through scores of applications when she happed upon one young man from Florida named Carlos Alfaro. Few were as qualified as their exaggerated claims. But when Carlos arrived with his handsome features, mesmerizing dark eyes, and boyish grin, Marguerite could do no more than blush pink cheeks as he smiled at her, and she hired him. "I will just have to train him," she told herself. And for months, she did.

Carlos was eager to learn the techniques of making sweet treats. Yet he was not a good baker, and his pastries were lifeless, flat, and tasted like they either had too much flour or too little sugar or both at the same time. Marguerite ended up doing most of the work. She did not mind much. She had secretly fallen in love with the much younger man, and one afternoon he told her that he loved her too.

However, could he have just a little raise in his wages and a new suit and hat? Of course, Marguerite agreed as he kissed her lips and caressed her shoulders. It would not be long before they shared a bed. She pampered Carlos. Marguerite bought him anything he wanted—expensive clothing, trinkets, and a small apartment. Carlos lived in the apartment alone, as he told her it would not be good for business if the straitlaced families who visited her shop knew her baker was her lover. She poured makeup on her cheeks, chin, and eyes, and even if she did not look twenty-years-old in the mirror, Marguerite felt like it inside. She even set up an account for him to buy whatever he wanted.

There came a time when Marguerite began to notice she was working later nights, and she could not find Carlos anywhere when she needed him in the shop. His kisses were less, and sometimes, he would not come home for days at a time. And a couple of times, he had winced when he looked deep into her eyes and when the lamplight was on as if the old face that he once said looked beautiful and young was not so beautiful and young at all. And she wondered if her lover had a wandering eye. But she loved this man with all her heart and soul. Surely, he loved her too. Marguerite knew she could not live without him, and so she let his follies go. She told herself that he was just out for the night with friends.

But the question of his whereabouts began to eat at Marguerite like a hawk uses its sharp beak to tear open the warm belly of a squirming, screaming bunny—it gnawed and tore deep and made her bleed. She felt the jealous pangs of a lover scorned. One day, while she had just exited the shop and was heading to order sugar from the market, she saw Carlos in a crowd walking the sidewalk. By his side was an incredibly beautiful and noticeably young woman with pale hair and dark eyes, and everything Marguerite was not.

She followed them, keeping to the shadows, along Bourbon Street, Toulouse, then to Royal and finally St Ann Street. She watched as their fingers twined when the two skipped up the stairway to the very apartment she paid for, and they kissed on the top steps—just as Carlos had passionately kissed her. Ach! Why did she think he did not see how old she was? Carlos had made a fool of her with that damn wandering eye. Marguerite Sauvé, the famous pastry shop owner, realized she was through. She returned to her home, put a gun to her head, and shot herself dead.

It was not long after that Carlos and his lover were found dead in the apartment on St Ann. The police deemed it an accident as the stove's gas had been left on, killing them while they slept. They scoffed at the young lady who also rented in the building and swore she saw the dead Marguerite Sauvé walking up the steps the night the two had died. She had moaned and mewled with each step she made to the apartment, then slipped inside.

The corner of Bourbon and Toulouse where the Old French Opera House once stood since 1859. It burned down December 4, 1919.

The Old French Opera is gone. It was lost in a fire and replaced by another building along with the sweet shop. Nobody today remembers Marguerite Sauvé or the pastries she created. But some still catch a glimpse of a pale woman with thick makeup covering her pale dead flesh—gobs of makeup on her cheeks, chin, and eyes. And an especially large amount of pink pearl paint on her wrinkled lips. She drifts around Bourbon Street, Toulouse, then to Royal and St Ann Street. It is Marguerite Sauvé. Because it is not just the eye that may wander, but also the heart, and then the soul after death.

Along Royal Street near St Ann where Marguerite's spirit is seen. Because 'tis not just the eye of a lover that now wanders, it is Marguerite's ghost and her dead feet plodding along the streets.

And in passing, if for any reason she thinks that *you* might have a straying eye or you are dishonorable to your lover, she will follow you back to wherever you are residing. She will wait until you sleep and take out a little vengeance for simply being who you are. Because it happened to her, she is now dead, and no longer who she once was.

Joseph Adolphe Tricou House
French Quarter

Bourbon Heat
711 Bourbon Street
New Orleans, LA 70116
29.958877, -90.065544

The Fallen

The Tricou House—

French architects built a home for Doctor Joseph Tricou on Bourbon Street in 1832 with a large, extravagant sitting area and a tightly curling stairway leading to the third floor. In those days, it was typical for doctors to have an office in one section of their home and reside in another area, so the house was quite large. A porte-cochere, a covered carriage entrance sheltering those entering or leaving his dwelling by vehicle, greeted guests. An ornate fence guarded the beautiful home courtyard.

Doctor Tricou became somewhat of a legend to the inhabitants of his neighborhood. In 1855, police began to enforce laws against the constant dueling in the streets; not a day went by without the sounds of their shots filling the air. However, the law could not stop men from fighting for their honor with passion in their eyes and pistols aimed at their adversary. After a particularly heated clash in the street, Doctor Tricou treated one of the contestants, nursing his wounds. When questioned by authorities, though, he refused to testify a duel caused the injury.

One day around 1874, while family stayed in the house, a grand-niece of the doctor took a misstep at the top rung of the narrow stairway on the third floor, tumbling down to her death. Heartbroken, the doctor moved from the home. Later on, families living in the house would talk of seeing a girl standing on the steps or wandering on the second floor. When the building became a local nightclub, it was not uncommon for staff to hear complaints of glasses disappearing, then appearing again, and lights turning off and on.

The deadly stairway.

French Quarter

Café Lafitte in Exile
901 Bourbon Street
New Orleans, LA 70116
29.960381, -90.064193

Sipping Cocktails

It's touted as the oldest gay bar in the United States, and one with ghosts!

When a landlord forced the bar owners to vacate the original location from Lafitte's Blacksmith Shop years ago, the owner of Café Lafitte made a move up the street. The new bar, which is touted as the oldest gay bar in the country, was aptly renamed Café Lafitte in Exile. Over time, many personalities have frequented the bar, including playwright Tennessee Williams, who makes his ghostly presence known at the far end of the bar sipping cocktails.

French Quarter

Lafitte's Blacksmith Shop Bar
941 Bourbon Street
New Orleans, LA 70116
29.961040, -90.063565

Dark Chill

Lafitte's Blacksmith Shop, a haunted bar on Bourbon Street.

While stopping at the Lafitte's Blacksmith Shop Bar, a couple sat down for drinks. The woman felt a cold chill, even though the air was hot. Then an icy hand slid along her back. No one was around, and she shook the incident off. Excusing herself to the restroom, she returned with a strange feeling someone had not only followed her across the room but was watching her.

Not long after, she glanced across the bar and into a dark corner where people were chatting. An attractive man with a long mustache and a curiously shaped hat was staring hard at her, smiling. She turned to address her husband to point out the odd feeling, and when she turned back to the dark corner, the figure had vanished.

Lafitte's Blacksmith Shop around 1934. *Image: Library of Congress.*

Others have encountered the ghostly figure at this circa 1772 building generally believed to be Jean or Pierre Lafitte. Old-timers recount that while the infamous Jean Lafitte sailed the Atlantic pirating slave ships, his brother, Pierre, used properties like this one on Bourbon and St Philip streets as bases for their smuggling operation in Barataria. This one was under the disguise of a "tuerie" or butcher shop.

The Corner of Orleans and Dauphine
Site of the Traitor's Date Palm

835-837 Orleans Street
New Orleans, LA 70116
29.959560, -90.065954

The origin of a certain but long-gone date tree has always been shrouded in mystery in New Orleans. Several legends surround the tree—Père Antoine was said to have planted it. It was also thought to mark the grave of a Turkish traitor hiding out in New Orleans in the 1700s—

The Date Palm—Mysterious Tale of the Sultan's Disappearance

Gardette-Le Pretre House (right) is settled across the street from the area an old legend was passed down for centuries, and has become a part of that tale. The second house on the left sits on the place a peculiar date palm once stood. *Image: Adrian Chevalier*

A legend grew in New Orleans, years before it was related as a part of traditional lore by Charles Gayarré (1805-1895) in *The History of Louisiana. Gayarré* had grown up on a plantation outside New Orleans and as a boy, an 80-year-old man related the story to him as passed down by his father—

In 1727, a haughty man donning Turkish attire with a single servant arrived in New Orleans by a French warship. His visit was mysterious and his presence seemed to require both a great amount of decorum and also secrecy from the governor, Etienne de Périer. He was secured a modest home near the northeast corner of Orleans and Dauphine streets, across from where, now, is the Gardette-LePretre House.

Those who saw his arrival and noted the subsequent seclusion given him on the outskirts of the town proper were certain he was confined for some political offense. Regardless that neither the Turk nor his servant had given any reason to doubt his honor, the fact that he could not speak the local language was fodder for many rumors. Most believed the stories that he was a Sultan from far away who had escaped his country for reasons far beyond the imagination and taken up refuge in France. As not to mar any goodwill with the man's home country, but not wanting to give up a political game piece it might use in the future, France had shipped him to Louisiana to live out his days.

It was those same townspeople who summoned the story who would also hear not long after that a Turkish ship was seen floating in the bay of Barataria as the dark clouds began to pile up in the sky. When the storms finally came, bursting with winds and lightning, shadows of these pirates were seen lurking around the streets by the home on Orleans and Dauphine streets. The next morning, as the rain passed, the Turk and his servant had disappeared. The house was vacant. All was as it had been before his arrival, except one thing. There was a mound of dirt in the garden and certainly a grave. A marble tablet was found with the inscription— "The justice of heaven is satisfied, and the date -tree shall grow on the traitor's tomb. The sublime Emperor of the faithful, the supporter of the faith, the omnipotent master and Sultan of the world, has redeemed his vow. God is great, and Mohammed is his prophet. Allah!"

Not long after, a tiny date tree began to grow from the spot where the grave was dug. Over the years, it grew to be 60-feet high before it died in 1886. The owner of the lot eventually had the rotting corpse of the tree hauled off. But for many years while it was alive, people would pass the spot and look up at the tree, telling and retelling the story of the Turk and his servant and this tree of the dead for it was cursed to forever grow over the heart of the traitor. But no one ever solved the mystery of what great mischief that the Turk had caused to incense his enemy enough to induce such wrath.

The Corner of Orleans and Dauphine
Site of Père Antoine's Date Palm

835-837 Orleans Street
New Orleans, LA 70116
29.959560, -90.065954

The Date Palm—Père Antoine's Date Palm—From the Heart

Father Antoine's Date Palm (Phoenix dactylifera)
as it appeared in 1841

An 1841 etching of Père Antoine's Date Palm.
Image: Old New Orleans: A History of the Vieux Carré, Its Ancient and Historical Buildings.

Just across the street from the Gardette-Le Pretre House (835-837 Orleans Street) is a cottage built on the property that was the location of a date palm tree. Many tales grew from the palm, including that of Père Antoine as it was later known as Père Antoine's Date Palm and the plot where he placed his hut.

This corner lot on Orleans and Dauphine was once a part of Père Antoine's property between 1811 and 1824. The site where the second building on the left sits was known as the site of Père Antoine's date palm. *Image: Adrian Chevalier*

A little brick cottage with wooden pillars and hand-made shingles once stood on the northeast corner of Orleans and Dauphine. It was the building where the mysterious Turkish man stayed, and a banished French nobleman, De Beaulieu, once owned it. After De Beaulieu returned to France, the home changed hands until, in 1811, a parishioner offered the land title to the beloved monk Père Antoine.

In 1841, notable Scottish geologist Sir Charles Lyell visited New Orleans and interviewed locals about a certain date tree growing near the cottage. At the time, the tree was seventy to eighty years old, and the old monk had been dead for nearly twelve years. Neighbors of the property relayed this story—

When Père Antoine was a young man, a childhood best friend named Émile Jardin was nearly always by his side.

The two never parted, and both were studying to enter the priesthood. Upon arrival to the city and the young men's neighborhood, a woman from the Pacific Islands had taken ill. While sick, Père and Émile had provided what aid they could bring to her, but the immigrant woman died suddenly. She left behind a daughter called Anglice, an exotically beautiful girl of only sixteen or seventeen years. Père took Émile aside and, knowing the girl had no family or friends to care for her, formed a pact that the two would act as brothers to the girl and watch over her.

Before long, though, both men began to secretly wrestle with feelings of not-so-brotherly love toward Anglice. For many months they fought back urges, knowing their vows denied this kind of love and then marriage, desperately meditating and praying to ward off the longings. And then one night, Émile and Anglice vanished. No one felt more pain than Père himself as he had finally decided he would profess his love to the young woman and beg her to leave with him.

He found a scrap of paper in Anglice's handwriting with words that seemed so small at the moment—"Par-donnez-nous, car nous aimons." *Forgive us, for we love.* Père Antoine thought that surely at that moment, his heart had broken. And yet, he picked up the pieces and went on with his life. He entered the church and got a little bit of land where he grew a garden not far from St Louis Cathedral.

Perhaps three or four years went by before he received word about his old friend and the young woman who had broken his heart. It came in two hastily written letters. The first was in shaky writing and sent by Anglice. She divulged that Émile had died of sickness earlier in the year, and she was certainly following in his steps. The two had a daughter, and Anglice begged Père to take in the child until she was old enough to enter the convent of the Sacré Cœur.

Père opened the second letter with shaking hands. His heart had been broken once by the woman, and she would break it again. Anglice had died. Authorities had placed the child on a ship that sailed toward New Orleans.

The little girl arrived only days later as storms, and a downed ship delayed the letters reaching him. Her name was that of her mother, Anglice, and Père Antoine marveled at how much she was like his old friend Émile and her mother. It was like having both of them given back to him.

Anglice was not so happy. She missed her homeland and cried miserably for it—the sun and the palm trees and the wild places she ran. As the days passed, she seemed to wilt the more she stayed there like a pretty wild rose in full bloom that had been plucked from its stem, then slowly left to die without the soil and rain to nourish it. The priest called in doctors who could find no cure for her illness, saying that what ailed her was in her mind and the heart. She yearned to be home on her islands.

Père Antoine asked her again and again if there was something that could make her feel better. Finally, she did answer one afternoon while she sat on the porch and stared out at the vacant street. "I suppose I miss the date palm trees from home. I used to sit under them for hours, staring up at their leaves. I long to be home and with them."

There was nothing he could do for her right then, even if he wanted. Within the week, the child grew listless; then she died the next. He dug a shallow grave in his garden and buried the little girl within. His tears would fall on the lonely mound for many days. Then, he noticed a stem with emerald leaves springing from the center of the grave. Curiously, he nurtured the plant, and it grew and grew until it formed a sapling, but Père had not a clue what particular seed had grown this strange tree.

Then one day, a sailor passed by and pointed to the plant, telling the man that he had never seen a date palm tree growing on this type of land. "A date palm!" Père exclaimed, and he felt a warmth he had not felt since he had met Anglice and then her daughter. "Bon Dieu, vous m'avez donné cela!" *My God, you gave me this!* After that, Père nurtured the date palm and refused to cut it down because he knew it grew from the very heart of little Anglice.

Etching of *Père Antoine's Date Palm.*
Image: Historical sketch book and guide to New Orleans and environs—

PÈRE ANTOINE'S DATE PALM

Père Antoine owned that plot until 1821, when it was sold to Philippe Avegno. Some writings state that Père wrote in the notes of sale that any owner who should take down the tree would give up rights to the property. It changed hands until it fell into that of the Claveries who owned a woodyard there. Everyone abided by the old priest's words. It was not until 1886 and long life, the tree died. On the morning of July 12, 1886, it was pulled down and towed away. New owners built a house atop that still sits here today.

Père Antoine's date palm-1884/85 *Image: George François Mugnier New Orleans Scenes, Louisiana Digital Library, Baton Rouge, La.*

French Quarter

Sausage Factory
725 Ursulines Avenue
New Orleans, LA 70116
29.961768, -90.062190

The Ghost Who Walked the Sausage Factory

This pretty private residence may or may not have been a sausage factory during its existence, but it has become the background for a staple ghost story throughout the years. Perhaps it is due to the murders of sisters Theresa and Leonide Moity, who were married to brothers Henry and Joseph Moity. The sisters were found just up the street at 715 Ursulines October 27, 1927, butchered, and parts of their bodies were placed into trunks. The newspapers dubbed it the "Trunk Murders." Courts sentenced Henry Moity for the crime. He had been a butcher's assistant.

A curiously morbid story comes from Lyle Saxon, Edward Dreyer, and Robert Tallant from *Gumbo Ya-Ya: A Collection of Louisiana Folk Tales*. It goes like this—Many years ago, the Mullers owned a popular sausage factory in New Orleans. The husband, Hans, worked hard to keep the business going, but his job was demanding. His wife, from overwork, had become old and wrinkled before her time. Hans also had eyes for a younger woman. One night, Hans threw his wife into the meat grinder. He thought the grinder had pulverized her to nothing, but customers complained of bits of bone, cloth, and hair in their sausage soon after. The woman he loved heard of the words spoken about the bad meat and refused to be around Hans.

There came a night when Hans heard a strange thumping sound, *thump-thump-thumpity-thump* near the boiler vat. Suddenly the bloody ghost of his wife rushed toward him. Hans screamed in fear and ran from the building. The neighbors awakened and asked the man why he was yelling, and he said he had nothing more than a bad dream. Then the women on the street noticed his wife was not around, and they began to whisper. One day, a customer was eating some of the sausages and bit down, only to find a gold wedding band in the meat. She called the police, they rounded up Hans Muller, but he had gone insane. And the ghost of Missus Muller still haunted the sausage house for many years, even after another family bought it.

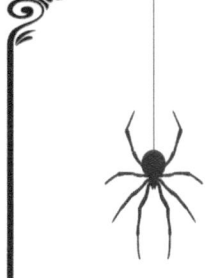

French Quarter

Place d' Armes Hotel
625 St Ann Street
New Orleans, LA 70116
29.958728, -90.063449

Old School

Place d' Armes Hotel

This 1856 brick townhouse, now a hotel, sits on the original site where Father Raphael, Rector of the St Louis Parish Church, held the first school in French colonial Louisiana in 1725—a one-room building for boys. It was there for only a few years, but the ghosts who haunt this building may have been from this short period. Guests staying at the hotel have heard ghostly children's voices and footsteps in the night.

St Ann—A Creole House Hotel
French Quarter

Inn on St Ann
1013 St Ann Street
New Orleans, LA 70116
29.960982, -90.066889

Knobby

Inn on St Ann

A young woman who stayed at the Inn on St Ann had a peculiar experience. While spending the night in one of their well-kept second-floor rooms, and as she placed her hand on a doorknob, it began to jiggle furiously on its own. Shaken, she had asked the staff what could have possibly caused this odd incident. It was an easy answer because guests ask this question often. In the early days, a daughter's bedroom was upstairs by the parents' chamber for safety. It also kept girls from sneaking out to meet a courter. Their resident ghost must have thought the girl was trying to steal away into the night, and it was giving a warning! The staff nicknamed the ghost Knobby, and sometimes the overly-protective spirit even takes the knobs right off the doors!

Marie Laveau (aka Widow Paris)

Where the home of Marie Laveau once stood
1020-22 St Ann Street
New Orleans, LA 70116
29.961009, -90.067210

Vodou Queen of New Orleans

Marie Laveau. *Image: by Frank Schneider, based on a painting by George Catlin (Louisiana State Museum)*

Although Marie Laveau has much mystery surrounding her day to day life, historical records suggest she was the first of her maternal line to be born free. Her great-grandmother Marguerite is believed to have come from Senegal to Louisiana aboard one of the last French slave-trading ships.

Marguerite would have a daughter named Catherine (Marie's grandmother), who was held in slavery through at least four owners before purchasing her freedom, where she took the name Catherine Henry. One of her children was Marguerite Henry (Marie's mother), released from slavery in 1790. From a union with a successful business owner, Charles Laveaux, Marie was born in September of 1801. Although his name was not on her birth certificate as the father, Charles Laveaux would later claim Marie Laveau(x) as a natural heir in his will. She most likely grew up in her grandmother's home on St Ann Street.

Marie Laveau and her children lived from 1839 to 1895 in the vicinity of what is now 1020-22 St Ann Street. The actual home where she resided was demolished in 1903.
Image: Adrian Chevalier

Marie Laveau has been described in many ways—as a mother, savvy businesswoman well ahead of her time, and powerful Vodou Queen, taking control and devising religious rituals. She is seen in paintings wearing a modest black chemise top, dark skirt, and a brightly colored shawl.

She also dons a tan and brick-red tignon, an initially bland and oppressive headwrap Louisiana Creole women of color were required to wear by law in the 18th century "as not to attract the white men's eyes." It would later become a fashion statement and a form of empowerment as women added brightly colored material and accessories to make them stand out.

Others described Marie Laveau quite differently— Alberta Jefferson, a neighbor during childhood, portrayed her as "a tall, thin, very pretty woman who wore her hair dressed with curls falling on her shoulder and never wore a headdress or tignon." Despite the many ways she was perceived, what would appear a typical life at the beginning would take a profound shift to extraordinary and mystical over the years.

On August 4, 1819, Marie Laveau married Jacques Paris, a carpenter from Saint Domingue—well-known priest Père Antoine performed the sacrament. From this union, two daughters were born—Felicité and Marie Angèlie Paris, but both died in childhood. Although there is no documentation of her husband's death, around 1824, records about him cease, and Laveau took the title of Widow Paris. A couple of years later, she would become the common-law wife of Louis Christophe Dominic Duminy de Glapion from a wealthy and prominent New Orleans family.

The relationship would span nearly 30 years, with seven offspring born from 1827 to 1839. Only two of their children lived past childhood—Marie Heloïse Euchariste Glapion, born in 1827, and Marie Philomène Glapion, born in 1836. Marie Philomène became Laveau's successor. Their likeness was so uncanny that it was quite often mentioned the daughter shocked passerby along the streets after her mother had died, many believing that it was Marie Laveau, herself, arising from the grave.

The family lived in a cottage on St Ann Street. Laveau became a hairdresser early on to make ends meet and catered to both the wealthy white and Creole women of New Orleans and those of lesser means. She became their confidante and also gave sound advice. When exactly Marie Laveau became the well-known healer and overseer of spiritual rites is hazy. Some believe her mother's death drew Laveau to search out the roots of her ancestors' African beliefs, culture, and religion. Yet it was not just through her job that she became acquainted with and trusted by wealthy and politically affluent clients, and eventually offered spiritual protection and guidance. She was trusted by the Africans, free or not. They had learned quite early that they must hide their traditional religion by using Catholic faith elements in their religious practices. She combined both Vodou beliefs and Catholic traditions and introduced statues of saints, crosses, and candle burning as common ground between the two.

But there was also a certain trust among those who share beliefs; Marie Laveau was a devout Catholic throughout her life, had been baptized by Père Antoine at St Louis Cathedral, and had her children baptized. The community also witnessed her compassionate work as a charity worker and a healer of sick prisoners and the needy. Such her pious duties made her respected among people of all realms of life. And if those were not enough reasons, most surely feared Marie Laveau. She was known to be quite powerful and offered up a certain theatrical flair to gain her attention and respect; many stories crept to ears of the evil that would befall those who offended her. Rituals occurred at three main sites—Congo Square for worship and dance, her home on St Ann Street (now 1020 St Ann, but the actual house was demolished in 1903) where she would meet with clients offering medicinals and charms, and Bayou St John's on Lake Pontchartrain where larger special events occurred.

Marie Laveau was surrounded in mystery and still is today—Just as she was described differently in many ways, she was also called by many names. Her three-vault tomb inscription reads: Famille de V ve Paris née Laveau (Family of the Widow Paris born Laveau).

Marie Laveau (aka Dame Christophe Glapion and Widow Paris) died June 15, 1881, at 8:00 p.m. at her residence Number 152 St Ann Street (per her death certificate). The church buried her in St Louis Cemetery No 1 in the middle vault of the family tomb opened by order of her daughter, Philomene Laveau. Newspapers with reporters who had met her acknowledged her kindness and charity. In contrast, the uneducated who watched her rituals from afar (or simply not at all), with the close-mindedness of prejudice, deemed her "the notorious hag who reigns over the ignorant and superstitious." Followers and the curious still revere her tomb, although to see her grave, you have to pay a tour guide. A tiny fee from the tour charge goes to the church. Perhaps, though, you will walk away with more than you think upon the visit. Some have seen the spectral side of Marie Laveau walking among the graves. They have even felt touched by her spirit.

Bourbon Orleans Ballroom/Theatre
French Quarter

Bourbon Orleans Hotel
717 Orleans Street
New Orleans, LA 70116
29.958980, -90.064691

Bourbon Orleans Hotel—The Phantom Dancer

Bourbon Orleans Hotel, now.

Orleans Theatre, then.

The Orleans Ballroom was originally constructed next to the Théâtre d'Orléans. Both were destroyed by fire in 1816 and rebuilt to become a well-known social center for the rich. It also has been used as a convent and school and is now a hotel.

It was the grandest theatre when it opened in 1819, catering to only New Orleans society's well-to-do. Sometime later, a ballroom was built alongside to entertain operas and elegant masquerade and carnival balls.

Bourbon Orleans ballroom.

It was not enough to accommodate the cultural fancies of the rich. It became popular for area ballrooms to offer dances for free women of color, especially those of mixed heritage, to meet rich French men looking for mistresses or simply a rendezvous for a night. During the early 1800s, when many Haitian refugees poured into the streets, some women needed to be resourceful to survive. Meeting with men at these balls would be a place where women could endure from day to day, or if they played their cards right, maneuver their way into the social ranks of Louisiana in exchange, of course, for a fleeting or a lifetime liaison. The Creole called these women who entered into these relationships plaçée or ménagère.

Something remains of the ballroom's popular past. A woman staying at the hotel decided to peek at the elegant room when no one was around. She pulled open the doors and slipped inside. It was dark with only a pale light creeping through the windows making shadows dance across the floor.

She caught the faint twinkle of the chandelier and decided how wonderful it must have been to dance beneath its light long ago. Caught up in the moment, she scurried out to the center of the floor. Then she began to twirl around and around in the silence beneath the chandelier. Then a rustling caught her attention at the far wall. She stopped abruptly. One set of curtains was moving, swaying back and forth. She could see a faint bulge behind the drapes the size of a person—someone was watching her! She gasped and fled the room, embarrassed. But when she peered back in moments later, nobody was there.

Visitors to the ballroom also began speaking of a ghostly dancer twirling around the floor beneath the crystal chandelier. She has sad almond eyes and dark hair adorned with a beautiful hair comb. She appears, circles for only moments then vanishes. Guests also witness something skulking behind the curtains and get the feeling someone is watching them. For those who dare to take the steps across the room and push aside the curtains, nothing is there.

Shadows played across the floor around me when I took pictures like dancers working their way around the room. You can see my own shadow behind me, and perhaps a spectral one or two across the floor.

Bourbon Orleans Ballroom/Theatre
French Quarter

Bourbon Orleans Hotel
The Stairway to the Ballroom
717 Orleans Street
New Orleans, LA 70116
29.958980, -90.064691

Bourbon Orleans Hotel—Dueling Twins

The bloody stairway.

A duel took place between two hot-headed Creoles, twins Stephen and Louis Charbonnet, over a beautiful woman on the double stairway leading up to the ballroom. Both were fatally wounded during their battle, and their blood ran heavily on the wooden floors that were of a unique construction of oak and cyprus. Blood continues to stain the wood, and it still seeps into the carpet, leaving it tinted a mute brownish-red. It is hardly obvious, but enough that the carpet has been changed a few times over the years.

Bourbon Orleans Ballroom/Theatre
French Quarter

Bourbon Orleans Hotel
717 Orleans Street
New Orleans, LA 70116
29.958980, -90.064691

Bourbon Orleans Hotel—Soldier in the Hall

The sixth floor of the Bourbon Orleans where a ghostly soldier walks.

In April of 1862, the Union Army attacked New Orleans, a vital port and manufacturing center for the South. Before the Union Army occupied the city, the Confederate Army had troops stationed in the harbor. They roamed the streets around the Orleans Ballroom and Theatre, which still held plays and ballroom dances during the war. Many years later, when the old theatre and ballroom became a hotel, guests staying on the sixth floor began witnessing a ghostly Confederate soldier strolling through the halls.

Bourbon Orleans Ballroom/Theatre
French Quarter

Bourbon Orleans Hotel
717 Orleans Street
New Orleans, LA 70116
29.958980, -90.064691

Bourbon Orleans Hotel—The Orphanage

The Bourbon Orleans when it was a convent. 1881 to 1964.

Visitors to the Bourbon Orleans have heard ghostly children's giggles in the building and have watched, with curiosity, as a nun appears then vanishes on the grounds. In the courtyard, the sound of chatter and laughter oozes out of the air when no children are around.

In the late 19th century, the Orleans Ballroom became the convent for the Sisters of Holy Family, the first African-American religious order. Henriette DeLille founded the order. DeLille was a free woman of color born of the plaçage system where young females of mixed descent were bound to rich men as mistresses. Her family expected her to follow the same path as her mother, but she was raised strict Catholic and denied this destiny to start a small unrecognized congregation or order of nuns. After the Orleans Theatre went up in flames, the order built an orphanage on the lot along with a courtyard and playground, now the hotel's courtyard and swimming area. During their time on the property, the sisters struggled through epidemics and took in the elderly and sick.

Years ago, while my family was checking into our room at the Bourbon Orleans, we eyed a forty-something couple shuffling along the carpet of the hallway, looking tired and muddled as they dragged their carry-on suitcases behind.

We greeted them with a friendly "Good morning!" The man looked up, "Good morning? We didn't sleep a wink last night. That wasn't your kid making all that racket last night, was it?"

I mumbled, "No, it wasn't," thinking by his scowl at my two-year-old son that certainly he felt I was not telling the truth. But sure enough, that night, we thought we heard children playing outside or somewhere in the hallways. No children were there.

Don Manuel Gayoso de Lemas House
French Quarter

Le Petit Theatre du Vieux Carré
616 St Peter Street
New Orleans, LA 70116
29.957596, -90.064226

Primping Ghost

A long-time theatre in New Orleans.

In the late 1700s, the last Spanish governor of Louisiana built a majestic home on St Peter Street. After he sold the building, it had more than a few owners before the structure was purchased in 1922 for a theatre and has remained in that capacity since. It might seem strange that the ghost of a Yankee soldier is seen walking the hallways and, at times, preening himself in front of a long-gone mirror. However, during the time the Union army occupied New Orleans during the Civil War, the building housed soldiers.

Dr Yves Le Monnier House
French Quarter

Café Beignet
Former Old Coffeepot Restaurant
714 St Peter Street
New Orleans, LA 70130
29.958198, -90.065162

The Sordid Tale of Etienne Deschamps

This charming café is home to a horridly true story of lust and murder.

About 1889, a French dentist Etienne Deschamps took up both his residence and his business in a single room along St Peters Street in the French Quarter. To make ends meet, he also offered cures using the early forms of hypnotism called magnetism—he believed that an unseen magnetic force running through the body united all things.

If something disrupted the flow, it could cause grave problems like diseases. By holding, massaging, or staring deep into his client's eyes, he could rid the obstructions and heal them. To aid in his endeavors, he would often use chloroform. His clients were many who were looking for remedies that ordinary doctors were unable to cure.

Fifty-nine-year-old Deschamps was new to the area and could not speak English. It was not a problem as most of the neighborhood, too, spoke his native language. He was well-liked in the community with his polished manners and refinement. He became quite close to one neighbor who lived just around the corner—a poor carpenter/upholsterer, Jules Deitsch, widowed and who supported his 90-year-old mother along with his two little girls—Laurence, nine-years-old, and Juliette, twelve-years-old. Deschamps seemed to have a special interest in the two youngsters, often taking them for walks to buy candy or trinkets and inviting them to visit him in his room, which always offered fresh fruit. It was difficult being a widowed father as Juliette was getting to the age where she began to notice boys.

Deschamps had seemed to see it too as he scolded the girl one day after finding out she had been in the company of a young neighborhood boy. The girls' father permitted this grandfatherly doting. Not only did he appreciate that the older man encouraged better behavior of the girls, but Deitsch enjoyed seeing Juliette and Laurence receive the small gifts Deschamps offered them that he could not afford.

Then on a January day of 1889, the two girls went to visit Etienne Deschamps. Juliette and Laurence were not gone long when Jules Deitsch heard hard steps clambering up the old stairway of the family's room. Laurence was sobbing when she burst through the door, telling her father that the old dentist had killed her sister. Of course, Deitsch bolted to Deschamps's apartment with neighbors following in pursuit, banging on the locked door. It eventually yielded to their force, and when it was open wide, a horrible scene played out. The child lay unclothed on the bed. Deschamps lay beside her, also naked. He had killed her with a chloroform towel across her face and had stabbed himself to near death.

Etienne Deschamps lived but was convicted of his crime and hanged in 1892. Shortly after, boarders in the building began to see an apparition of a young girl wandering through the rooms and halls, seeming lost, then she would vanish.

The café is a great place to visit for the local powdered sugar delight, beignets. And perhaps, for running into a ghost.

John Garnier House
French Quarter

Pat O'Briens
718 St Peter Street
New Orleans, LA 70130
29.958228, -90.065246

Spirits of a Building's Past

Pat O'Brien's bar.

John Garnier built this townhouse in 1817 as a home. In December 1942, what had been a speakeasy during Prohibition on the corner of Royal and St Peter streets, moved into the building and became Pat O'Brien's. Local bartenders invented the Hurricane at this location during World War II. After difficulties importing whiskey and scotch, to acquire small amounts of the liquor, bar owners were forced to purchase rum in bulk. A drink with rum served in a hurricane-shaped glass was created by bartenders to eliminate the surplus, and the Hurricane was born. That said, the bar has more spirits than just the drinking kind—shadow figures walk about the building, and footsteps are heard in the hallways and upstairs.

Old O'Flaherty's Irish Channel Pub
French Quarter

New Orleans Creole Cookery
508 Toulouse Street
New Orleans, LA 70130
29.956158, -90.064019

Fountain of Youth

The courtyard that hid a murder.

Around 1806, Mary Wheaton Sevre Marre acquired a substantial fortune along with a feed store with a residence above, an oyster-shucking house, and a double courtyard along Toulouse Street when her husband died from yellow fever. Mary was a hard-working woman and continued the business on her own until a few years later when she married a man named Joseph Baptandiere. The marriage was troubled from the start. The couple bickered often.

Not long after the wedding, Joseph began having a secret affair with Angelique DuBois, a pretty young woman who worked at the feed store and who lived in a small attic apartment of the shop.

It was not long before Angelique became jealous and wanted Joseph all to herself. She begged him to divorce Mary, but he refused to leave since his wife handled all the money. Not only would it cause a scandal, but he would be destitute. But he did not tell Angelique that he would never separate from his wife. Instead, he told her it would only be a short period before they would be together forever. After some time, Angelique became impatient and outraged, and the pleading changed to fits of anger. Then one night, Angelique threatened to tell Mary about the affair. In a frenzy, Joseph strangled his young lover. Knowing police would arrest him for her murder, Joseph dug a shallow grave in the courtyard and covered her with dirt. However, as he stood back to take in what he had done, he heard something from above the enclosure. His eyes worked upward to the darkened interior of a window. A face was peering down at him! Knowing someone had seen his foul deed and authorities would have him executed for the crime, Joseph went to the top of the building and hung himself.

It was a young slave who had been looking out the window. When he knew the man was dead, he revealed what he had seen, leading the police to a recently-dug grave in the courtyard. Angelique was interred and given a proper burial. Later, building owners erected a fountain in the area where Joseph hid her youthful body. Mary lived in the home and continued the business for many years, dying in 1817. Not long after she died, those visiting the property witnessed an older woman in a fit of anger, tossing objects at those within her reach.

This building has been long known to harbor ghosts.

Some unfortunate guests once saw a man hanging on the third floor before suddenly, he vanished. Others have seen Angelique wandering through the courtyard near the fountain, wringing her hands in disbelief of her young life cut short. Guests have also spotted her listening intently to music in the former Ballad Room.

The Olivier House
French Quarter

Olivier House Hotel
828 Toulouse Street
New Orleans, LA 70112
29.958179, -90.067072

Woman in Black

Olivier House Hotel.

There is a hotel along Toulouse Street. It is haunted by a woman dressed in a modest, black frock who wanders the building, mumbling what most deem indecipherable words.

If her seemingly odd rambles are interrupted, she grunts a reprimand or two.

Some attribute the ghost's existence to an owner who died in 1884. The building was once a residence owned by the Locoul family. The matriarch of the home was Elisabeth Locoul, who owned a sugar plantation outside New Orleans. She was a devout Catholic and would spend time each day with her rosary clasped in her hands praying. Now, the rosary has fifty-nine beads, a crucifix, and a medal. There are specific prayers for each piece. The rosary is fed through the fingers to the point where the next prayer is chanted. It requires concentration—there is a certain rhythm involved in praying the rosary with emphasis on focusing on the meaning of the words. Interruptions tend to break up that concentration. Such, if you accidentally run into a lady in black roaming the Olivier Hotel, do not provoke her. Kindly let her pass and finish her prayers.

Pierce Edmond Foucher/Alciatore House
French Quarter

Antoine's Restaurant
713 St Louis Street
New Orleans, LA 70130
29.956731, -90.066425

Watchful Eye

Antoine's Restaurant.

In 1840, Antoine Alciatore came to New Orleans with a vision—to start a fancy restaurant for the affluent. With hard work, he was able to fulfill his dream. By 1868, Antoine had established enough business that he outgrew his small restaurant and moved to a larger building where Antoine's Restaurant still stands today. But when Antoine's health began to diminish in the 1870s, he left for his home country of France to live out his dying days. Later on, after Antoine Alciatore died, family members and staff would often encounter his ghost, leaving them with a sensation he was keeping a careful watch on the restaurant.

Bienville street Shell Road
Basin Street
French Quarter

(Intersecting Basin)
New Orleans, LA 70112
29.957939, -90.071970
Bienville Avenue (intersecting Robinson)
29.960152, -90.075339

Ghost of Shell Road

Old Shell Road in New Orleans. *Image: Library of Congress*

In the early days, shells were used as a paving material for roads. The road was built up from piles of white clamshells, raising it above the swampy land. Horse hooves, carriage wheels, and foot traffic wore the shells down to a smooth surface that made a pleasant whirring sound when wooden wheels drove over.

When the 6-mile New Basin Canal (now Pontchartrain Boulevard) was built, a shell road was laid down alongside it for carriages. Traders, travelers, and even people living downtown could use it to find respite from the city and enjoy the lakefront, Mannessiers Pavilion, hotels, and restaurants along Lake Pontchartrain. Other roads in New Orleans also used shells as their base as they tended to be bordered by swampy areas. One such street was called Bienville street Shell Road that ran through what would later become the Storyville area (New Orleans' red-light district that already had a bad reputation even in 1852) and all the way to Lake Pontchartrain. And at that time, there was a ghost along this road. It was seen quite often by the prostitutes in their carriages while they were heading along the path drumming up work. Their carriage drivers were prone to watching the road carefully for certain lights that looked out-of-the-ordinary. Although each hansom cab had a lantern to illuminate their course, occasionally, an oncoming glow was not a carriage with a lantern at all. Instead, a tiny glow would form into a pale figure gliding along with noiseless steps. It would slip across the road and stop at one point to gyrate here and there. Then the form would disappear behind a tree or brush or even the top of a roof. But not before it spooked their horses into a ditch and joggled everyone in the carriage.

The ghost's story had been that it was a California miner who got rich panning for gold in the rush of 1849. Traveling through the city, he was ambushed, robbed, and his throat slit ear to ear. Although two men passing by found the corpse, before police could make it to the scene, the dead body had disappeared. The murdering thieves had dragged his body to the muddy waters of the nearby canal and dumped it in. There was no physical evidence, so the law never completed an investigation.

The ghostly shenanigans began to occur so often that a surly policeman named Officer Bolonsa took a cab to the Bienville street Shell Road. Armed with a pistol and a club, he hid in the brush awaiting the ghost. It was not long into the evening when a carriage passed, and a pale, shadowy figure waylaid it. The form danced and gyrated in front of the horses, wild arms waving in the air. Officer Bolonsa called out, then strutted straight across and confronted the ghost. Soon enough, he recognized the *spirit* as a certain and quite human resident of the streets who spent most of his time at the local asylum for the insane. The poor man had been scammed and played the fool, having paid some conman one dollar and fifty cents to purchase all the land between the city and the river. He believed he was chasing off trespassers. He was quickly arrested and carted away.

Another Old Shell Road in New Orleans. *Image: Library of Congress*

The tale should end right there if the ghostly acts stopped after the man was safely tucked back in his bed at the asylum. They did not. Sure enough, it was only one night before the light showed up again, along with the spectral figure. But somebody could have easily explained it if the police had just asked the right people.

You see, in 1851, Mentor Quigley was a young clerk at a local apothecary. Not only was the pay meager for his job, but he had set his heart on making extracts. At the time, the average home cook had few options for flavoring their meals. He wanted to offer more choices and commercially produce extracts and spices for resale that would be easily available to anyone and could be found at all the grocery stores. His wife, Delie, a pastry-maker, thought his idea was just splendid and was as eager for him to begin his venture. The only thing stopping him was the lack of money.

On Sunday, late afternoon, it was his day off, and Mentor went for a walk. The young man was so focused on the thoughts of starting his business that he did not realize he had meandered past the safer side of town and into one known to harbor thieves and murderers. When a carriage full of rowdy women passed him by who whistled and called out flirtatiously to him, Mentor realized his feet had stepped far along Bienville street Shell Road. He shook his thoughts away, started to turn toward home, and just as he did, he felt a hard thump on the back of his head.

Mentor awakened in dewy grass in darkness and to the call of someone's voice, "Hey, you alright there?" He sat up and watched the light of a lantern weave and bob towards him. As Mentor rubbed his head, the lantern stopped in front of him, exposing the face of an old man with a long white beard and pale blue eyes. "You look familiar. Do I know you?" the old man asked, holding the lantern higher.

Mentor stared at the face. He looked almost exactly like his grandfather. "I'm Mentor Quigley." Before he could say more, the older man guffawed loudly. "Well, I do know you! You are my brother Israel's grandson! You look just like him when we were young." He stretched out a knobby-knuckled hand and helped Mentor rise. "I'm your great Uncle Adam."

Mentor's pockets were inside-out and empty, and he had a hard knot on the back of his head. Somebody had robbed him. The old man took him to a little shack hidden in the woods by the road and bandaged his noggin. Mentor had looked around the abode—there was not much there but a mat for sleeping, tin dishes, and a battered hat. His Uncle Adam's old burro greeted them both with a snorting bray while the elderly man told him of his great gold-mining adventures in California and how well they had done.

Mentor left not long after and made it home safely. But it would not be long before his uncle began to visit Mentor and his wife, and they, too, would call on him. Every time he came for supper, Delie made Uncle Adam's very favorite meal of gumbo. When Uncle Adam left, he tucked a ten-dollar bill in the Bible outside the kitchen and would not take it back no matter how hard the couple tried to convince him it was unnecessary. They thought his mining stories were made-up. "Aw, I've got plenty. I should probably bury it out by my shack. I got a mockingbird out there, though, that keeps trying to talk me out of it. But nothin' is ever gonna know where it is except the beetles and the worms."

In late December, Mentor read in the newspaper that someone had brutally murdered a gold miner named Adam Quigley for his money along the Shell Road. The killers had nearly severed his head from his neck. His little burro, too, had been killed. There were two men, unidentified, who swore they found Adam Quigley lying there. But by the time they had contacted the police, the corpse had vanished.

They pointed to a mound in the road. When the men found old Quigley, it was a hole. City workers had patched it since.

After came the stories of a ghost near the place Mentor's grand-uncle died. When the police found out it was a man from the asylum playing the haunt, Mentor drew a sigh of relief. He did not want Delie to think the old man was a ghost; she was so fond of him. He still fretted over what happened to Uncle Adam's body. It clung to him like moss to stone. Then the stories of a ghost showing up *again* on Bienville street Shell Road left him no choice but to talk to Delie before she heard it from a tongue-wagging neighbor.

That Sunday, they made plans. They hired a horse and buggy, packed a lunch, a lantern, and a shovel. Then they took off for Bienville street Shell Road. They waited until night, hiding the horse and buggy in the woods, avoiding the carriages of prostitutes with their drunken catches. Then one large black carriage came to a screeching halt, the horse whinnying loudly and shying back. Before it, a white figure wiggled and waggled across the road. The carriage driver whipped the horses hard, so they passed. Mentor and Delie hurried up to see the white form—it had a long beard like Uncle Adam, and it raised a pale finger and pointed to a huge gash in its throat. The stench of death rode the wind, an awful reek of a corpse long left to rot. Mentor lit the lantern and held it aloft. The ghost suddenly vanished into the shells. Then came the cry of a mockingbird in a tree by the side of the road.

Delie knew it was Uncle Adam, and she pointed to the mound in the road where the ghost disappeared. "I know the ghost is Uncle! He has to be buried there!" The two hurried to the mound, Mentor holding the lantern above it, exposing a handful of black beetles scrambling away from the light and into the earth. Worms squirmed away, melting into the shells too.

"The beetles and the worms—" Mentor mumbled. "Uncle Adam told us the beetles and the worms would be the only ones who knew where his money was!"

Mentor snatched up the shovel, and he dug a hole where the hump had been. Just a couple of feet down, he hit a box. In moments, the two had lugged it up, and within were hundreds and hundreds of gold coins. On top was his will carefully signed and witnessed: "I bequeath all my worldly possessions to my grandnephew, Mentor Quigley and his wife, Delie, all that I possess when I die including the mockingbird in the tree if he can be caught, my burro, and the beetles, and the worms."

That night, they dug a little farther and found the body of Uncle Adam. Before morning, they were able to contact the police. They later discovered that the men who had murdered Uncle Adam had also been the men who had witnessed his last will and testament. They had conspired to kill the man, hide his money, then come back and split it six ways. The police apprehended them after Officer Bolonsa hid in the shack two days later and waited for them to return for the money.

Delie and Mentor were able to start their extract company. It grew extremely popular over the years. And what happened to the ghost of old Uncle Adam? It would seem he would find eternal rest as most spirits do when they have gotten a message across and found justice in their death.

It was not so with the gold miner. It appears the old man had a sense of humor because once in a while, the ghost of Adam Quigley returns along the old Bienville street Shell Road, even if it does not have shells anymore. It is just like he did in the old days. He pops out at unwary travelers as a white light forming into a hazy ghost, gyrates about, and disappears behind a tree or a bush or even the top of a roof.

But now, after he scares those walking down the street and sends them running in a frenzy, there is a full and deep-bellied laugh right after.

A section of Bienville street Shell Road in New Orleans today where the story took place, now not so remote as it used to be.

Old Parish Prison
Tremé / Lafitte

Orleans, St Ann, Tremé and Marais streets
29.962760, -90.070242

Red-Headed Ghost of Parish Prison

The Old Parish Prison was bounded by Orleans, St Ann, Tremé and Marais streets, behind what is now the Municipal Auditorium at the present-day Louis Armstrong Park. *Image: Miscellaneous Photographs, Southeastern Architectural Archive, Tulane University Special Collections, Howard-Tilton Memorial Library*

The city built the old Parish Prison from 1831-1836 on Orleans Street between Marais and Tremé. It was in use until 1894 and razed in 1939. The jail was long known to hold ghosts in its grasp—shadows wandering the courtyard, ghastly remnants miming wicked lost souls, clambering like hideously deformed four-legged spiders up the walls.

A story came from a 15-year-old boy who observed one of the hauntings with his own eyes. Both his parents fell sick and died of yellow fever within a few weeks of each other. They were poor and left nothing for the boy—no place to live, no furnishings to sell, and no food. Nearly starving, he stole a loaf of bread from a baker one morning. The fresh, warm bakeshop good never made it to his lips before he was arrested and carted off to the Parish Prison with the murders, thieves, and worse.

From the very first night, the boy could not sleep. He was usually a good boy, not one to lie or steal. Wrestling with his guilt, he tossed and turned. Finally, when the night was at its darkest, he fell into a fitful doze. Yet he was awakened by the puff of cool breath to his bare neck as he lay on his mat. Aroused, he sat up and blinked. He was sure someone had been watching him. He shivered and laid back down. Just as his eyes closed, he felt something cool and hard slip along his scalp like a bony hand with bony fingers caressing his hair. Again, he sat up and felt eyes staring at him. No one was anywhere nearby.

He laid back down, wanting to stay awake, begging his eyes to remain open. Nevertheless, sleep finally washed over him, a deep slumber but one with horrible nightmares. In his dream, the boy was somewhere near the ceiling of the room. He was looking down, and he could see himself sleeping on his back with his hands clasped on his belly in the same way he had fallen to sleep. His eyes were closed, and his lips slightly parted. From the darkness near one corner, a man hobbled across the floor and stopped beside his bed. The boy felt his heart lurch in terror as the man stood over him, hunched over, and eyes bulging grotesquely. He wanted to scream and could see his body twitching and his mouth trying to contort into a screech. But nothing came out.

He could not move. He could only stare at himself as the man leaned closer and closer. The young inmate thought he was human until the man's head rolled abnormally forward and dangled from the neck like a pig swaying from a butcher's hook. He knew it had to be the ghost of one of the inmates the guards had hanged here. The ghost's arms raised, his hands reaching out to the boy's body. The boy lay there unable to move, to run, to scream, and just as the ghost's shadow covered him completely from view, there was a dreadful, loud shriek like one an old woman would make along with a second shadow and a flash of red-gray hair flying from the center of the room. With that, he awakened with a start and was back in his cot, his screams melding into the shadow's cries.

More ghosts appeared that night, and the next couple of days, others cruelly awakened him with every snore he made, every fitful toss and turn on the mungy cot. He was always bound to the ceiling by some unknown force and looking down on his sleeping form. Each time they were about to grab his body in their hands, the screams would peal through the air, shaking him from his deathlike sleep.

He begged the guards to get him another room. He was so terrified after three days, the trembling boy was released. As guards escorted him from his chamber, he looked back to the door of the cell he had slept within. A woman stood there with gray-red frizzed hair sticking about all over her head. Her eyes were wild and wide, and her pale, shriveled lips set to a grimace, white froth dribbling down to her chin in rivulets. "*Thbbbbat,*" she grunted, one arm flying up in a violent wave toward the door, forefinger poking at the doorframe. He was too shocked to say anything. She looked up, and the boy's own wide eyes followed to see NUMBER 17 marking the cell door. He took it in, then let his chin fall to the woman once more. What was she trying to tell him?

"*Thbbbbat*," she mumbled once more. She pivoted on her feet and, with high-knee marching steps, worked her way to the center of the cell. Something wrenched her arms awkwardly behind her. Her head flopped behind as if she was readying to keel backward. The old woman's body glided five feet upward, and she dangled there, her head tipped to one side, hanging from an unseen noose above. "*Thbbbbat*," she gasped one more time, then vanished.

Cell 17. It was called The Haunted Cell. It was well known that an old red-headed woman was confined within that very chamber many years earlier and committed suicide. Everyone who stayed in that cell would awaken to her shrieks and yells. Those who did not heed them would be found the next morning dead. The prison authorities attributed the deaths to suicide. Nobody was ever able to decipher what her muffled words meant.

The Old Tremé Street Bridge Over the Canal
Tremé / Lafitte

Lafitte Greenway Trail
New Orleans, LA 70112
29.961376, -90.070854

A Ghost at the Old Basin Canal

Old Basin, where a ghost rose from the deep. *Image: Library of Congress*

In mid-April of 1874, a ghost began to show at the Old Basin near the Tremé Street Bridge as the bell struck twelve, and its last dying echo began to fade. Up from the dark and dismal water of the canal, a beautiful young woman would rise. Some nights, she would wear a soft white gown and stand still and pure with a sweet smile barely parting her lips and a flag clasped to her breast.

Her long hair, twined with dried flowers, would blow lightly in the wind. Hither and thither, to and fro, she paced silently with sweet longing on her face. Other nights, though, she would burp forth from the canal wearing a black mourning dress dripping with green slime and a large worm wiggling from a gaping hole in her neck. In her hands, she held a drab, flickering candle. Each of her eyes glowed a tiny but brilliant green fire. While she drew the flame aloft, it would expose the same girl, but one whose life had taken a bleaker path of sin. Her face was haggard, and her eyes darkened with resentment and shame. Her frizzy hair had little creatures like beetles and water bugs and maggots wiggling within. She contorted her lips in a dreadful frown, exposing toothless gums and a bloody, drooling ooze. For only moments, she would linger there as her hands worked upward as if pleading toward the heavens while her expression changed to agony and defeat. Hither and thither, to and fro, she would walk back and forth. Just as she sank back down into the waters, her breast would heave up and down in convulsive, silent sobs.

People thronged to the bridge to see the event. They were not disappointed. Some speculated that the apparitions were two separate spirits—one a pure virgin arriving to give a grand revelation and the other, a scorned woman of some brothel who had committed suicide there.

Toward the end of the month, a crowd had gathered expecting to see one ghost or the other—but which would it be? Neither! At midnight on April 26th, as the last bell tolled, a woman in white slithered up from The Basin, and in her arms, she closely-held a tiny baby. She looked gaunt and worn with hair pulled back tightly to her head. The chubby worm had come from her neck and now slithered inside one of the baby's ears and came out the other side. There was green fungus on her shoulders, her dress, and on her face.

The vile reek of death surrounding her sent most covering their noses with a wrist before she sank straight down and disappeared.

The Old Basin. *Image 1910: Library of Congress.*

Everyone offered up ideas about who the ghost had been in life. But only one man knew the truth, although he only admitted it when he was eighty-five years old and knew he would not live much longer. "I saw the ghost when I was twenty-five in 1874," he declared. "I knew she was a real ghost because I knew the girl. Her name was Helen Rockworth, and her family was acquaintances of my family. She was beautiful with golden ringlets of hair, brown eyes, and puffy lips and engaged to Jerome Gail. He went to war in 1861 and came home four years later. There was talk that she had some scandal, saw a few men while he was away. Jerome married another, and Helen ended up as a prostitute working the streets." He paused, sighing before going on.

"Sometime in April of 1870, Jerome was passing along Old Levee Street, and out comes Helen from one of the filthiest and wildest bars. She was drunk and carrying a baby, and when she happed upon Jerome, she began tossing her fist and yowling at him that because he jilted her, she had turned out like this. Helen had reached out towards his chest like she was going to push him. Instead, her fingers softly alit on his coat. Her palm lingered there for just a moment as if something were still alive in her. It was just a touch, but he had recoiled. She saw his face all twisted in a grimace. That night, she drowned herself in the Old Basin. Her family never claimed her body, and the city buried her in the Potter's Cemetery."

Life would go on for Jerome, but his wife could not have children and became very depressed. They decided to adopt and found a little girl in the orphan asylum that seemed perfect. As the little girl grew, Jerome became greatly attached to her. But there was something about the child that seemed so familiar in her golden ringlets of hair, brown eyes, and puffy lips. Curious, he went to the Orphan Asylum and asked about the little girl. He was dumbfounded to find out it was Helen Rockworth's baby. It was not long after that the little girl fell from an open window at their home. Jerome had so fallen in love with her, he walked to the Old Basin and drowned himself in the dark waters.

"That was in the middle of April of 1874," the old man continued. "It was right about when the ghost showed up in the form of the pure and young Helen that Jerome had known before the war. Then she came as the woman scorned and, lastly, as what she had become—in the end." The old man had said little more as his voice cracked while the tears welled in his eyes. He waved a hand as if he wished to never speak of it again. Then he sighed deeply, muttering something about the ghost stopping after a few more weeks.

He hoped it was because she reunited with Jerome, and the baby had been the connection that brought them together. But only time would tell if she would show up again—

The Old Basin is now gone. I walked the Lafitte Greenway Trail to the Basin Parking lots near the Old Basin. Or you can check out the Basin Street Station (501 Basin St, New Orleans, LA 70112 (29.959880, -90.070725), which is right there and offers tourist information.

Congo Square
Tremé /Lafitte

701 N Rampart Street
New Orleans, LA 70116
29.961340, -90.068679

Congo Square and the Tale of the Haunted Tree

Congo Square—within Armstrong Park.

In the early 1700s, the Compagnie des Indes, Company of the Indies, held France's colonial trade monopoly. France's Louisiana Colony, adjoining the Gulf Coast, had expanded with population increases, and French settlements popped up in places like Natchez, Missouri, and New Orleans. The agriculture industry of tobacco and indigo and later cotton and sugar thrived. In 1718, La Nouvelle-Orleans would be founded on the Mississippi River banks by Jean Baptiste Le Moyne de Bienville.

Then around 1721 and with the collapse of the Company of the Indies, planters in the region were struggling to feed and clothe their slaves. To survive, they set aside patches of land unsuitable for their crops and assigned their enslaved Africans to plant gardens so they could become self-sustaining. Even though the land was of poor quality, the Africans could maintain food sources both there and collect them from the wildlands around the places they lived. For some, it was enough that they could sell and trade their surplus on a few streets and along certain parts of the riverfront on Sundays. The Code Noir (The Black Code), a policy for monitoring slavery, forbade slaveholders to force the enslaved to work from midnight to the following midnight on Sundays and religious holidays.

Dance in Congo Square—*Image: E. W. Kemble*

It was a day to do what they pleased, and authorities made no laws to stop the slaves and freed blacks from congregating in certain areas. Although there were restrictions on the places they could meet, one abandoned commonplace on the outskirts of town became quite popular—"Circus Square" or Congo Place, named for a small circus with gymnasts, a trick horse, and performing dogs settled there.

It was here at the city's very fringes on a bit of unwanted land where earthen fortifications kept out the unwanted Indians and pirates, both enslaved Africans and freed persons of color could sing and dance and hold spiritual ceremonies from their own culture. Music and dances like the Bamboula, Calinda, and the Congo would spring up from these gatherings, eventually paving the path for New Orleans' own unique jazz and rhythm and blues.

Marching brass band at Congo Square. *Image: SydQuackArt*

Curious people of the city would come to watch with a sense of fascination and trepidation at the display of faith that was so unrestricted and diverse than their own rigid religion. From these visits, stories arose of a haunted Sycamore tree settled there with a scarred and hollowed trunk. Legends declared that when it rained on moonlit nights, the ghosts of Vodou queens of the past would appear. They would emerge from the darkened storm clouds and fall with the droplets of rain to the tree. And they would dance around the Sycamore in the moonshine until dawn.

Marigny/Bywater

Marigny/Bywater District

House of the Sirens
2606 Royal Street
New Orleans, LA 70117
29.964742, -90.051209

Madame Mineurecanal and Her Little Terrier

There is a cozy two and a half story townhouse just outside the French Quarter in the neighborhood of Faubourg Marigny. It is privately owned, and it has been through many tenants. In the mid-1900s, no one would buy the home, so the owners rented the structure to tenants.

The renters did not stay long, complaining of hearing moaning in the upstairs and high-pitched yaps of a terrier.

After a while, the Ruez family took over the home. They were a large, extended family, including grandparents, aunts, uncles, cousins, and children. All the neighbors were curious to know what was keeping them there because surely, they had seen the spirit. And they had—a ghostly woman displayed herself usually wearing a white dress and stepping from the attic. Her neck was cockeyed with the most gruesome and unnatural tilt to one side, and her hideously large and blue tongue protruded from her lips as if someone had thrust a decayed dead fish in her mouth.

One night, while Grandma Ruez was sleeping in her bed on the second-floor landing, she was awakened by the sound of one of the family member's baby whimpering just down the hallway. She arose and padded down to the room, stopping in the doorway to peer within. By then, the baby's sobs had turned to wails. Seeing a silhouette hovering over the bed, but the baby still crying, she waited a moment and wondered why the mother was just standing there and had not picked up the screaming child. "Rita," she started to call out the baby's mother's name, but the shadow did not move. Grandma Ruez made a loud stomp with her foot to catch the mother's attention, but Rita still did not move. "Rita!" A moment passed when she heard a voice coming from the room to her left, which was the baby's parent's bed-chamber. Rita's sleepy voice echoed from within *that* room and not from the area of the crib at all! Rita stepped up beside Grandma Ruez and looked at her before following the stunned gaze back to the crib. The form of the woman was walking past the baby and into the wall on the other side!

A neighbor explained the ghost as this—In the early 1900s, a Creole woman named Madame Mineurecanal lived a solitary life with her beloved little terrier in this dwelling.

Her neighbors knew little about the woman other than her husband had died fighting in the Spanish-American War in 1898. She had a son, but he had not visited his mother for some time.

One day, for perhaps those very reasons, she took the steps to the third-floor attic, strangled her terrier to death, then hanged herself by tying a rope around a thick ceiling beam and then her neck and stepping off a chair. After, people living nearby would see Madame Mineurecanal walking her dog along the street. Sometimes the dead woman looked into the windows at the tenants, which spooked them greatly. And one time, when a little boy was making fun of her name, taunting *Mini-Canal* over and over, he was awakened abruptly in the middle of the night with a red cheek from a ghostly slap!

Mid-City

Slattery House
Mid-City

The Old Mortuary and nearby Gates of Prayer
4800 Canal Street
New Orleans, LA 70119
29.979299, -90.108051

Dead Man in a Top Hat

Mausoleum beside Gates of Prayer Cemetery.

There is a well-dressed man in a top hat wandering the Gates of Prayer Cemetery and Hope Mausoleum next to an old mortuary. He is very protective of the tombs there, lashing out when someone disrespects the graveyard. Some believe he has ties to the building next door. Originally, Mary and John Slattery built a mansion along Canal Road in 1872. They would live there until selling the home in 1905.

It would pass through hands before becoming a funeral home in 1928 for nearly eighty years, skillfully run by PJ McMahon and Sons, who had such grand amenities as an embalming room, crematorium, cooled storage for the dead, and an autopsy room. There were also rooms on the above floors for grieving families. Many passed through the doors, both dead and alive. *Where* the man came from who haunts the nearby yards of the dead, we may never know.

Lower Garden

Griffin House
Lower Garden District

1447 Constance Street
New Orleans, Louisiana 70130
29.934983, -90.071180

Yankee Soldiers Who Just Won't Rest

An old ghost story leads back to a building on Constance Street. However, the exact location and description conflict. The Griffon House, built in 1852 by Adam Griffin at 1447 Constance, is a popular site for the story—taken from the book Gumbo Ya-ya.

In the 1930s, there was a lamp factory in an old mansion on Constance Street. The building was two-stories with a spacious display room on the second floor. In December of 1936, the business owner, 38-year-old Isadore Seelig, ordered factory workers to stay late at night as many customers did not get off work until just about suppertime.

It was the Christmas season, and orders were getting backed up. When the time came for closing, a young man named Calvin was cleaning up the showrooms on the second floor, restocking, and shuffling displaced items back to where they belonged. He swept the floor and readied himself to turn out the lights, his fingers tickling the string that flipped the switch. Something moved in a dark corner at the back of the room. His belly jumped, and he hesitated, frozen in terror, turning his head to squint past the well-lit room and to the darkness beyond. He observed a pair of shiny black boots walking toward him, their soles clacking and clattering on the wood floor. Then a second pair of boots fell in behind. But there were no legs or body to hold them! While he held his breath in fear, his legs wobbled like Jell-O, and eerie chuckles split the air along with the sound of a man singing, "Mine eyes have seen the glory of the coming of the Lord—" Calvin did not wait to hear the rest of the song. The young man tore out of the room, screaming.

No amount of wage increase could get him to return to the haunted place. But Isadore Seelig, himself, could hardly blame the young man. Although he seldom talked of it, when unpacking materials one early morning with his brother, a massive concrete block was flung at the two men from the stairway, barely missing them both. It had shaken them deeply.

Everyone knew there was a haunting in the building. Often, people walking the neighborhood had seen two Yankee soldiers peering out the windows. Neighbors said that an old widow had moved into the building some years earlier, making ends meet as a seamstress. While sewing downstairs one evening, she felt something warm and sticky dribble on her wrist. She looked down and blinked at three tiny red droplets. It was blood. She followed the path of the *drip-drip-drip*, and her eyes stopped at the ceiling.

Nothing was leaking from above. Unable to find the source, even after lugging out a ladder and carefully examining the ceiling, she sighed and assumed she must have pricked herself with a needle and the puncture was too tiny to detect.

She sat back down and continued her sewing. This time, she listened to someone singing in the street. "Mine eyes have seen the glory of the coming of the Lord; He is trampling out the vintage where the grapes of wrath are stored; He has loosed the fateful lightning of His terrible swift sword; His truth is marching on." Louder and louder, the singing blared in the room, and she realized whoever was singing was not outside at all. It was right above her on the second floor! And then came the *drip-drip-drip* of blood on her arm that dribbled to the apron she wore. The woman took in a breath and screamed, running from the room, down the steps, and into the street.

Family members had to come and pack her bags as she refused to go back inside. At first, her relatives shook their heads in disbelief. Then as they locked the door behind them, their eyes shifted to windows upstairs, and before them, they watched as two soldiers in blue Yankee uniforms peered down at them.

A local New Orleans patrolman, William Fleming, recalled exploring the home when he was young. There were three boys, along with a couple of dogs. The walls and doors were still in place, but the upper floor was nearly gone, so the boys walked the beams like a tightrope. Suddenly, a door swung open by unseen hands, and a chilly breeze flowed into the room. One frightened dog jumped and fell to its death to the first floor. The other howled and carried on before he finally ran away. Behind them, the boys all heard singing. They took flight themselves, not looking back as they fled into the street.

The story of the restless soldiers can be traced back to the Civil War. When the Union army occupied New Orleans, Captain Hugh Devers, and Quartermaster Charles Cromley, by General Benjamin Butler's orders, settled themselves into the mansion on Constance Street. They sent for their wives in Boston, who came quite swiftly and unpacked their chests and hired servants to tend to them. They settled in well for some time until money came to pay the Yankee bills in New Orleans. Cromley and Devers, seduced by the amount of cash stored in the building, began to devise a scheme to divide it among themselves and make it appear stolen. Of course, they could not tell their wives.

However, the general had placed a spy within the home for several days to guard the money. He overheard the men talking and reported the plot to his commanding officer. It was not long before word had spread that the general knew of the ploy, and it came to the thieving men's ears. The men knew the authorities were going to arrest them. Instead of facing their families with the truth and understanding that the army would imprison them, they sent their wives ahead of them to a party at a colonel's house they were supposed to attend that evening. They also sent the servants home. Then Cromley and Devers went to the upstairs room.

Both men peered out the windows making sure no one was around the home. They bolted the door behind them and took the long steps to the bed with their boots clacking and clattering loudly on the floor. The men lay down on the bed and lifted their revolvers to their heads. Then they began to sing, "Mine eyes have seen the glory of the coming of the Lord; He is trampling out the vintage where the grapes of wrath are stored; He has loosed the fateful lightning of His terrible swift sword; His truth is marching on."

Both shots came at nearly the exact moment. The blood from their skulls crushed by the bullets flowed over the side of the bed. It dribbled down to the floor and the rooms below—*drip-drip-drip*.

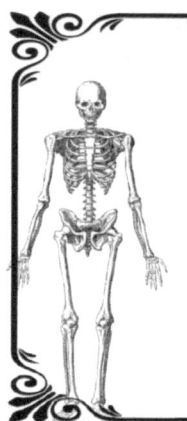

St Vincent's Infant Asylum
Lower Garden District

Saint Vincent's Guest House
1507 Magazine Street
New Orleans, LA 70130
29.934365, -90.072781

Giggles

St Vincent's Infant Asylum

About a mile and a half from downtown New Orleans on Magazine Street, there is an aged, massive brick building complex with ornately constructed iron galleries on its exterior. Within, there are bedrooms after bedrooms. In the 1990s, Peter Schreiber and Sally Leonard purchased the dilapidated building, renovating it as a guest house, calling it St Vincent's Guest House.

A hallway where children's voices are heard.

A picture was on the wall displaying children who had stayed at St Vincent's Infant Asylum

After lodgers began to stay in the rooms, some would see ghostly children roaming around the hallways, hear the sound of giggles and soft chatter. An easy explanation of the ghosts is that the building was once an orphan asylum and home for unwed mothers. In the 1800s, yellow fever epidemics killed many in the city, leaving children orphaned. St Vincent's Infant Asylum was built and run by the Daughters of Charity, an order of nuns to house those little ones in need. It served the city until the 1970s.

Lower Garden District

Josephine and Rousseau Streets
New Orleans, LA 70130
29.925308, -90.071531

Headless Woman in a Drab Gingham Dress

Along Josephine Street—not far from where this story begins and ends with a headless ghost. *Image: Library of Congress.*

Around 1847, there was a family consisting of a husband, wife, and two children living in a two-story home on the corner of Josephine and Rousseau streets. If the wife was pleased with the house, her husband did not notice. He did note with a sour and disapproving frown, however, the fancy lace curtains with delicate and pretty pink bows that she carefully sewed and placed in every window one afternoon. The smirk was so dark that she had drawn back. Still, she did not remove the curtains or the lace or the bows.

The wife, whose name was Alice Vesey, always appeared tired and worn. Her face wrinkled at only age twenty-seven, and her hair had started to gray. Her once bright blue eyes were dim and gray. "We certainly cannot afford to hire servants to help you, but you are starting to age and not very gracefully," her husband Charles told her. "In the morning, I will place an advertisement for a domestic to cook and clean."

She had taken the shabby words he hurled at her matter-of-factly and shook her head. "I don't need help. I am perfectly capable of keeping the house," she replied blandly. Alice knew if she did not cook and clean and sew and care for the children, she would remember the past, and she certainly did not want to do that. Staying busy pushed away the memories of her younger days so she could put aside her youth. "I must not ever remember my past," she told herself because Alice had a secret from her younger years, and his name was Jeminy Crews.

Jeminy was a dreamer. He sometimes studied to be an artist, and sometimes he took classes to become a doctor, and other times, he was determined to study theology. But none of his efforts lasted too long, and Jeminy always ended up living in a room at his parent's house. There, he would joyfully paint beautiful works of colorful art for his beloved and write Alice boundless sheets of poetry and rhymes. His inability to make a living did not stop Alice from falling hopelessly in love with the boy, and he dearly cherished her in return, but he also loved his gin. Of course, her parents did not approve of the boy. Alice worried how they would survive if they married and he could not keep a job.

When it finally came time, Alice drew Jeminy aside and broke the news that she would not marry him. "You are probably wise in your decision," he sighed. He believed it. "But we could have written beautiful sonnets, you and I."

It was not long before Alice caught the eyes of Charles Vesey, and the two married. She was about twenty-years-old. Jeminy soaked himself in gin. He stopped painting vibrant works of art, and his landscapes looked more like gray, desolate deserts. He covered his canvases with strange headless women and splotches of wicked, bloody creatures. He wrote no more of his eloquent verses.

Then one afternoon, Alice ran into Jeminy at the busy market with her two children in tow. She was picking out bread, and the grocer of the shop was wrapping it in paper. The two old lovers' eyes met for just a moment; then, his gaze dropped as if to take her in before he turned away.

"Do you know him?" The grocer asked. But before Alice could answer, the man shoved the bread at her and said, "He is quite famous for his paintings, as strange as they are all dark and twisted. He has his studio in France." Alice blanched. She thought of her drab gingham dress with the gray lace collar and the tawdry apron she wore from dawn to dusk and her wrinkled skin, her untidy hair. Although his face was serious, she could tell he had quit drinking many years earlier. He was tall and handsome and wearing fine clothing. She was wearing a frumpy dress, and her hair was unkempt. She had replaced the nice French heels she once wore with flat, ugly pumps.

Alice ran home and looked at herself in the mirror. How had he seen her? She knew because the woman staring back at her was now an old and worn woman. Desperately, Alice wanted to bring back those years. She threw open an old chest of clothing of her youth—a sleek dress and pale slippers and pretty, ear baubles and jewelry. Alice dressed up, then went back to the mirror. She sobbed into her hands; it made no difference; she was still old and shabby beneath the dress. In a burst of shame, she threw the clothing back into the chest.

Yet, she wanted to be the girl who used to write poems with Jeminy. On a whim, she set up a small table and chair in a room on the top floor and began to write again when her husband was gone to work. Perhaps they were not sweet poems of her youth; they tended to be outbursts of rage and anger and sometimes hurt and anguish of the woman she had become. Then one day, she put pen to paper and wrote a most delicious letter of love, pouring out her heart to Jeminy with compelling tales of what they could have become. But she was unknowing that her husband had found out about her little hideaway and her strange thoughts to paper. He was standing in the shadows that day and read what she had written to her old lover.

It was two decades passing when another family moved into the home in 1867. One of the servants named Wilhelmina climbed the steps to the attic to clean. A woman dressed in drab gingham and tan pumps appeared before her, fingers frantically writing on paper like she wanted to divulge something to the girl. But as the girl stared at her, she saw no head above the gray lace collar! The headless woman took one step forward, and the servant screamed, running down the stairs. Wilhelmina wondered for weeks why the woman had come to her. Everyone had an opinion, but no one knew for sure. A year later, Wilhelmina died.

Time would pass, and every twenty years, the ghost would appear to a young woman. Not long after, each would die from some sickness or an accident. A grocer had seduced one, and she later died in childbirth. Although some would surmise it was the ghostly presence causing the deaths, others believed that the headless spirit was warning them of their impending death to come soon after. Neither was the truth. The day that Charles Vesey came from the shadows and read the sordid love letter Alice wrote to Jeminy, in a furious jealous rage, he snatched a dull axe by the fireplace.

He beat her head until it was nothing but pasty pink and pulpy remnants of brain, teeny pieces of skull, and red, red blood puddling on the floor. She was not trying to divulge who killed her; her husband had dragged her body to the stairway and tossed her down the steps. He told the police she died while falling down the stairs. But they did not believe him, so he was arrested and charged, and he ended up dying in jail.

Instead, she was trying to warn them of the wake of death that comes with love. Her message was not to save them because she had not been saved. Instead, the sadness, loss, and anger she lived out her life followed her to the grave. But Alice came back without a head because there was little left but what they could scrape off the floor with a shovel before her body was set in a casket. Without a head, she could never fully express herself in the same way that she could not write beautiful poems anymore after she left her lover.

In the 1920s, the house burned to the ground. Those who watched the blaze swore they saw a woman in a drab gingham dress with a gray lace collar standing in the middle of the flames, desperately writing something before she disappeared with the smoke.

Irish Channel

Seaman's Bethel on St Thomas
Irish Channel

2218 St Thomas Street
New Orleans, LA 70130
29.925196, -90.073599

Lost Boys

Seaman's Bethel once catered to the sailors.

A church on Saint Thomas Street was once the Seaman's Bethel. It was a place of worship catering to the many seamen coming to New Orleans on merchant ships. The building also provided a place to stay, with the notion the men using it would avoid the areas of ill-repute many sailors visited, squandering their money in brothels and taverns.

During this time, sailors staying in the building began to see and hear peculiar things—two hazy forms climbing the stairway before each went from room to room as if searching for something or someone. Those within the chambers were roused from sleep by the creaking of iron hinges as the door opened wide. Then the tapping sound of booted footsteps crossed the wooden floor—*tap-tap, tap-tap*, and would stop at the end of the bed as if pondering who was lying there. While the quivering sailor tugged the sheets to his chin, the mist would twist and turn, bend and weave in a strange, macabre dance above him. Unusual mewls and cries like a hungry kitten searching for its mother's teat slipped from somewhere within them. For those unlucky enough, there was a tugging of bedlinens, the sheets and blankets pulled while the ghostly forms begged for a closer glimpse of who lay there. Staring down at the frightened seaman only a fingers-width from his face were two gruesome, pale heads with mouths opened wide in an eternal black gape, and dark eye sockets nothing but hollows. They appeared to be searching for someone they could never find. But what or whom, no one knew.

These ghostly visitations occurred for a long time. One day, a seaman tired of being awakened as the vague forms hovered over his bed, making their little mewling cries, and staring at him with dead eyes. "What is it that you search for?" he demanded as he rested upon his mat. "Answer or begone with you!"

"Mother, mother!" the voice cried. "Where is my mother? I have brought Julian back to Mother! Mother, are you there?" The seaman, surprised he received an answer, propped himself up on an elbow. Before him, he could make out a young man in oilskins dripping with water smelling of the sea. To his side, there was a tiny boy with seaweed for clothing. The man blinked, and the two vanished.

Quite the braggart, the seaman who had seen the ghosts awakened the other men. He told them they had been cowards. He was brave enough to confront the ghosts, and they spoke to him. Strangely, though, within a day, the seaman who called out to the spirits the night before choked to death. He was staring with wide, terrified eyes into the air as if witnessing something behind them the others in the room could not see. Among them was a seaman who made it his work to find out about the building's ghosts. Asking around the neighborhood, he found that during the 1840s, the house belonged to the Weaver family. There were five children, with the youngest boy named Julian. Julian was a sweet and pretty boy who rarely knew a stranger. He would chat with anyone passing along the street and entertain guests who entered the home with his silly antics. The little boy was quite fond of his mother, more so even than his beloved papa, who Julian would greet by bursting through the doors with kisses when papa was returning from work. He always saved a few last and special kisses just for mama too. She pampered the boy greatly in return. He rarely left her side. Except once when Julian was about four-years-old, and a stranger kidnapped him. The family searched frantically and endlessly for the boy, but they never found him. The mother grieved so for her little boy. She often cried and walked the streets searching for his little face and visited the docks staring out at sea for any ships that might hold him. And she seldom smiled. She felt cheated and closed her heart so she would not be hurt again.

Years passed and the eldest son named Edward went to sea on the Steven Gaunt. It wrecked and there was only one survivor. This lone survivor, a sailor, ended up making his home in New Orleans. He told the story of a boy named Edward Weaver who, upon becoming a seaman, had found his little brother who had been spirited away as a child.

The two became inseparable while they awaited the ship to return to New Orleans and a reunion with the family. They would talk all day and night about how they would approach their mother with this wonderful news, surprising her with the story of crossing paths. They would give her gifts and kisses and hugs and make her smile again.

Yet, they would not return in human form as they met a watery grave, their bodies left to rot in the ocean and flesh nibbled by turtles and fish. Only as misty ghosts could they come to their home and visit her. And they did. "Mother, mother!" the voice said. "Where is my mother? I have brought Julian back to Mother! Mother, are you there?" But their mother had turned a cold gaze to not only the family but also to God. When they rushed up the steps, opened the doors to every room to find her, then skittered across the wood floor to the beds to see if she lay within, she did not see their spirits. Try as they might, her eyes were cold and dead to them, and she saw nothing but the air.

They still waited for her to come around. At times, the boys would crouch on the rooftop with their skinny arms and legs covered in a green sea slime and their hair a moldy olive. Their once boyish faces had chunks eaten off them from settling on the bottom of the ocean so long and being eaten by crabs and fish. Sometimes, the two would squat by the front door with elbows on knees and the stench of rotten seaweed and the stagnant scent of a shallow puddle of seawater. Those walking past the house would see them and run away, shrieking. The whispers got so bad, the Weavers moved away and did not return. The home was made into the Seaman's Bethel because nobody else would buy it. Startled passersby can sometimes see Julian and Edward's ghosts perched on the roof or crouched in front of the house, always searching for their mother.

Central City

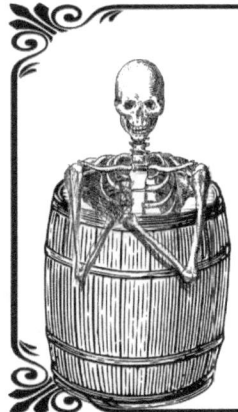

Central Business District— Downtown

**100 Block of Chartres Street
New Orleans, LA 70130
29.952850, -90.068022**

Misfortune in a Keg of Rum

Chartres Street in early 1900s. *Image: Library of Congress.*

French-made canopies for hanging curtains above the bed, *Ciel-de-lits*, were all the rage in the mid-1800s, especially extravagant ones. Monsieur Dufau owned a shop on Rue Chartres with art and paintings. He also specialized in these Ciel-de-lits for brides, ornate ones with pale blue silks, satin, and decorations like chubby dancing cherubs for the wealthy, and those of calico and satin for those not-so-wealthy. But for all, he used the finest materials available.

He was renowned locally for his exquisite designs that embodied eternal love and the sweetest of dreams for newlyweds. Well, that is, until he ran into a bit of misfortune. He had a following of wealthy, upstanding men in the community, Le Comité des Bon Amis, who took turns having parties in their homes. When it was Dufau's time to entertain, he was lucky to have a sailor flag him down near the docks and offer a keg of rum at an incredibly low cost. Of course, he purchased the rum and invited his friends to his home. But as he passed around the drinks from the keg, everyone's mouths pursed at the curious taste. It was unlike anything they had ever swigged before. It was so incredibly horrible; they brought out an axe and popped open the lid. Curiously, they peered inside and found themselves staring at an old man with whiskers, and he was perfectly pickled!

The authorities cleared Monsieur Dufau of any criminal connection to the preserved man. However, the poor shopkeeper was kicked out of his club and did not receive any more orders for the Ciel-de-lits. And he never bought a keg of rum from a sailor again!

100 Block of Chartres Street today.

Central City

Fourth Street
New Orleans, LA 70130

Fourth Street Ghost

Fourth Street homes. *Courtesy: Library of Congress.*

Two elderly women moved into a house on Fourth Street, and the ghostlike creatures there were unbearable. The kitchen door would creak open at night, and misty human-like forms would crawl inside on hands and knees. Their hair was covered in matted blood, and one even tore off his leg and threw it at one woman. They broke plates, smeared the parlor sofa with filth, and vomited in their shoes. The horrible creatures tore things apart so badly that the women had to leave. Later, the owner pulled out the wooden floor and found skeletons beneath. Once the remains were properly buried, they did not return.

The Devil's Mansion
Central City

Site where Maison Saint Charles Now Stands
1319 St Charles Avenue
New Orleans, LA 70130
29.940284, -90.075117

The Devil's Mistress

At one time, the Devil had a mansion on St Charles Avenue along with a mistress. *Image: Fourteen depictions with devils, Charles Ramelet, 1833- Le Charivari 2 (1833). The series "Petites macédoines d'Aubert"*

The Devil had a stately mansion erected on St Charles Avenue in the 1820s for his beautiful, coquettish French mistress. Her name was Madeleine Freneau. There is not a single record of the home, and if you had asked anyone when he built it, they would have given it a little thought and mumbled something like, "It just seemed to appear overnight like a mushroom after a rain."

Others would reflect that it had taken six days. It should have been seven, but as the Devil could not work on Sunday, he had to finish too quickly and bungled the floors from one room to the next, so throughout the house, there were too many uneven stairways, short and tall. No matter, the elegant furnishings, and carpets were a sight to behold and made up for any inconsistencies in the building itself. On the outside, the Devil barred the windows on the bottom floor with wrought iron rods. He furnished it with tiny demons who made sure it was spotless all the time.

A busy St Charles Avenue where the Devil roamed—*Image: Library of Congress.*

He made sure Madeleine Freneau always dressed in the finest silks and velvets, with priceless jewels adorning her neck and slender wrists. He was away most of the week attending business and came and went whenever he pleased. When he did return, instead of coming through a door in the front of the house, he entered through the front gable high on the roof, where he had a secret balcony built.

Image: Eleven depictions with devils, Charles Ramelet, 1833.

Here, he would linger and peruse the streets and homes and sidewalks beneath him. Those who dared to pass the house at dusk could see him standing there with moonlight shimmering on his horns and leaving a dark shadow on the wall behind him. If they squinted hard enough, they could make out his puffy lips twisting and contorting with an evil sneer and his tiny eyes glowing red-orange and wicked in the dark.

Soon his mistress became bored being alone all week. It was not difficult with her raging beauty to find a lover in a handsome Creole man in the city. His name was Alcide Cancienne. The neighbors gossiped about the two coming and going all hours of the day and night until one day, they disappeared altogether, and the house stayed empty and abandoned. Most believed the two had run off.

After a few years, another family resided in the home. Then they moved out within a month. A couple with two children bought the house, and they left quite quickly too. Tenant after tenant refused to stay long at the mansion. The last finally demolished the building. It seems because it had ghosts.

Every evening at dusk, as the families readied to eat their supper, they would enter the dining room, and the table they were preparing to use was suddenly laden with silver trays and China plates and golden goblets. Many ghostly servants set two places on either side of the table along with a feast for a huge celebration. Above, a crystal chandelier would materialize on the high-peaked ceiling. Then, a man and woman entered the room in a ghostly procession and sat down at two exquisitely carved wooden chairs as if to eat. The unseen hands served the meal to them. Suddenly, the woman would rise, and her face would contort into a hateful sneer. She would strut across to the man and strangle him with a napkin in her hand. She would look to her hands drenched in blood that she could not wipe away no matter how hard she tried. Then the ghost woman would begin to howl and wail before both vanished from sight.

Tradition tells that one night, Satan had returned and perched himself upon the gable. He watched with piercing eyes his mistress's lover work his way up the sidewalk then open the gate to the lawn. Alicde Cancienne stepped to the front door of the mansion, opened the latch, and disappeared inside. Each night, the two would dine with plates piled high with the finest foods from the best chefs and desserts of sugared sweet treats from the greatest bakeries. The wine flew freely, and Madeleine Freneau told silly jokes which her lover would always guffaw like they were the best jokes he had ever heard, and they laughed and chattered for hours. But not so one night. Alcide was moody and grim. Her jokes were not so funny as he would not laugh.

"What is wrong, my love?" she purred to him. She prayed he had not found out she was the Devil's whore. But he would not answer at first, and it took some time for her to coerce it out of him.

"Two nights ago, when I left, a man was leaning on the post along the street. He was quite tall and handsome with piercing eyes," Alcide told her. "He told me he was a stranger to the city and asked if I knew Madeleine Freneau. I was taken aback, but I told him I did know you. Do you know this man?"

"No," she lied.

"Well," Alcide mumbled, something stirring in his eyes. "He made this strange laugh and asked if I was in love with you. He offered me a million pounds of gold, and we could leave. The only condition was that we must be known as Monsieur L and Madame L." The Devil's mistress felt the blood run from her face. She knew what the "L" meant. It was Lucifer.

"But what did you say to him, my love?" she asked with bated breath. Then she looked at the door. "Let us leave—"

But Alcide chuckled blandly. "I told him of our affair, how sweet your taste, and how soft your skin was to my fingers. I also told him the truth that I did not love you." Madeleine Freneau gasped. She ran across to Alcide, scratching and clawing him, then strangling him with her napkin, looking down to see his blood on her hands. She wailed and howled her high pitched screams into the air.

Later that night, the Devil came to his perch on the gable then slithered into the house. He snatched up Madelaine in one hand and Alcide in the other, dragging them up to the secret balcony on the roof. There, he sucked the insides out of the man, letting Madelaine listen to the gruesome crunch of bone and the sipping sound of blood and visceral sifted through his teeth, leaving nothing but the skin which he tossed with a sickening thud to the lawn. Madelaine was too frightened to scream when the Devil did the same to her. He threw her skin to the ground beside her lover's pale hide and watched animals of the night fight over the meal.

The cats, with their sharp claws, were especially fond of the meat around the noses and mouths. When they had finished, there was little more than gummy clumps of bloody hair. But something strange came of it. For a long time, people staring up at the gable would see a devilish face. It was the Devil himself. In his jealousy, he had forgotten not to work on a full moon and was punished for his foolishness. His head was fixed to the roof with the sticky flesh of the two lovers.

An inn sits on the spot where the Devil once had a residence.

Uptown/Carrollton

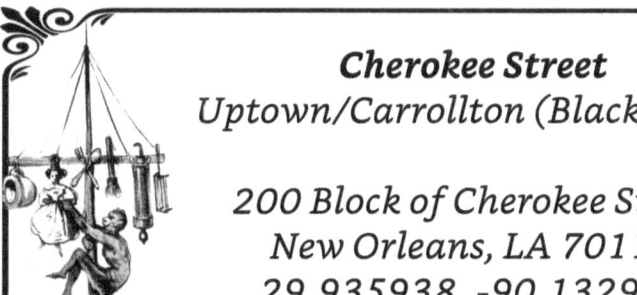

Cherokee Street
Uptown/Carrollton (Black Pearl)

200 Block of Cherokee Street
New Orleans, LA 70118
29.935938, -90.132976

Flying Bricks of Cherokee Street

The 200 block of Cherokee Street where ghostly shenanigans played out in the 1800s.

In the 1800s, a family lived in a small house along a quiet street called Cherokee. One day, a volley of bricks, stones, and wood hailed down in the backyard. The owners ran outside to locate the hooligans who could have caused such a raucous, and sure it must be naughty neighborhood boys or someone holding a grudge who wanted to even up the score on some wrongdoing. However, no one was around, and the adjacent yards were empty.

It did not happen just once, but many times. After a while, it became too dangerous for the family to venture into the backyard for fear of getting hit by a stone or wood or even a piece of iron flying at them. For days, neighbors and police tried to help the family find the cause of the hurled objects, but there seemed to be no source from where they came, and they appeared to come from unseen hands.

But the old-timers knew the origin of the flying bricks and stones and wood. Many years before, an ill-tempered old man named Abner White lived in the house next to where the troubled family lived. He was irritable, unfriendly, and detested little boys and girls, always complaining that the children playing on the street would call him names and throw stones at his windows.

One day while Abner was walking along the sidewalk near his home, he came upon three little girls. As he passed, they began to cluck their tongues, roll their eyes, and make funny faces at him. One little girl cupped a hand and began whispering behind her palm to another little girl's ear. Furious, he stepped forward, let out a streak of curse words, and grabbed one of them by a skinny arm, a girl named Ollie Voss who lived next door to him, and shook her hard enough that her teeth chattered. The girls began to scream at the top of their lungs, and the doors to the homes opened wide. Heads peered out to see who was causing all the fuss. Abner grunted and released his fingers from Ollie's arm and walked away. It was not long after that someone found old Abner dead of natural causes in his bed, and everyone sighed in great relief to have the cantankerous man gone.

A week later, Ollie was standing in front of the fireplace wearing a cotton nightgown. A piece of lit charcoal flew from within the grate. It caught her dress afire. While her mother and father were desperately trying to save her by putting the flames out, she screamed, pointing at the fire.

"It's Old Abner who did it!" she cried. "He's in the fireplace laughing at me!" And then, she died.

They entombed her in a nearby cemetery in their family's ancient mausoleum, and after a time, the vault began to fall apart. Such, the parents reburied her in another cemetery. Soon after, the barrage of bricks, stones, and wood began to fall at the old Voss house, which was next to Abner White's house. One old woman came forward. She knew why the objects were flying—the family had reburied Ollie Voss next to Abner White in the cemetery. Abner still held his grudge, and he had collected everything he could to throw at the yard where the Voss family once lived.

Ollie Voss, within her tomb, got word of the old man coming back and causing trouble. She arose, too, and began to hurl rocks and bricks and the likes back at Abner's ghost. Things went on until the old-timers spoke up and told them the story of Abner White and Ollie Voss. The family reburied the little girl far away from Abner's grave. Since then, no more wraiths have battled in the 200 block of Cherokee Street, and no unseen hands have thrown such thing as bricks, stones, and wood there.

The Old Carrollton Jail
East Carrollton Neighborhood

Site of The Old Carrollton Jail
Corner of Hampson
and Short Streets
New Orleans, LA 70118
29.943126, -90.132569

Ghosts of Old Carrollton Jail

Right, Ninth Street Precinct and jail. *Left*, Old Carrollton Courthouse. *Image: New Orleans Police Department's History*

Carrollton developed as a rural subdivision of New Orleans with mostly middle and upper-class families. As it grew, it was not without crime, so it was only a matter of time before the governing agencies built a city hall and around 1850, a jail (Ninth Ward Prison or Carrollton Jail) next to it and on the corner of Hampson and Short streets.

Before the city demolished the old prison in 1937, it had always remained under particular scrutiny of being haunted. The police officers who worked there divulged some peculiar spirits inhabited the building.

The hauntings peaked around 1898, and when Sergeant William Clifton was the commander there. Clifton was highly respected, a veteran officer, and had served on the New Orleans police force. At Ninth Ward, his staff included a clerk, deputy, two doorkeepers, and eight police officers. Clifton's office was just inside the entranceway along a wide hallway and had a desk, several chairs, framed pictures on the wall, and a sofa. He knew from the start that something undeniably weird was going on. "We had been bothered off and on by strange noises, things falling without apparent cause," he told reporters from a local newspaper. "Here in my office, our attention was first attracted to an old sofa in the corner. Frequently at night, one of our men would lie down on it to rest, and invariably, something queer would happen. Sometimes the man would be thrown violently off, sometimes he would feel hands touching him, and several times the sofa would be moved bodily several feet from the wall." Chairs would move on their own, objects would be thrown through the air, and a washtub flew across the room, smashing into a wall. Sergeant Clifton was an admirer of Confederate General Beauregard, who bravely led the attack on Fort Sumter. He had the general's picture hanging on the wall of his office. One night while speaking to another officer, he remarked how brave Beauregard was and gave the portrait a salute. BAM! The picture crashed to the floor.

In 1899, Joseph Crowley was the night clerk and operator of the prison. A no-nonsense man; he scoffed at the officers' ghost stories. That is, until one September evening of that year, when he was working intently at his desk.

Crowley had an incredible urge to look up, feeling like someone was watching him. He raised his eyes to see a tall, gaunt man with a dark beard standing just outside a railed enclosure. He noted the stranger appeared sick, and the clerk stood to inquire if he could do something for him. The man glided away silently to the door. Thinking that surely it was a prank, Crowley rushed to the door, but the man had vanished. Neither the doorman nor police officers chatting in the hall had heard or seen a thing!

This is the old Ninth Street Precinct and jail location, and the courtyard where the city hanged many criminals.

When workers demolished the Old Ninth, they told of ghastly shapes forming from the dust, sweeping upward and changing into those who were executed there—necks twisting grotesquely sideways and bobbling on shoulders as they stood there with eyes wide and bulging.

Area of the Old Dairy Stables not far from the Mississippi and heading toward New Orleans Proper

Uptown/Carrollton

Near the Old Dairy Farms

S Carrollton Avenue

New Orleans, LA 70118

29.947466, -90.129352

Milk Stable Ghost

11855   A NEW ORLEANS MILK CART.

At one time, Carrollton had dairy farms on the outskirts of town that supplied much of the milk to New Orleans. One just off Carrollton Avenue had a ghost. In 1881, a local milkman died of unknown causes. In August of 1884, his little child died too. For weeks after the little one's death, dairy women making their way along Carrollton Avenue with their loads laden for sale in the city and passing the dairy stable would see the dead man lying prone on the floor with candles at his head and feet. He clasped, within his arms, the dead child.

City Park

Mona Lisa Drive
City Park

Lover's Lane—City Park
1 Palm Drive
New Orleans, LA 70124
29.995012, -90.098766

The Legend of Wandering Moaning Mona Lisa

The area in City Park where a statue stood along an old lover's lane—with a haunting.

In the early 1900s, a wealthy man donated several statues to the city around the area that is Popp's Fountain at City Park, one commemorating his beloved daughter who had died in one of the lagoons. The statue was bonze and made to look like Venus. Yet, she also carried the likeness of the girl with a soft, Mona Lisa smile parting her lips. Park officials created a walkway so visitors could stroll past the statues.

Legends say that the girl had fallen in love with a seafaring sailor who had come into New Orleans on a ship. Her father did not approve and forbade the girl to see the man. Devastated, she walked into one of the lagoons at the park and drowned herself.

Years later, this area became overgrown, and the cul-de-sac where the statues ended was a lover's lane for local teens. A speeding car went off the road and hit the young woman's statue, knocking it down. A story arose that a misty figure resembling the man's daughter would rise from the location where the monument stood and trudge the area moaning sadly, the Mona Lisa smile on her lips. She would scratch at the windows of cars parking there. Eventually, the statue was vandalized and its ruins removed. But the ghost still visits the area. She has been heard all over City Park—moaning, screaming, and scratching the windows of cars.

Dueling Oaks
City Park

Dueling Oaks—City Park
29591 Dreyfous Drive
New Orleans, LA 70119
29.985655, -90.094183

Deadly Clashes at the Dueling Oaks

Dueling Oak at City Park—

In the mid-1700s, when one hot-headed man robbed another of some honor, a duel was fought to reclaim it in St Anthony's Garden behind St Louis Cathedral. Still today, some have heard the clash of swords within, the gasp of surprise as a ghostly sword is thrust into long-dead flesh, and witnessed the delicate wisp of shadows flitting around.

Yet, the old garden is not the only place ghosts are seen and heard because of duels. By 1855, the townspeople had enough of the spilling of blood within sight, the noise, and the occasional bullet soaring past their buildings. City officials outlawed dueling inside the city limits. Most of these disputes over honor were held outside the city on Esplanade Avenue at what is now City Park and was once the Allard Plantation.

Dueling Grounds in New Orleans. *Image: Library of Congress.*

Hundreds of onlookers would come to witness the duels, as many as ten occurring in one day in 1839 beneath two old oaks—of many; one was Micajah Lewis, who was the private secretary and brother-in-law to Governor Claiborne. At only around 25 years old, he was killed in 1804, defending his brother's honor during a duel at the oaks.

Then there was the legend of an arrogant French scholar known as Chevalier Tomasi. He not only insulted the Americans by stating they were ignorant tribes who were expelled from Europe for crimes and stupidity and knew nothing of science, but he also called the Mississippi nothing more than a tiny rill compared to the great rivers of Europe. Unfortunately, he made the latter remark in front of a proud Creole who promptly offered to defend the Mississippi's honor with one swipe of glove to Tomasi's cheek. For this, the Creole escorted the Frenchman to the dueling grounds. Tomasi was wounded, but not mortally. The Creole had justly found a way to keep the arrogant Frenchman from uttering insults without excruciating pain by cutting him from cheek to cheek and across his lips. Tomasi had to wear a bandage over his mouth for days.

On March 13, 1892, the Times-Picayune wrote this, *"Here nearest the roadside are the 'duel oaks.' Once this was the green field of honor. The old cavalier, with sword in hand, came here to find his rival's heart. Politicians and statesmen have had here their final arbitrament. In a hundred duels has blood been shed under the old cathedral aisles of nature. Why, it would not be strange if the very violets blossomed red of this soaked grass! The lover for his mistress, the gentleman for his honor, the courtier for his King; what loyalty has not cried out in pistol shot and scratch of steel! Sometimes two or three hundred people hurried from the city to witness these human baitings. On the occasion of one duel, the spectators could stand no more, drew their own swords, and there was a general melee—"*

Only one of the famous oaks remains because a hurricane uprooted the other. There was a crypt beneath the remaining Dueling Oak—the grave of plantation owner Louis Allard, politician, and poet. Sometime in 1829, Louis Allard mortgaged the property to gain funding for crops.

Unable to repay the banknote, by 1845, he had lost the property at a sheriff's sale to John McDonogh.

Allard stayed on as overseer of the property. As his health began to decline in the next two years, he would sit beneath the tree writing poetry. Before he died, he asked the new owner to bury him beneath the tree, and on May 18, 1847, as far as everyone knew, they entombed Allard's body in a crypt there.

However, his story is not over. Years after his death, when the city developed the land into a park, workers found no coffin within the vault, but someone discovered a casket lock and handles at the site. In 2011, the park arranged for sonar imaging to be completed on the gravesite. They found no casket within. No one is sure what happened to Allard's body, and the mystery of the empty crypt has never been solved.

Old oak with crypt to right. *Image: Library of Congress.*

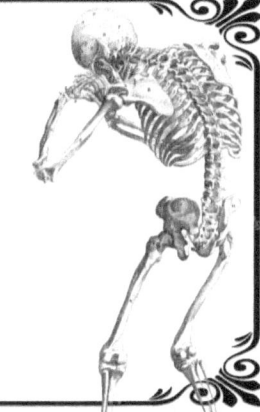

Suicide Oak
City Park

Suicide Oak—City Park
Stadium Drive
New Orleans, LA 70124
29.986038, -90.101334

Suicide Oak

Suicide Oak in City Park, New Orleans. *Image: Adrian Chevalier*

The legend is that within twelve years, sixteen men committed suicide beneath the branches of this tree in City Park.

Third District

A Stately Mansion in the Third District

The Witch of Casa Rosa and the Gay Caballeros

Casa Rosa was a stately mansion once majestically standing along the streets in the lower part of New Orleans' Third District. Don Juan Luis Angula of Spain painstakingly built the home with the old money he brought with him when he moved there. As years passed and after his death, although kept within the family, it started into ruin. Many began to call it haunted. Those walking the streets would stop to peer curiously through the bent and gnarled gates to see if they could find a ghostly face peering out windows with dusty and dreary torn velvet blinds or hap upon a being crouching on the worn roof cupola. Once in a while, an old mangy cat slinked from the bushes. A story would evolve around it implicating some grisly creature living there with fangs covered in blood and drippy drool dribbling from its chin and snatching up little children as they passed with a paw and dining on their tender flesh.

On a slow week of news, reporter William Dawson seized on the story, making his way to Casa Rosa to interview the owner, Señorita Mercedes Antonia Angula. He was young and tall, pleasing to the eye, and smartly dressed in a suitcoat. William spoke eloquently to the somber servant woman who opened the door and grudgingly let him enter.

"I don't know why you want to talk to her," she muttered and shook her head. She took a large key from her pocket and bolted the door behind him—*click-click*. "I've known her all my life, and we both are about dead. Sooner or later, we'll be buried out back by the old wall like all the rest." She walked the reporter down a long, dark hall. It reeked of old things, dust, and mildew, and maybe a mouse or two that had died, but before they expired, slithered into a hole in the wall and laid there shriveled and unfound.

As William entered a great room, he felt a burst of cool air in the solemn darkness as the curtains sucked in with the opening of the door, not unlike the unsealing of a tomb long closed. The servant faded away, and he was left standing there alone, or at least, so he thought. His eyes took a moment to get used to the dimness, then worked around the room to the once spectacular, painted ceiling that was now leaving plaster flakes all over the ragged floor rugs. He could barely make out the velvet seating couches and old artwork of former family members on the walls, a cracked bust, and three statues—all grand at one time but now looking like a church graveyard long forgotten.

In the center of the room on a faded, red velvet settee, was a woman. William squinted into the oozy shadows and saw a bit of pale face. Was she young or old? That is what William wondered as he gazed there, letting his eyes adjust as he took in the fringes of a beautiful satin dress. Then he blinked and saw her as she was, a woman who could have been a thousand years old. Her face was yellowish, dried, and crinkled. Her head had tufts of gray hair here and there with teeny lice wiggling along the strands. A boil bulged above the bridge of her nose, a brown lump looking like a rat had shat upon her forehead. The aged creature was wearing an ancient, red bell-shaped gown with puffy sleeves and festooned in pearls, some missing in great numbers.

A diamond necklace wrapped around her too-long, too-thin neck, and her skinny wrists and knobby-knuckled fingers were donning gold bands with rubies and diamonds. She had tied the ends of each with pieces of twine to keep them from falling off, and she kept bringing them to her lips to suck on noisily. Each dribbled with pus-green slobber. William tried not to cringe or gag or both. But he simply could not drag his eyes away from her.

"Have you come for the jewels?" a creaky voice squeaked from the settee. William jumped startled. He had been so mesmerized by the repulsiveness he had not torn his eyes away. She twirled a finger at him, and for a moment, William decided she must be a witch and had tried to cast a charm spell upon him. Then he realized his folly and adjusted his stance, working up a fancy smile. "No, Señorita Angula," he cleared his throat. "I have come to talk about this beautiful house, the flowers in your garden, your family, and especially—*you.*"

She smiled and seemed satisfied that he wanted to talk about *her.* She pointed to a dusty chair nearby, and William shook his head. "I have been sitting all day. I would rather stand." He watched a cockroach slither across the armrest. Señorita Angula settled into the settee, and the two chatted of petty things like the weather and the old places of New Orleans. "And you have never married?" William asked as he had grown bored talking about matters he already knew—it was going to rain, and this mansion or that mansion was getting torn down. Everyone she knew was years into a tomb. He changed the subject, and although he understood his question was rude for a spinster, the Señorita giggled much like a schoolgirl.

"No, none of my suitors were good enough for my father. He is gone now. I mean, he is away in Barcelona at our estate there. He wrote to me the other day."

William began to realize she was not in her right mind. Her father was long dead; his bones were dust. He shifted awkwardly. It did not appear there was much of a story in this rundown old house, just an old lady who had lost her wits. However, she was not going to let him leave so soon.

"Did you know Señor Blenco?" Señorita asked, not waiting for him to answer. "No, you are too young to be acquainted with him." The old woman wagged a pale, veined hand lazily, and her rings clanged and clattered before she began to prattle on about her many old loves that he wondered existed at all. She spoke of her beauty and desirability, of at least twenty young men from Spain who had competed for her hand in marriage. After each one, she would drag her toothless gums together, making a gruesome squeaking sound, not unlike a finger rubbed up and down on the wet glass of a window.

William began to realize that not only had Señorita Angula lost her senses, but she was also concocting stories. "Señor Blenco found me quite to his taste," she rambled on while William tried not to cup a palm to his lips and stifle a yawn. "He poisoned his mother to give me her rubies, then died not long after being poisoned himself. And then there was Señor Villesca, a pretty man, indeed. He doted on me, gave me everything he had—until he broke his back." She cackled. "They came, all of them, bringing me gold and jewels to tempt me to wed. My father was clever. He invited many men from across the ocean to court his daughter here. He arranged their leaving from our house at daylight, so everyone saw them leave. Then later, they returned for a liaison with me. And not one of them ever wanted to leave my house because I was so pleasing." she chuckled. "And they never left once they called—" She paused and coughed a spittle-filled, throaty hack. "What was I talking about? Oh, yes, you must dine with us tonight—"

"Never left?" William had interrupted, perked up. "What do you mean by that?" But she had fallen asleep in the middle of the sentence, mumbling indecipherable words before grumbling snores filled the air.

William had nearly cheered in relief, but his mind was whirling. What did she mean that all those suitors never left? Certainly, he would stay for dinner. He had to find out. And what about the gold and rubies they gave her? Were her ramblings of a murderer or just an old woman who had lost her senses? He tipped his head and decided to sneak off and take a peek around the musty, dusty old mansion. He crept down one hallway, then another. The interior of the estate seemed just as odd as the woman who lived in it. He heard a scuffle near a stairwell and paused his steps. Was it the servant noting he had slipped away and was nosing around the place? Or was the skitter the fleeting passing of a rat?

William shivered, but nothing could have stunned him more than seeing what suddenly appeared before him—*a young man*. He certainly was not of this earth as he wore old-fashioned clothing. His face was deathly pale, and his legs wobbled when the man walked like his back was not attached to his waist. He extended his hand to William, who took it more out of shock than wanting to clasp the ice-cold fingers. The ghostly man led him up a flight of steps, and they came upon another spirit that appeared as if someone had smashed his head to a bloody pulp, one side flat from a horrible beating. And on they went up the stairway, each step seeming to have another dead man—one holding rubies in his bloodied hands while his mouth frothed as if someone had poisoned him, and others who were bludgeoned or had their faces smashed. William wavered, then looked to the man with the strange unattached spine. "You are Señor Villesca," he gasped aloud, realizing the truth. "The man whose back was broken."

Suddenly there was an appalling stench. He released Señor Villesca's hand, and around him, all the men began to melt in puddles of green snot-like slime, deep red blood, brittle bones and yellowed teeth. Like a flood, this gooey sludge ran down the stairway as William slipped and slid, trying to escape. He ran straight to the door. As he got there, he stopped in terror. The servant had bolted the latch! William pounded desperately on the door for help, then heard the *cluck-cluck* of a tongue and saw the old servant coming up behind him, wiggling her clanking keys in the air. "Ah, you've done it! You've set them free!" she screamed at him while she came up beside William and wrestled with the key to lock. "Now, they're going to kill her and get their revenge." William did not answer. Instead, he slid through the gap as quickly as he could when she opened the door.

Just as he got to the front gate, he saw that someone had bolted it shut too. Would he ever escape this place? The moment the thought crossed his mind, William saw the same man with the wobbly back appear before him. He took one hand and pushed the gate, and it opened wide. William burst through, and stopped in the street to catch his breath, sweat rolling down his temple as he turned to look back. To his surprise, the gate was closed and locked. The man who had helped him flee had fallen to the ground in two parts, the top rolling one way and the bottom rolling another. Then he vanished.

Señorita Angula died. The family sold the home, and new owners decided to move a wall by a very old rose garden. As workers knocked the barrier down, the bottom exposed a three-foot deep hole that went all the way across the courtyard—beneath, they found fifty skeletons of men, poor love-sick wretches who had fallen prey to the charms of a woman and a murderous scam. Among them, one skeletal hand was still clinging to a ruby necklace.

Around New Orleans

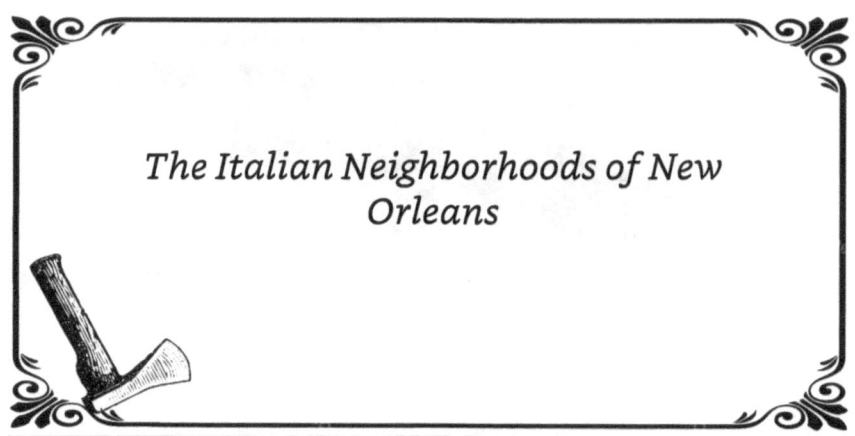

The Italian Neighborhoods of New Orleans

The Axeman

This illustration, "The witching hour—12:15 A.M.," is from the March 19, 1919 issue of the Times-Picayune. During 1919, New Orleans had its own Jack the Ripper—one with not only a fondness for striking fear into the hearts of those living in the city but also with a soft spot for Jazz. *Image: The New Orleans Advocate*

A man in a shop once scolded me for offhandedly repeating a saying I read that New Orleans was built on Vodou, Jazz, good Creole food, and sin. "Well, you're wrong," he grunted. "You're leaving out a whole lot of culture and flavor when you say that. It's like making gumbo and forgetting the crabmeat and shrimp."

He was right. But I was not so wrong. The city has always been home to a diverse crowd, often not agreeing on one thing or another, just like the two of us. But there was one night that just about everyone came together, no matter their background or traditions or where they lived. On March 19th, 1919, folks from Storyville to the Garden District, rich or poor, played jazz because a mysterious murderer who hacked up residents with an axe wrote a letter stating he would spare the occupants of any place that played the music that night.

Italian-American neighborhood—its occupants living in New Orleans were nearly held hostage from fear of a serial killer in their midst in the early 1900s. *Image: Library of Congress*

On March 14, 1919, the Times-Picayune published a letter signed by "The Axeman." An excerpt from the letter reads—

Hottest Hell, March 13, 1919

Esteemed Mortal of New Orleans: The Axeman

They have never caught me and they never will. They have never seen me, for I am invisible, even as the ether that surrounds your earth. I am not a human being, but a spirit and a demon from the hottest hell. I am what you Orleanians and your foolish police call the Axeman.

When I see fit, I shall come and claim other victims. I alone know whom they shall be. I shall leave no clue except my bloody axe, besmeared with blood and brains of he whom I have sent below to keep me company. . . Now, to be exact, at 12:15 (earthly time) on next Tuesday night, I am going to pass over New Orleans. In my infinite mercy, I am going to make a little proposition to you people. Here it is: I am very fond of jazz music, and I swear by all the devils in the nether regions that every person shall be spared in whose home a jazz band is in full swing at the time I have just mentioned. If everyone has a jazz band going, well, then, so much the better for you people. One thing is certain and that is that some of your people who do not jazz it out on that specific Tuesday night (if there be any) will get the axe. . .

—The Axeman

And so, they played. No one wanted to take the chance and die if they did not. Because people did die. It started with 42-year-old Joseph and 36-year-old Catherine Maggio, who were sleeping side by side at their home on the corner of Upperline and Magnolia Streets on a warm May 23rd night. Their residence adjoined their grocery store and bar, which they had owned for six years. The Italian couple lived in the home with Joseph's younger brother, Andrew, a barber.

His bedroom was next to theirs. When Andrew came home that evening, the couple was still awake. He shuffled off to bed, but a strange sound of moaning issuing from the couple's room awakened him. He banged on the wall, certain they would return with a knock. There was no answer. It was around 4:45 a.m., and panicking, Andrew ran up the road to a family member's home and returned with two brothers.

When they opened the door to the couple's room, the grisly sight nearly brought the men to their knees. Still alive, Joseph was lying diagonally on the bed with his throat slashed. Catherine lay lifeless; the killer had severed her throat so deeply he or she nearly cut it clean from her body. Someone had slashed both their throats and smeared blood around the room. Police would discover that the razor used to murder the two belonged to Andrew, who they initially believed had committed the crime. Police later released him.

Over time, the Axeman murdered twelve people, mostly Italian grocers or bakers and their families. Each time the murderer chiseled the door open and left an axe or chisel near the house. Folks believed he was either a serial killer or some demon from Hell, this Axeman. Neighborhoods organized guards to patrol the streets. Those who were wounded and lived related that a phantom-like form awakened them hovering over their bed. Some described the killer as a chubby man with white wings.

But on the night of March 19th, 1919 when everybody played jazz, nobody died from the killer's hands. Not long after, he struck again. Then in October of 1919, the spree completely stopped. Police never caught the killer. And so far, he has never returned. On certain nights, though, something remains. Pedestrians walking near the home of the first couple murdered have reported hearing muffled groans.

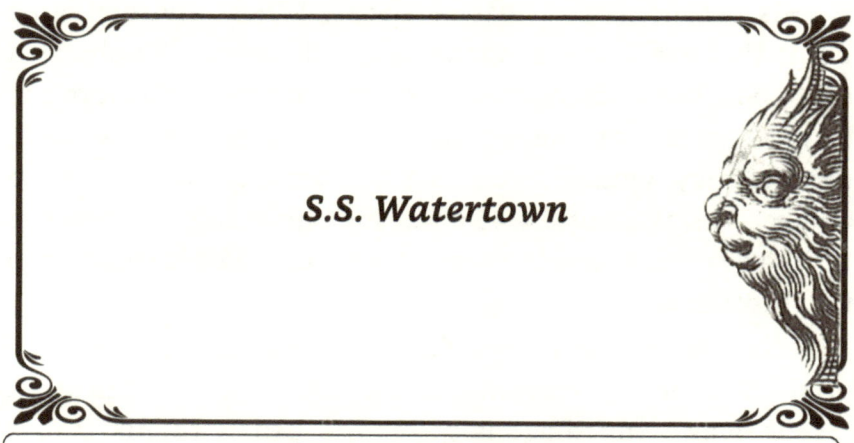

S.S. Watertown

Ghost in the Photo

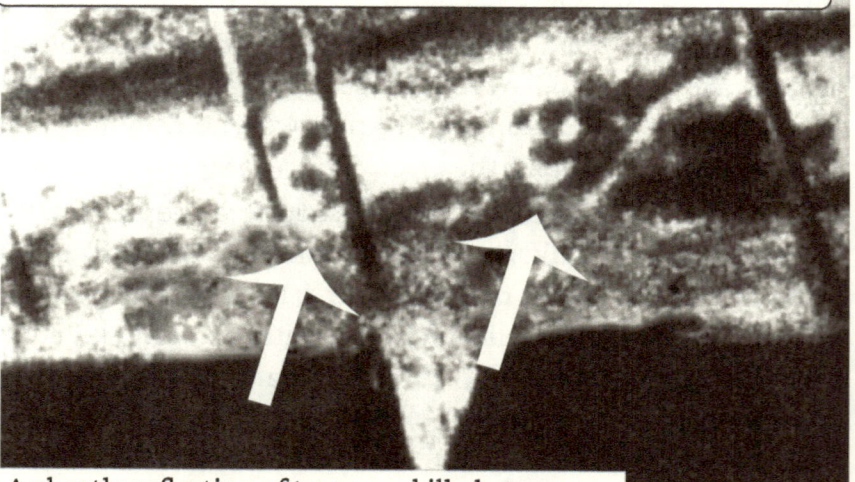

A ghostly reflection of two men killed at sea—

In 1924, James Courtney and Michael Meehan, two crewmen on the tanker S.S. Watertown, were killed by gas fumes when scrubbing an empty cargo tank. Meehan was lying on the floor, and Courtney was sprawled on top of him as if Meehan had passed out first, and Courtney had attempted to drag him to safety. Following their burial at sea on December 4, 1924, their faces appeared in the water next to the ship. It occurred many times and for about 10 seconds before disappearing.

When docked in New Orleans, Captain Keith Tracy purchased a camera and took pictures of the strange happening. On the return trip, Tracy's crew alerted him each time they spotted the faces, and he continued to take pictures. Only one image showed the faces. The photo stood up to heavy skepticism, and nobody could definitively prove it was a hoax. Members of the crew also saw the men's faces in the water, and many like to believe James Courtney and Michael Meehan were giving their final farewells to their crewmates.

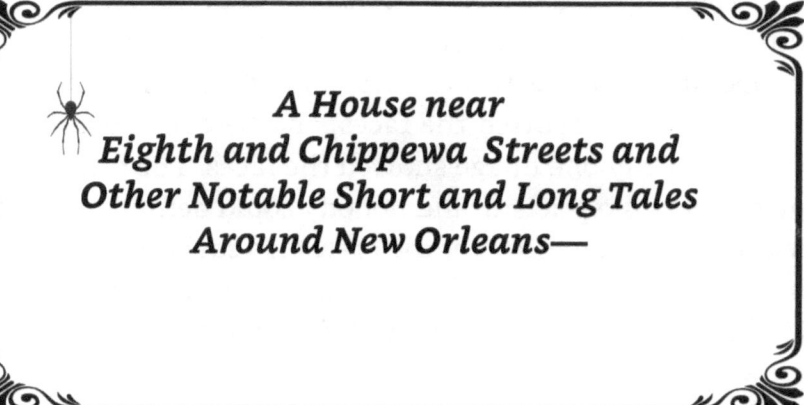

A House near Eighth and Chippewa Streets and Other Notable Short and Long Tales Around New Orleans—

Delightful Short Tales of the Dead

A home near Eighth and Chippewa streets had ghostly happenings near a fireplace. No one knew the cause. Then owners removed the hearthstones and found the bones of a woman and child beneath.

One night, a dandy quite full of himself asked a pretty lady on the street if she would like him to escort her home. Without hesitation, she jumped on his back and forced him to carry her around the town all night. Then she jumped from his back, breaking the spell, and vanished.

There was a headless phantom of the Irish Channel that came every twenty years and was only seen by women.

No cab driver wanted to transport riders near St Louis Cemetery No 1. More than one complained that he had given a lift home to a woman wearing a white dress. When he got to her address, she would disappear. A man would come out to greet the driver and tell him that the woman was his wife, and she had been dead for ten years. And she had been buried in her wedding dress.

Plantations Nearby

The Myrtles Plantation
7747 U.S. Highway 61
St Francisville, Louisiana 70775
30.803454, -91.388026

Faces in the Mirror

The Myrtles Plantation is haunted and you can stay the night!

David Bradford was a successful lawyer, businessman, and Deputy Attorney General of Washington County, Pennsylvania. However, his reputation there, although not short-lived, would come to a jarring halt. In 1794, George Washington placed a bounty on his head after Bradford led a series of protests against high taxes during the Whiskey Rebellion. To escape arrest from the militia, he fled to Louisiana and built an eight-room home that he named "Laurel Grove."

Bradford lived in the mansion with his wife Elizabeth and children until 1899 when he received a pardon, then returned to Pennsylvania to become a judge and, at times, mentor young law students, teaching them the business. One of those students, Clark Woodruff, would later marry his daughter Sarah Matilda.

In 1808, after Bradford's death, Sarah Matilda and Clark returned to manage the Louisiana plantation along with their three children, Cornelia Gale, James, and Mary Octavia. Not long after, his widowed mother-in-law Elizabeth joined them. Although the farm built on indigo and cotton flourished, some family members eventually succumbed to the terrible epidemics raging through Louisiana. In July 1823, Sarah Matilda contracted yellow fever and died. A little less than a year later, 12-year-old James also caught yellow fever and died, followed by 8-year-old Cornelia Gale only two months after. When elderly Elizabeth died in 1830, Clark Woodruff moved to New Orleans and worked in public service while his only living daughter Mary Octavia attended finishing school in Connecticut. In 1834, Woodruff sold the property to a local, wealthy plantation owner, Ruffin Stirling, who would restore the property and rename it as Myrtles for the flowers blooming from June through November.

Stirling traveled to Europe to bring elegant furnishings to the home, including obtaining specialized craftsmen and artisans who painted and created the plaster moulding. He continued to build both the house and a family, having somewhere between seven to nine children (documents differ), most of whom lived to adulthood except for possibly two known, both between the ages of one and two and around 1872 and 1873. He died in 1881 at age 54 from tuberculosis. His wife took over managing the plantations.

Sarah Mulford Stirling, a daughter of Ruffin Stirling, would marry William Drew Winter. The two would take over the management of the Myrtles. In January of 1871, an unnamed man summoned Winter to the door and shot him. Winter collapsed and died. Through the 1890s, the home would change hands but remain stately and beautiful with tall oaks draped with Spanish moss, stone statues dotting the property, and ghosts around every corner.

This famous image of what appears to be a slave was photographed in 1992 by the Myrtles' proprietress when taking pictures of the plantation buildings required by an insurance company. *Image: Myrtles Plantation*

In the 1950s, people began whispering about the ghosts there. Marjorie Munson, then the owner, spoke of seeing the spirit of a woman in a turban or hat roaming around. In 1992, while taking photos for fire insurance underwriters, the owner caught a startling image of what appeared to be a slave woman wearing a turban. But they were not the only owners who have experienced ghostly happenings. When owner Teeta Moss moved into the Myrtles with her family, they lived in the upper section of the mansion while the lower quarters remained a bed and breakfast for guests.

Soon, the family began hearing their name called out, and their two sons caught glimpses of children roaming about the house. The most captivating story occurred in 1993 when Teeta worked at her desk while the nanny watched her ten-month-old son Morgan. A raspy voice whispered in her ear, "Go check your baby." Thinking little of it, she continued with her project when the voice came back with a more urgent tone, "Check your baby." Teeta had jumped up from her desk and hurried into Morgan's room only to find it empty. In a panic, she ran from room to room, finally ending up outside. There she found her son scuffling close to the pond. Once safely in her arms, she felt a wonderful warmth surround them both.

More experiences have happened here that remain unexplained—

George Hesser, a former manager of the mansion, claimed to be a skeptic but still could not figure out why the upstairs windows flew open after carefully closing them. He is not the only one who had strange and unexpected events occur to them at the inn. Furniture has moved, and tour guides have listened to footsteps pound on the floor when no one else is around. Visitors have heard the soft sound of a violin played in the evening. Doors open on their own accord, and guests have taken numerous pictures with long-dead occupants showing up on the images.

When no one is in a room on the first floor with a grand piano, it has repeatedly played a cord. When someone comes to see who is playing, it stops, only to begin again once the person has left.

Guests staying in a children's room have awakened with a doll lying next to them on a pillow. When I stayed at Myrtles Plantation, a mother and daughter overnighting in one of the rooms had a baby doll and several other objects move from the dressers and bed.

A grand piano plays by ghostly fingers.

A baby doll in one of the well-appointed chambers once used as a child's room moves on its own accord.

And there is a legend surrounding a certain mirror in the mansion. When a few of the family members died, the living were so grief-stricken that they forgot to appropriately

A ghostly face appears in this mirror.

cover the mirror with black linen. By tradition, the grieving have believed a recently departed and confused spirit searching for the beyond could get trapped inside if a cloth did not cover the mirror. Such, those who died in the home remain, and faces and handprints appear on the surface.

And visitors to the inn have heard the dreadful knocks and dragging sounds of someone struggling along the porch floor where William Winter was murdered in cold blood.

There is a portrait of a previous owner on the wall of the stairway. If he smiles at you, you are welcome in the home. If he is frowning when you peer at his face, well—you are not!

The ghostly image that I took of a child playing inside the back door of the plantation home. The child appears to be leaning on one arm while hugging a doll or a dressed up dog with the other.

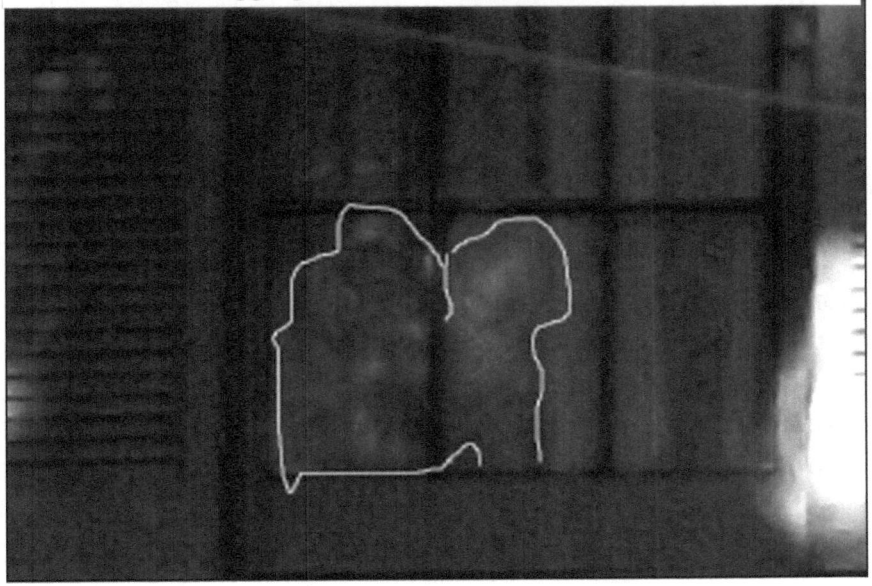

Myrtles Plantation is a sight to behold with a period veranda and ten guest rooms with five inside the home. And even better, ghost-loving guests are welcome. The lawn is expansive and dressed with a gazebo and statues. Do not forget to take a tour to learn the history and the newest stories guests have given.

Prepare to have some contact with ghosts if you visit—although nothing to be alarmed about, you may come face to face with an older woman in a green turban or fancy green hat. A little child may show up in your pictures, and you realize that ghostly kids were running between your feet, and you did not see them in plain sight. A deep spectral voice might whisper in your ear. Or you may have something shadowy show at the end of your bed at night after something gently awakens you with a playful tug on your toes beneath the blankets. I did. Just as quickly as it came, it disappeared. Look over the wrought iron fence on the porch to the shaded windows—take a few shots with your camera. Perhaps you will see a ghost! And that, too, I did!

Destréhan Plantation
13034 River Road
Destrehan, LA 70047
29.945038, -90.364233

Wandering Stephen

Destréhan Plantation—has a ghostly presence and paid historical tours that support the preservation and upkeep of the property.

About thirteen miles from New Orleans, Destrehan Plantation is the oldest documented plantation home in the Lower Mississippi Valley. Since its beginnings in 1783, it had up to 200 enslaved people at any given time before the U.S. abolished slavery. It was built on indigo and later sugar farming and mainly known for its second owner, Jean-Noël Destréhan.

During Destréhan's ownership, there was a regional slave rebellion in 1811, the German Coast Uprising, and Destrehan Plantation became one of three tribunals resulting in the execution of eighteen rebels. The trial was not impartial as the judges were all slave owners.

Destréhan's 16-year-old daughter, Marie Elénore Zélia, married 42-year old Stephen Henderson in 1816. In 1825, two years after Destréhan's death, Stephen bought the plantation from the estate. He lived there with Zélia until she died in September of 1830 at only 29-years-old with an unknown illness while traveling to New York.

An eerie shadow dancing (bottom right) beneath a tree makes a macabre appearance on the Destréhan Plantation lawn, offering those who saw it sway momentarily a creepy peek at its past.

Stephen Henderson never found another love after his wife died, and he missed her even beyond the grave. He died in 1836. Witnesses have seen his ghost roaming the drive, on a back stairway, and sitting in a chair in one of the rooms.

Bayous Nearby

A Bayou near New Orleans

Singing Bones

A family along a bayou not far from New Orleans. *Image: Schomburg Center for Research in Black Culture, Jean Blackwell Hutson Research and Reference Division, The New York Public Library.*

A large family with 25 children lived in a bayou below New Orleans and all within one small, palmetto-roofed shack. Food was scarce, and the mother had to divide even the tiniest bit of fish or meat between all of them. Many nights, the little ones would go to bed crying because their bellies growled with hunger. It made the wife always sullen and angry. She yelled at her husband for this and that and even the smallest infraction like smoking his pipe.

One winter was particularly hard, and the father came home one night without any food for the children. He stood outside the rickety house and pondered how he would explain to his wife and children that he had no food for them. Tears welled in his eyes as he imagined the sad faces that would look up at him. Still, he took the hard steps to the door and readied his hand to push it open. Yet, just as he entered, a wonderful scent of cooking meat tantalized his nostrils, and his happy children surrounded him. One snatched up his hand and pulled him inside, and his usually ill-tempered wife was smiling as she threw out her hand to expose the eating table. There was a feast of boneless meat sitting in front of him piled high in the center.

Home-sweet-home on a bayou near New Orleans. *Image: Lee, R., photographer. (1938) Fisherman's home along the bayou, Akers, Louisiana.*

That night, the family enjoyed the finest meal they had eaten in years. But it would not be the last. For the next three days, the family indulged themselves in the delicious meat. The man thought about asking his wife where she got the meal, then decided it was not worth getting yelled at or putting her in a bad mood.

He also noticed that his wife was not eating with them, and he worried she was ill. So, he decided to use that notion to end his curiosity as he sat down for another supper. "This meat is delicious," the man said as he took a bite of a particularly tender, juicy piece. "But it must be expensive as it has no bones." She replied that she bought it that way, and without the bones, it was less weight to carry.

"Ah, I see. How about you sit and eat with us tonight?" the husband asked the wife. "I haven't seen you eat in days."

"I eat before you come home," she replied, "so I can care for the children."

He felt satisfied with her answer, but as he looked around the table, one of his favorite sons was missing. He did not want to enrage his wife, so he did not mention anything aloud. But two weeks passed, and two more of their children did not greet him when he came home. He asked his wife where the children were, and she shrugged her shoulders, "I took them to their aunties house to visit," she answered. "They will be back in a while."

But they did not return. Another week passed, and still, another child disappeared. The man went for a walk and then returned, wondering how he would approach his wife. Something was wrong. He sat down hard on the back porch step, lit his pipe, and thought for a while.

As he sat there, he heard a low humming nearby. At first, he thought it was a bird, then mosquitos. Yet it got louder the longer he listened. It was the sound of children singing, and it was coming from a rock near his foot. "Our mother kills us. Our father eats us. We have no coffins. We are not on holy ground—"

The man dropped to his knees and towed up the stone. Beneath it, he could see so many small children's bones! He gasped. Now he certainly knew where his children had gone. He knew where his wife had gotten the tender meat.

He went inside the house, took up an axe, and killed the woman. He would not listen to her protests that there were too many children anyway. Then he buried the children in a cemetery, and he never ate meat again.

Frenier
Manchac Swamp
Cajun Pride Swamp Tours
110 Frenier Road
Laplace, LA 70068
30.095049, -90.436380

The Warning

A storm on the horizon in the ghost town of Frenier.

The community of Frenier was once a logging town when early immigrant Martin Schlösser settled in a region around 1836 between the Mississippi River and Lake Pontchartrain. Loggers cleared the trees, and barges filled with lumber headed to New Orleans. Around 1849, 25 families lived in the area. When timbering became less profitable, the settlement began farming cabbage in the dark, fertile soil and then selling Frenier sauerkraut to the French Market in New Orleans and Chicago.

Once the railway opened up nearby, the community prospered because they could deliver their harvest to Chicago markets before other producers in the southern states. However, early settlers laid out the town on a narrow piece of land between the river and the lake. It was prone to flooding, which was then locally known as "crevasses," the break or crack in the levee. Still much worse, though, were the storms hitting the area. It seemed Frenier was always just one hurricane or flood away from catastrophe, even if townspeople built homes eight feet off the ground to withstand the constant threat of walking knee-deep in water from the kitchen to the bedroom.

And that storm would come, though many scoffed, saying that it was just another storm like the others. It was not. On September 21, 1915, the New Orleans hurricane began as a weak tropical storm over the Windward Islands of the West Indies before it headed to the Gulf of Mexico, entering on September 28. The Weather Bureau desperately began issuing warnings for the Louisiana coast.

Back in the day just like today, the railway runs through Frenier. And so, too, do the storms.

Those in the town of Frenier were isolated, barring the railroad tracks that ran past the settlement. Perhaps they knew about the impending hurricane from a kind flagman or engineer in a passing train who might toss a newspaper out while rolling through as they often did. Yet, those in Frenier did not need some outside newspaper or weather agency telling them something bad would happen. They knew. Because you see, they already learned it from a song.

Julia (Bernard) Brown was 70-years-old and had the tidy sum of 40 acres, which had been passed on by her husband of 32 years, Celestin "Celis." They had owned the land since 1900 when Celis was given the property for farming. He had come from Texas. She had originally hailed from New Orleans.

Tucked between Lake Pontchartrain and the Mississippi River is the Maurepas Swamp, the town of Frenier, and the land where Julia Brown once lived—and died.

Being an elder in the community, Julia Brown had collected enough wisdom on the workings of curing that she had become what was called a *traiteur* or traditional healer.

She used Catholic prayer and medicinal remedies, midwifed, and cared for many in the community that was too tiny for a "degreed" doctor. Like many from her time in Southern Louisiana, she probably had some Vodou background also.

After Celis died between 1910 and 1915, Julia had hardly strayed far from home, and those who passed her house saw her, most often, sitting on her porch and singing little songs she would make up. One such ditty went something like this "—and oh when I die, I'll take half of Frenier with me."

Julia did die. It was on September 28 of 1915. Everyone had some ties with Julia, so when they laid her in a coffin box and set her out for folks to visit, many mourners came from near and far to give their last respects. But by 4:00 p.m., the wind was so powerful that all those who attended headed for cover. Some would later say that while running for shelter, the rain was coming down so hard it was like getting hit by buckshot.

Many were not so lucky—those who could not get away clambered up on tables as the water rose, then as it surged higher dragged themselves to the rooftops. There, they slipped or were blown overboard and pulled into the rushing and dark depths. One man desperately clung to a tree, pushing his palms to his ears to block out the screams of the dying around him. Many did die. Up to 28 perished in the area, their bodies found in the swamp and the trees and beneath soggy lumber. The hurricane had no compassion—it took the old, and it took the babies, it took newlyweds, and it took the strong, the weak, and mamas and daddies.

Some in the area were able to survive by clinging to the railroad tracks on a little higher ground. Others hopped a passing train and rode until the ties started disappearing underwater and with the storm. These poor souls would barely make it out alive, praying on their knees for hours.

But those who survived the hurricane passed down that Julia Brown's casket floated out into the water not long after her wake. Later, her body was found, as was the coffin, but both far apart. And they remembered her warnings and what happened on the day she died, "Oh, when I die, I'll take half of Frenier with me."

Those who heal us or ward off death have some power over us and against the evil who would take our lives. Such, some would ask themselves, had someone angered Julia Brown? Is that why this came to us? And they would always wonder if she was trying to warn them, or if she had, in some grand finale, brought on that storm.

You can take a boat ride through the area Frenier once stood with Cajun Pride Swamp Tours and get a view of the old cemetery/mass burials of the dead. Legends say that ghosts still walk there and some have seen Julia, herself. Others have heard the mournful cry of the dead and dying.

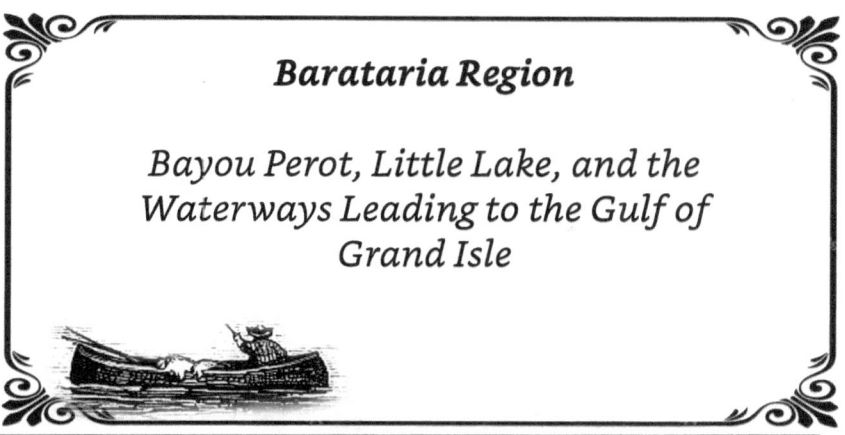

Barataria Region

Bayou Perot, Little Lake, and the Waterways Leading to the Gulf of Grand Isle

The Phantom Canoe

There are not just alligators lurking in the bayous outside New Orleans. Phantom canoes can be found there too.

The Barataria region lies south of New Orleans, a place of wetlands and bayous, lakes, and islands. Most of it has always been lonesome and cut off from the rest of the world. It is where all sorts of spirits can be summoned up in a vision while boating far off in its waters. And sometimes, those ghosts need no beckoning from a fanciful imagination at all—they quite easily come on their own.

Fisherman's home and pirogues in a bayou near New Orleans about the time as hapless folks came across a specter canoe.
Image: Library of Congress

Many years ago, Gaspar Fericheau lived on the shores of Lake Salvador in a shack not more than 20 miles from New Orleans by the way the crows fly. An old man, he had lived there for nearly 75 years and still took his boat out every day in the swamp setting traps for turtles or fishing with a cane pole. When he was home, he liked to stop passersby and tell them stories of the old days. One story was his favorite, and when a boatload of city fishermen came through one evening, he waved them over to his place. While they settled down on his little section of beach, he lit a fire and sat back and told them of the ghost canoe that haunted Bayou Perot, Little Lake, and the waterways leading to the gulf of Grand Isle. The story went like this:

Pierre Noir, Black Peter, had been a gunner for Lafitte's ship before the Battle of New Orleans. But after the war, he settled down to a quiet life in a little town as a fisherman, nothing more and nothing less. Pierre had what many would call a Cajun canoe, a pirogue that was a wooden boat.

It was much like a canoe, but it sits lower on the water, so the wind does not catch it easily and throw it around. It also has a flat bottom that skims easily across the shallow water and through the swamps' thick reeds. One late autumn afternoon, Pierre Noir took out into the waters of Lake Perot in his pirogue. He was checking his turtle traps, and lo and behold, he found them full of three turtles, which he quickly snatched from their prison and lay them flopping and floundering on their backs at the bottom of his boat. He realized it was getting late, and darkness had already started coming early in the fall, so he started back with hearty strokes of his paddle and his voice singing old songs of his pirate days loudly into the air.

It was as Pierre belted out a second song that something seemed amiss. Goosebumps slithered up his arms, and he quivered. The fisherman was not one who feared, not even in the heat of battle. His voice came to an abrupt halt mid-verse, and he dropped his chin feeling miserably afraid. It was then that he heard what sounded like a low, dull chant. The sound crept through reeds, and he followed the water to where it rang from—the bayou near Little Lake. His arm had been poised in the air, waiting to push the paddle into the soupy water to ease himself forward. But he stopped and swallowed hard, forcing it past a dry lump in his throat. He held his breath, and while he stared into the bayou, he saw before him a boat he had never seen before on the waters, an ancient Native Indian craft with figures and animals carved into its sides. This canoe had no one within. The bow was illuminated by some strange light until the center of the boat disappeared into the darkness. And it moved on its own accord as if pushed by unseen hands upon a paddle. Pierre was terrified. The craft came closer and closer until it passed within feet of his boat. The song wavering from within did not stop and was low and deep.

Then the boat paused. It just wavered there equal to Pierre's pirogue, and a stench like the rotting of a corpse issued out from it. Pierre stifled a gag with his palm. As he did, from the darkness that was the center of the boat, a long arm extended out. Flaps of dead, dried skin hardly clung to moldering bones. The specter had clenched his bony hand until this point, a fist that suddenly opened as one forefinger pushed out past the others pointing directly at Pierre. And Pierre screamed, his lungs wrenching out the most God-awful screech that echoed so far people on nearby shores would later claim they heard as clear as if the man was standing in their yards. He stared with dumbed eyes as the canoe went toward the misty shoreline and vanished.

With that, Pierre leaned hard to his left and shoved his paddle into the water. Now, as I failed to mention earlier, pirogues are much tipsier than canoes. They wiggle and waggle at the slightest movement, and those who are careless often end up either drowning or in an alligator's tight grasp when they misjudge their weight a little far to the left or a little far to the right and end with a splash into the swamp. On this night, Pierre did keel a little far to the left when he dug his paddle into the water; however, he was lucky. He was able to right himself and make it back to the village to divulge his horrible tale. But the old man was not so fortunate a month later when caught in a storm that snuck into the bayou. He was caught off-guard, and during the squall, he leaned on his paddle too hard and went into the water and drowned.

Pierre was not the only one to be doomed by the ghostly canoe. A sailor came across the boat. A few weeks later, a hot-headed deckhand slashed him with a knife in a duel. Three Creoles fishing on the waters saw the strange sight—one was bit by a rattlesnake, another dragged into the marsh and eaten by an alligator, and a shark devoured the third.

Old Gaspar would end his tale like that, telling the fishermen that he, too, had seen the specter canoe. Everyone who saw it would die some horrid death or come to serious injury. He had expected some terrible death to come to him, but he had yet to die from the curse—he had only been beaten nearly to death by four men he had angered.

Gaspar warned them that if they go out on the bayous, lakes, and islands, they might come upon the harbinger of death too. The fishermen had listened as most do, rolling their eyes at the spooky story and chuckling to themselves as they left. They should have heeded his words. A storm came that evening, and although a boat was found empty floating on Lake Perot, nobody ever found the men who had been fishing within.

Vodou

A Brief Background of Vodou In New Orleans

Congo Square—On Sundays, the slaves and freed blacks escaped to the outskirts of town to celebrate their religion and traditions.

When the French and Spanish brought enslaved West Africans from areas like Benin and Togo and into New Orleans, the traditions, healing practices, and religious beliefs (Voudou or Vodoun) came with them. Voodoo/ Vodou utilizes rituals and ceremonies and one supreme being similar to the Christian, Islamic, and Judaism God. Just like these religions are diverse with multifaceted and distinctive individual practices, Vodou has unique ways to worship, some even kept secret among those initiated into the faith.

The Vodou God (Bondye) does not interfere in the lives of humans. However, spirits (loa), each with its own character, responsibilities of everyday life, and ways of service, will intervene and act as intermediaries between the physical world and the divine world. Vodou practitioners do not pray to the loa like saints or angels and instead *serve* the spirits. Powerful practitioners (kings and queens) guide the religious community by leading ritual dances and ceremonies a few times a year, inviting the spirits to come by offering singing, percussion, and drumming. They lay out a table with the foods that the spirits enjoy, and then those attending and the poor share the meal at the end of the ceremony. They also perform healing, impart protective spiritual objects like powders and gris-gris, and offer private consultations.

A Vodou king or queen begins a ritual by calling upon Papa Legba with a chant. Papa Legba is the loa intermediary of the crossroads between earth and the spirit world—a gatekeeper who gives or denies permission to speak with the spirits. He is often depicted as an older black man in a straw hat and carrying a wooden walking stick. There is a bag at the top of the walking stick holding every souls' fate and destiny on earth. A vèvè or a symbol specific to the spirit made of cornmeal or flour concentrates the energies so that the loa will reveal itself and materialize within the queen or king's body in a spiritual form. The act will give the spirit a human body to speak through and also allow it to enjoy the gift given like rum, black coffee, cigars, or sweets, which are common offerings to Papa Legba.

In old New Orleans, Vodou would eventually blend with the main religion of the city–Catholicism, which the Arcadians and Spaniards introduced to become what most called Vodou-Catholicism. Some Vodou spirits even became associated with the Christian saints.

In the beginning, after church services on Sundays, by law, the slaves were able to have time to themselves. They headed to the outskirts of town and past the earthen ramparts that protected the city from attack to an old commonplace, now called Congo Square, to celebrate their freedom and express their religion and beliefs that were misunderstood and seemingly unacceptable to those who enslaved them.

The practice continues today in the city, a respected member of the religious community. So that everyone has a chance to empathize, learn, and experience the religion, there are events like Vodou Music and Arts Experience, St John's Eve Head Washing Ceremony, the Voodoo Spiritual Temple, and the Voodoo Museum.

VOODOO SPIRITUAL TEMPLE – 1428 N Rampart Street, New Orleans—Consultations, rituals, potions, tours, and lectures.

New Orleans Voodoo Historic Museum—724 Dumaine St, New Orleans—One of only a few museums dedicated entirely to Vodou art.

Carmel and Sons Botonica—1532 Dumaine Street, New Orleans

Events:

St John's Eve (June 23) Celebration, including a head-washing ritual, initiated when Marie Laveau hosted feasts in the 1830s on the banks of Lake Pontchartrain.

Mardi Gras

Mardi Gras

Of Celebration

Making enough noise to wake the dead, the Skull and Bone Gang walk the streets and awaken the neighborhood for Mardi Gras.
Image: Karen Apricot

Everyone knows ghosts walk the streets of New Orleans, long-dead entities that cannot find rest. But on one morning of the year, skeletons join them in a march around Treme.

But these entities are more than just old bones clanking around—they are people costumed as skeletons in a community masking tradition that has historical ties all the way back to 1819 and originated by a sailor and merchant marine from South Africa. On Fat Tuesday and before sunrise, the Northside Skull and Bone Gang walk door to door costumed as skeletons waking people up. Their message is not of fear or dread or wrath, but instead love and thankfulness of another day of life.

At Mardi Gras. *Image: Library of Congress.*

And that is how Mardi Gras starts even today. However, it had its beginnings in pre-Christian pagan societies, including the Roman holidays of Saturnalia (spring and fertility) and Lupercalia (winter celebration to the god Saturn). When Christianity came to Rome, leaders incorporated the tradition into its faith. Technically, it begins on Epiphany, a Christian holiday celebrating the three kings who visited Jesus. Christians traditionally celebrate on the Tuesday before Ash Wednesday, called Fat Tuesday, and the beginning of the Christian Lent season leading to Easter. Fat Tuesday is the day of eating fatty foods before Lent which is the time of fasting. This period between Epiphany and Fat Tuesday is also called Carnival.

The celebration would spread. Mardi Gras was brought to America and specifically New Orleans by the French who settled the region, Pierre Le Moyne d'Iberville and Sieur de Bienville. Upon arrival in an area about 60 miles downriver from New Orleans on March 3, 1699, the explorers held a celebration and named the area Pointe du Mardi Gras upon realizing it was the eve of the holiday. As time passed, those settling the region would hold elegant, masked balls and indulge in lavish feasts before they had to fast for lent.

Many donned the masks to hide their identity, rid their inhibitions, and mingle among other classes. There were parties in the streets until Spain took control of the region from 1762 to 1800 and banned many celebrations. It was not much better after the U.S. claimed New Orleans in 1803. Officials forbade disguises and masks for quite some time.

Mistick Krewe of Comus– from an 1867 print. Mardi Gras has long been celebrated as a time of debauchery, parades in the streets, and wild rituals before the calmer days of Lent. *Image: Library of Congress.*

The Pageant of Rex began in 1872 to honor a Russian King visiting Mardi Gras. It has, since, become a tradition. Circa 1907.
Image: Library of Congress

In 1827, students who had visited France returned and mimicked the celebrations there, wearing colorful costumes and masks and parading along the streets. Soon, carriages and horseback riders would join them, marching and dancing in the streets. In the late 1850s, gaslight torches added a certain mystique and magic by a secret society called the Mistick Krewe of Comus. They held a parade themed "The Demon Actors in Milton's Paradise Lost" and began having lavish balls.

-Purple, gold, and green are the most common colors of New Orleans' Mardi Gras.

-A cake, called King Cake, made with brioche dough, braided, and laced with cinnamon and colored sugar, is eaten during this season. A tiny plastic baby is hidden inside -whoever finds it might get a surprise or host the next party.

-Women exposing their breasts during Mardi Gras in New Orleans have been documented since 1889. It has escalated to the baring of breasts in exchange for beads and trinkets.

-People partying in the street have noticed ghosts of the past mingling among the living. Whether dressed in Mardi Gras costumes or simply parading with the crowd, they appear as quickly as they disappear and sometimes, even to those who are not completely soused!

The Cemeteries

I pass on the stories of some of the typical ghosts for each cemetery. Many others are roaming the old cities of the dead who are less known or pop up once in a while to follow someone around; ghosts are drawn to the living, especially ones to whom they have something in common, who they would identify with when alive.

You might find one peering curiously at you from around a tomb or whispering something in your ear. You might pass someone, then turn, and discover you actually passed no-one at all, at least someone living. Or someone in spectral form may follow you like I was shadowed in St Louis Cemetery No 1. I could only hear the rumble of traffic along Basin Street and droning voices from other tours while I strolled along the shell path within. However, after I listened to a recording I had been taking, above the noises around me, a man's deep and wooing voice had been mumbling sweet words in Creole only a few steps behind—

Wall vaults to the right and *mausoleums* to the left.

A little about the tombs you may see—

Initially, colonists buried their dead below ground. In the early 1800s, burials followed the French and Spanish tradition of above-ground tombs. Most commonly used are the *wall vaults*—vaults stacked on top of one another. There are also, for those who could afford a family tomb, ornate *mausoleums* with crypts inside. Regardless of the construction, they all follow much the same process.

During a burial, cemetery caretakers temporarily remove the bricks or barrier at the front of the vault and place a curtain to cover the opening during the funeral. After, the undertaker (or in earlier years, the family members) lays the corpse in a casket, and caretakers slide the casket into one of the vaults. Then the bricks or covering are restored and the vault sealed. Bodies decompose quickly in the subtropic heat of New Orleans, but it is traditional not to move them for at least one year. When another family member dies, the vault is reopened, the body is pushed back into the chamber, and the new one takes its place.

Coping Tombs are made with sealed material like marble or granite and are covered with pebbled gravel to define a grave's boundaries.

Ledger Stones—a flat slab of stone with epitaphs are laid atop, placed flush with the earth's surface, and over the tomb to seal it.

St Peter Street Cemetery
New Orleans Catholic Cemetery
600 Block of Rampart and Burgundy
New Orleans, LA 70116
Within the Bounds of N Rampart, St Peter, Burgundy, and Toulouse Streets
29.96132, -90.06759

St Peter Cemetery—Underfoot

Site of the old St Peter Street Cemetery. *Image: Adrian Chevalier*

If you stand on the corner of Burgundy and St Peter near Congo Square, beneath the soles of your shoes are the bodies of the first citizens of New Orleans. In the initial development of the city during the early 1700s, New Orleans was only half the size of the French Quarter known today. During that time, a consecrated cemetery was created, called the *Campo Santo*, meaning the Holy Field, outside the city proper by the Catholic Church.

Since Catholicism was the only religion practiced in the territory during the Colonial era, nearly everyone had been baptized in the church and buried there—French, Spanish, whites, slaves, free people of color, and those of Native American descent. Even if a person was not Catholic, they were buried just outside the bounds.

To create the burial ground, the city dug ditches around the parcel of land, and the excavated earth was used to elevate the plot. A wooden wall was built around it. Here, families did not bury the bodies of their dead above the ground at the time, but below, wrapped in linen and laid in a modest coffin made of cyprus. Although historians believe that burials as early as 1718 were placed along the riverbank when New Orleans was nothing more than a fledgling outpost, this cemetery along St Peter Street was the first formal burial ground. It welcomed the dead in New Orleans from 1724 to 1789 (and even into the 1790s if St Louis Cemetery No 1, its replacement, had flooded). The people of the city called the graveyard St Peter Street Cemetery, and later, after new cemeteries were created, the Old Cemetery.

In the 1780s, the city began to expand. Physicians warned authorities that there was a true cause for alarm for the spread of disease from a graveyard so close to human habitation. The Spanish government opted to create a new cemetery, St Louis No 1, where bodies would be buried above the ground. Because the Catholic Church had not formally claimed title to the land, the Cabildo reclaimed the property and sold it at auction. Despite protest from the Catholic Church and the city's citizens, the government refused to dig up the old graves and move them. Instead, by the early 1800s, St Peter Street Cemetery was closed, the land was subdivided and sold for development, and homes and businesses were built overtop.

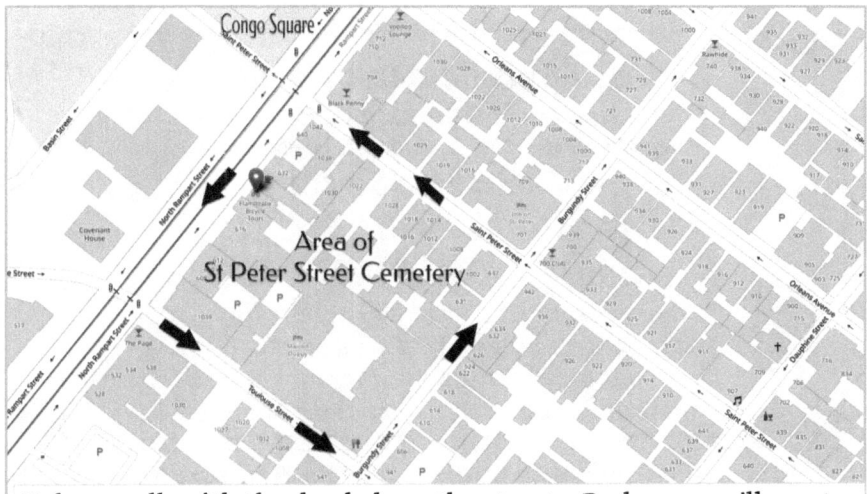

Take a walk with the dead along the streets. Perhaps you'll meet a ghostly reminder of the old cemetery's past.

Over the years, private property owners have discovered bones during remodels in the old cemetery area. Proper excavations and reburials were able to occur when feasible. Still, those who lay there can hardly rest with sidewalks and buildings settled on top of them. Step lightly. Do not be surprised if you hear moaning and groaning walking St Peter, Burgundy, and Toulouse streets. Not far below could be a spirit you have awakened. And hopefully, it is not an angry one.

St Louis Cemetery No 1

New Orleans Catholic Cemetery
Owned/Overseen by: Archdiocese of New Orleans

425 Basin Street
New Orleans, LA 70112
29.959605, -90.071465

To tour St Louis No 1, you will need to hire a tour
guide/join a tour group. It is recommended you
reserve/book online ahead of time. For your safety, do
not walk into the cemeteries alone or at night.

St Louis Cemetery No 1—The Background

St Louis Cemetery No 1—decorating the tombs on All Saints Day–
Image: Harper's Weekly, November 1885

The Catholic Church operates St Louis Cemetery. This old boneyard had its first burials in 1789 after authorities designated a marshy swampland outside the city proper for interments. When the cemetery opened, Spain was still governing the colony and mandated that graves would be built in tombs above the earth, following customs of using above-ground vaults especially popular in both Spain and France.

This practice also avoided watery graves because the water table is high in the city. During flooding, the air-filled caskets were forced above the surface along with the decaying corpses. Even drilling holes into the top of the casket helped little as the moldering body-liquids would leak into the soil and contaminate the land and water sources around them.

Not all are dead within St Louis Cemetery No 1. Unless, of course, this kitty isn't a kitty at all, but someone's familiar spirit out for a stroll. *Image: Backroads Boo and Brew*

It is still an active graveyard with a Catholic section in the front with a mixture of stately mausoleums, crumbling tombs, and narrow shell footpaths. There were also sections set aside in the rear early on for Protestants, assigned for Christ Church Episcopal, and burials of African-Americans and people of color. There is not much grass, or trees, or shrubs here; there is no room. The tombs are so tightly packed in the lot that, at times, visitors have to squeeze between the vaults to get from one area to the next.

It is a labyrinth of stone and brick tombs, once whitewashed, but now with dingy paint flecking away and exteriors falling into decay. Above the graves are angels and crosses, and sometimes along the path, you can see oyster shells and bits of old bone. Within the tombs, the old bodies have long rotted away, and not the faintest scent of death remains—the hot summer sun has cooked their bones and flesh away.

It has long been home to agony and tragedy. Once long ago, a man would visit his daughter day after day, sometimes opening her tomb to peer within. He would stare for hours at her decaying casket. Then one afternoon, wrought with sadness, he opened her tomb, climbed within, and wiggled the lid over as best he could. Then he pulled from his pocket the poison laudanum in a bottle and drank it down. Later, his wife worried about him. She followed his usual path to the grave and noticed the lid of the tomb partway open. Within, she found her husband, already in his grave.

For centuries, the living have come to visit their beloved dead here. It appears that some would stay. Now, many come to see the ghosts, walking through the cemeteries with eyes wide, waiting for some spirit to rise. And at times, they do.

St Louis Cemetery No 1
New Orleans Catholic Cemetery
Owned/Overseen by: Archdiocese of New Orleans
425 Basin Street
New Orleans, LA 70112
29.959605, -90.071465
To tour St Louis No 1, you will need to hire a tour guide/join a tour group. It is recommended you reserve/book online ahead of time. For your safety, do not walk into the cemeteries alone or at night.

St Louis Cemetery No 1—Marie Laveau Tomb

The grave of Marie Laveau in St Louis Cemetery No 1. Her ghost has been seen in many forms—one legend tells that after she died, she could turn herself into a crow and fly over the cemetery.

Marie Laveau, Louisiana Creole practitioner of Vodou, hairdresser, and healer, died on June 15, 1881, at age 79. Her daughter, Philomene, buried her in St Louis Cemetery No 1 in the family tomb's middle vault. Since her death, visitors claim to see her strolling along the gritty cemetery paths.

She wears a dark chemise top and skirt and a brightly colored shawl. She also wears a tan and brick-red tignon.

In earlier years, people walking near the cemetery saw her as a Newfoundland dog loping along. Several local legends recall that when she died, she turned herself into a crow that could fly across the cemetery and perhaps, over the wall and into the city. In the 1930s, Elmore Lee Banks, a person of color, had stopped at a shop near the old cemetery and caught more than a glimpse of something he would never forget. "I was in a drugstore right near St Louis No 1, and this wasn't no more than ten years ago," he told one writer, "An old woman dressed in a long, white dress and with a blue tignon come in and stood right next to me. I didn't pay her no mind but kept on explaining to the drugstore man what I wanted." Suddenly, Banks realized that the drugstore owner was not listening to his request at all, but staring right at the old woman with "eyes popping out like a frog's." The drugstore owner whipped around and shot into the back of the store, disappearing. "I didn't know what to do," Banks went on. "So, I turned around and looked at this woman. She looked back at me, and she started laughing, kind of like she was crazy. She just laughed and laughed and, me, I thought she was just some poor crazy woman that the druggist was scared of. God, if I'd known what was coming, I'd have died on the spot!"

Right then she asked Banks, "Don't you know me?" "No, ma'am," he answered, "Where the drugstore man go?" It seemed to spark something in the woman, and her eyes got fiery with anger. She lifted a hand and slapped Banks on the cheek! Before he could blink, the woman jumped into the air and whooshed out the door, soaring over the telephone wires. She passed over the cemetery and vanished. Banks passed out. "When I woke up," Banks would relate, "The drugstore man was pouring whiskey down my throat."

"You know who that was?" the drugstore man had asked Banks, who was still in shock. "That was Marie Laveau. She been dead for years and years, but every once in a while, people around here see her. Son, you is been slapped by the Queen of the Voodoos!"

The grave of Marie Laveau in St Louis Cemetery No 1. After her death, followers would leave offerings on the grave and draw crosses on the stone to ask her spirit for contact. The drawings were believed to be both an interaction of Catholic faith and African customs. In African religious rituals, the crossed lines represent the highest point of power between the living world and the spirit world. These were continuously noted into the 1940s and 1950s along with newspaper articles talking about the sextons at the cemetery cleaning up everything from pineapples and bananas to cooking tools and cakes left for Marie Laveau. Later, tour guides watered down this version telling tourists to draw three Xs and leave a silver coin or some trinket, to be granted a wish. The acts are prohibited now, not only because those who mark the tomb do not do it in respectful recognition of Vodou religion, but it is destroying the graves.

St Louis Cemetery No 1

New Orleans Catholic Cemetery
Owned/Overseen by: Archdiocese of New Orleans

425 Basin Street
New Orleans, LA 70112
29.959605, -90.071465

To tour St Louis No 1, you will need to hire a tour guide/join a tour group. It is recommended you reserve/book online ahead of time. For your safety, do not walk into the cemeteries alone or at night.

St Louis Cemetery No 1—Hex Tomb

The builder of the Italian Mutual Benevolent Society tomb, center, was said to be cursed by the very tomb he designed. *Image: Library of Congress, 1900.*

Pietro Gualdi was an Italian of many talents—artist, architect, and painter of panoramas. In 1851, he moved to New Orleans and, while living here, created an incredibly detailed and much-hailed panorama of the city. While completing another project, an ornate marble mausoleum for the Italian Mutual Benevolent Society at St Louis Cemetery No I, he caught malaria and died in January 1857.

He would be one of the first to be entombed in the same crypt he made. And it seems the use of "society" vaults were fleeting—during life, those with less wealth could still pay a stipend to a society linked to them by ethnicity or trade. Then they were buried in a communal mausoleum. Upon death, the members were customarily interred for only a year, and then their remains were placed in a collective area below or their bones sent back to their homeland. Some believe Pietro Gualdi sealed his fate by creating the short-lived home for the dead because his own life was cut short in New Orleans for creating a tomb where an eternal resting place was not so everlasting and instead, transitory.

Italian Mutual Benevolent Society tomb.

St Louis Cemetery No 1

New Orleans Catholic Cemetery
Owned/Overseen by: Archdiocese of New Orleans

425 Basin Street
New Orleans, LA 70112
29.959605, -90.071465

To tour St Louis No 1, you will need to hire a tour guide/join a tour group. It is recommended you reserve/book online ahead of time. For your safety, do not walk into the cemeteries alone or at night.

St Louis Cemetery No 1—Henry Vignes

The area of the cemetery once assigned to Protestants, paupers, African-Americans, and people of color. And where a ghostly figure rises searching for his family tomb.

As the population grew in New Orleans, so too did the original outline of the cemetery. With the arrival of Protestants and Haitians in the early 1800s, the cemetery was enlarged to accommodate more than Catholics. An area in the rear was added. Henry Vignes was buried here in the 19th century. A seaman, he lodged in New Orleans when his ship docked for any amount of time as he once had family here.

He trusted the boarding house lady where he stayed enough to leave his papers with her while at sea. Alas, when he returned one day, he found she had sold his family's tomb. Soon after, he became ill and died. His body was buried in the back of St Louis No 1 in an unmarked grave. At times, he rises from the bare ground and walks the rows of tombs, stopping passersby and asking if they can point him in the direction of the Vignes tomb. Then he disappears.

St Louis Cemetery No 1

New Orleans Catholic Cemetery
Owned/Overseen by: Archdiocese of New Orleans

425 Basin Street

New Orleans, LA 70112

29.959605, -90.071465

To tour St Louis No 1, you will need to hire a tour guide/join a tour group. It is recommended you reserve/book online ahead of time. For your safety, do not walk into the cemeteries alone or at night.

St Louis Cemetery No 1—The Widow

A widow once walked from her home to the cemetery every day to weep over her husband's tomb. Wrought with grief, she decided to end her life. During one visit, she fell into a deep, sad sleep over her husband's grave. When she awakened, it was in the dark of night, and with a start, she saw a pale form stepping from her husband's tomb. She recognized her husband instantly, and she was filled with joy. As she looked around, though, she realized she could see not only her husband but others who were mingling amongst the tombs, laughing and chatting. Then as she peered outside the graveyard, the woman watched in horror as ghastly skeletons rushed around, scrambling crazily to get from one place to the other. She gasped, and her dead husband grabbed her hand and said softly, "Do not be afraid, my love. Those outside are how the living, like you, appear to us. They are dead. We are alive." From that day forward, the woman no longer suffered so much grief, for she knew her husband was happy after death. And if you are suffering from sorrow and visit the cemetery, there may be just a fraction of a moment where all is nearly silent to you. Listen carefully, as you will hear the dead amusing themselves and chattering. It is their way of making you feel at peace.

St Louis Cemetery No 2

New Orleans Catholic Cemetery
Owned/Overseen by: Archdiocese of New Orleans

300 N Claiborne Avenue
New Orleans, LA 70112

Entrance: 1698-1650 Conti Street
New Orleans, LA 70112
29.961205, -90.075066
For your safety, do not walk into the cemeteries alone
or at night.

St Louis Cemetery No 2—Ghastly Moans

St Louis Cemetery No 2 where moans are heard—

St Louis Cemetery No 2 was founded in 1823 and is owned by the Archdiocese of New Orleans. New Orleans was struck by disease mostly caused by poor medical knowledge and lack of health regulations during this time. Cholera, diphtheria, typhoid, smallpox, bubonic plague, yellow fever, and malaria took a toll on both the rich and the poor, young and old. But the dead do not seem to want to rest here. Those walking its paths have seen apparitions wandering this old graveyard. If you listen closely over the sounds of the highway above, you may hear occasional ghastly moans or groans along with muffled chatter of the long-dead.

St Louis Cemetery No 2

New Orleans Catholic Cemetery
Owned/Overseen by: Archdiocese of New Orleans

300 N Claiborne Avenue
New Orleans, LA 70112

Entrance: 1698-1650 Conti Street
New Orleans, LA 70112
29.961205, -90.075066
For your safety, do not walk into the cemeteries alone
or at night.

St Louis Cemetery No 2—Wishing Vault

The Wishing Vault (center with votives) is in the corner formed by Iberville and Robertson streets (St James Aisle) and next to Jordan B. Nobel's tomb, 14-year old drummer in the Civil War and after, a notable fixture in the city. Image: *Libby Bollino, Lucky Bean Tours, public and private walking tours.*

In the back of St Louis Cemetery No 2 is a 3-tiered vault. There is one tomb that tends to stand out with trinkets and notes and plenty of Xs. It is called the Wishing Vault, and while some believe that a daughter of Marie Laveau continued with her mother's work and her family later buried her here, others believe Marie Laveau, herself, is inside. Even others suggest that Marie Contesse, who was a Vodou Queen before Laveau, is entombed within.

There used to be a crack in the bricks, and some would visit the tomb and make wishes, dropping coins afterward into the gap. "Nice looking young ladies come," the cemetery sexton divulged in 1931. "On many a bright afternoon, they come slipping through the gates and looking around, so careful to see that nobody is watching. They pass down that way, you see, and before every tomb, they stop and tap three times while they whisper the wish they want to come true. Then they come to the Voodoo Tomb and say their wish out loud."

The Wishing Vault. Another view from: *Libby Bollino, Lucky Bean Tours, public and private walking tours.*

Today, the tomb is intact, and visitors place tokens on the shelf instead.

St Louis Cemetery No 3

New Orleans Catholic Cemetery
Owned/Overseen by: Archdiocese of New Orleans

3421 Esplanade Avenue
New Orleans, LA 70119
29.983747, -90.087571

*For your own safety, do not walk into the cemeteries
alone or at night.*

St Louis Cemetery No 3—Disappearing Trick

St Louis Cemetery No 3 — Huge and haunted.

Louis Cemetery No 3 runs parallel to Bayou St John and was established in 1854, then outside the city limits. Visitors often speak of hearing ghostly voices throughout the cemetery. One tourist traveling with the history tours paused politely near a small mausoleum for another in her group to pass, only to watch the shadowy form stoop low and completely disappear into the closed-door tomb! But the most common experience here is the wiggly orbs of spirit lights even seen during the day.

Lafayette Cemetery No. 1
1427 Washington Avenue
New Orleans, LA 70130
29.928989, -90.085398
For your own safety, do not walk into the cemeteries
alone or at night.

Lafayette Cemetery No. 1—Just Passersby

Those who pass by may be dead or alive! *Image: MusikAnimal*

Established in 1833 in the Garden District, this early non
-denominational and city-run cemetery was once in the City
of Lafayette, a suburb of New Orleans and home to many
immigrants from Ireland and Germany. It is a beautiful
cemetery with magnolia trees lining the streets. Most often,
people remark that they see ghostly figures strolling among
the tombs. So lifelike, most assume they are folks from the
neighborhood on a leisurely walk.

Cypress Grove Cemetery
120 City Park Avenue
New Orleans, LA 70124
29.979424, -90.111472
For your own safety, do not walk into the cemeteries alone or at night.

Cyprus Grove—Up in Smoke

Cyprus Grove has many societies buried within, one is a fireman's association that offers a unique supernatural occurrence.

In 1840, the Firemen's Charitable and Benevolent Association founded Cyprus Grove to honor New Orleans firefighters through charitable donations. Not so strangely, some entering the cemetery catch a waft of smoke lingering in the air. Others have found images taken in the graveyard have a smoky or foggy appearance.

Greenwood Cemetery
5190 Canal Blvd #200
New Orleans, LA 70124
29.982668, -90.112153
For your own safety, do not walk into the cemeteries
alone or at night.

Greenwood Cemetery—Ambling Writer

Greenwood Cemetery.

The cemetery is one of the oldest in New Orleans and was opened in 1852 by the Firemen's Charitable and Benevolent Association after Cypress Grove Cemetery. Most people note the four huge monuments at the entrance: Firemen's Memorial, Confederate monument, the Elk's tomb, and the tombs of former presidents of the association, Michael McKay and John Fitzpatrick.

Among the ghosts that amble around this cemetery is writer John Kennedy Toole, buried here after committing suicide at age 31. His grave is on the Latanier path between the Hawthorne and Magnolia Walks and marked, *Ducoing*.

Charity Hospital Cemetery
5050 Canal Street
New Orleans, LA 70119
29.980019, -90.110742
*For your own safety, do not walk into the cemeteries
alone or at night.*

Charity Hospital Cemetery —Buried Alive

Charity Hospital Cemetery. Where you did not have to be all the way dead to find a final resting place.

The Charity Hospital purchased the cemetery in April of 1848 as a mass cemetery for unclaimed bodies and was formally known as Potters Field. Most of the bodies, unlike other cemeteries in the region, were buried underground. However, it appears that not all were *dead* when interred in the cemetery. A macabre story comes from 1875—

At one time, Charity Hospital hired a wagon to drive the dead to Potters Field. In May of 1875, during a smallpox epidemic, rumors began to fly around the city of a man buried alive in the cemetery. C.H. Beggs was in the Potters Field when Charity Hospital Wagon No 1 drove into the cemetery, followed by several women who seemed quite distressed. The driver stopped near a grave pit and began to tow the coffin from the wagon's rear. As he began to deposit the coffin into the hole, the occupant kicked the lid off, and an arm wiggled out. "For God's sake," a voice called out from within, "do not bury me alive!" With that, the driver picked up a brick and growled back, "I have a doctor's certificate, you are dead, and I am going to bury you!" The driver then struck the body in the casket, dumped it in the grave, and proceeded with the burial.

Believing it was a hoax, police did not investigate, so local reporters began canvassing the streets and interviewing possible witnesses. Melinda Smith, who was visiting a friend on Locust Street, would corroborate Beggs's story as she was one of the women following the wagon. She had stopped at a neighbor's house on Locust Street, between First and Second, when the hospital wagon stopped nearby. A friend hailed her. Thinking that the wagon had broken down, Smith walked out to the wagon, noting both a baby's casket and an adult casket within. Then she saw movement. "What do you want?" the driver, a tall white man with a red face and a white hat had growled at her. "Do you want to catch the smallpox?"

"I am not afraid of the smallpox. I want to see," Smith had demanded.

"Get away from here before I slap you in the mouth!" the driver threatened. She could see the adult coffin was open, and she distinctly saw a man inside moving his hand in a vain attempt to push off the lid.

The driver arose, took the cushion off his wagon seat, pushed it over the man's head, and sat atop it. When Smith called attention to the fact that he was taking a live man to the graveyard, he scoffed at her. Then he drove along for several blocks while the woman followed, stopping once to snatch up a hammer and attempt to nail the lid tightly shut. The driver, then, pushed the baby's coffin on top of the foot of the man's casket and then sat atop it while he carried on to the cemetery, refusing her entrance.

The place where thousands of souls are buried—many of them from smallpox epidemics, and some do not rest peacefully.

Another woman putting up her wash, Mary Thompson, had joined the march too after the wagon had caught her eye. She had seen the man in the casket struggle and watched the baby's casket slammed on top. The driver denied her pleas to stop the wagon, and she kept up a good pace only a step behind. She was sure the man within the casket was alive but too weak to put up much of a fight.

Rose Johnson, Ellen Burns, and Henderson Burch, all residing on Locust, had also watched with mouths agape, positive he was not dead. The trio became a part of the mass of women and young boys, blacks and whites pouring down the streets or watching with curiosity as the procession made its way along the roadway.

Walking through this cemetery leaves a chilling feeling in the soul. Moans and groans are heard at this old Potters Field.

A bystander by the name of William Harrison heard the news that they were burying a man alive. The sexton and the cemetery workers had stopped the others, refusing their entrance. But Harrison pushed through the crowd and into the gates of the cemetery, stopping before the grave. A young man asked him to look into the coffin, and Harrison removed the lid. He saw what the others had seen, but yet there was more—in the casket was a black man, naked and with cobblestone on his belly. His toes were twitching, and his chest still rose and fell.

When the news met the reporters' ears, they hurried to find the identity of the man buried alive—they found the death certificate of Tennessee native George Banks, a young man of color and only 19 years of age who had supposedly died of smallpox on May 25. On May 26, the young man, most likely in a coma, had been placed in a wagon by Jim Conners to be taken to the Potters Cemetery.

But even before they got to the muddy mound on the vacant lot where they had heard the driver had buried the young man, reporters caught the horrid smell of death and the ghastly sight of a mound of dead babies covered in flies and laid one atop the other five feet high left to rot in the sun. There were bodies laid out, a man and a woman with a baby lying between the two. Scattered around were layers of coffins of the still unburied after the smallpox epidemic.

Conners, a belligerent man who had a disreputable past, denied that George Banks had been alive, but he was arrested and taken to the workhouse, nonetheless. Schwartz, the cemetery sexton, said this, "The man was dead. I buried him. The coffin had fallen to pieces from the jolting of the cart. The lid of the coffin was off. The lid was divided into pieces. The driver of the wagon, in driving in the nail, had driven it in the outside, and the lid fell off. I do not know what happened before he got to the cemetery. I did not see a stone placed on the breast of the dead man. Jim is a man suited for his position, and of course, is not very good-hearted or tender. It is customary to admit persons to see bodies buried, but on this day, we kept everybody out because there was so much excitement."

St Patrick Cemetery No 1, 2, and 3
New Orleans Catholic Cemetery
Owned/Overseen by: Archdiocese of New Orleans
5000 Canal Street
New Orleans, LA 70119
29.981743, -90.109583
For your own safety, do not walk into the cemeteries
alone or at night.

St Patrick Cemetery 1,2,3—Photobombers

St Patrick Cemetery 1—with many coping tombs.

During the 1830s and 1840s, famines and poor living conditions in Ireland left thousands of Irish immigrants pouring into the U.S. and searching for work. In New Orleans, the newcomers took the only jobs they could find. Many were in dangerous labor positions like laying the bricks for streets or digging the canals in mosquito-infested swamps that even the slave owners would not hire out their slaves to do because of the incredibly high risk of yellow fever and malaria.

But the Irish population grew, and the opportunity to build a church for their community came in the early 1830s as St Patrick's Church. By 1841, the parishioners purchased land for the building of a cemetery. Canal Street and City Park Avenue separated the property forming three distinct cemeteries—St Patrick No 1, No 2, and No 3.

In the early years of the cemetery, when the Irish were coming into the country, the interments were placed in-ground and raised slightly by frames (coping). This type of burial was both cost-effective for the meagerly-paid newcomers and also customary in their homeland. But even these modest tombs and any semblance of forming a pattern of distinct rows for the burials in St Patrick No 1 would give way to desperate times and the sudden need of hasty burials in incredibly large numbers when yellow fever hit in 1853. Parishioners could do little more than bury their families in haphazardly placed, quickly dug graves—in August of that year, caretakers buried 1100 people in the cemetery alone due to the epidemic.

St Patrick Cemetery 2—with more above-ground tombs.

But as time progressed and the hard-working Irish moved up the ranks of the labor force and began to mingle and marry with other ethnic groups, the traditional New Orleans' above-ground tombs became more common. These burial types and cemetery rows and patterns are more evident in St Patrick No 2 and No 3.

There are ghosts in St Patrick Cemetery. You do not have to steal through the graves at night to see them (which is not allowed anyway); you might do better to walk with a camera during the day, randomly taking shots. Ghosts are sure to photobomb you. What is not to love about that? Of all the cemeteries I visit, this one leaves a certain and distinct feeling someone is walking with me. But it would probably be wiser of me to say the ghosts are all around every person who walks within—curiously watching or doing their own thing, passing by, or mingling with their own—or photobombing just to see how you will react!

Printed ghostly images seldom do the picture justice. But if you are skeptical, try it yourself!

Two little ghost girls were watching me curiously from afar.

A Civil War officer, perhaps? He was standing over a grave seeming to reflect upon his death.

St Joseph Cemetery No 1 & 2

(aka St Joseph's German Orphan Asylum Cemetery)
New Orleans Catholic Cemetery
Owned/Overseen by: Archdiocese of New Orleans

2220 Washington Avenue
New Orleans, LA 70119
29.936295,-90.090049

For your own safety, do not walk into the cemeteries
alone or at night.

St Joseph Cemetery—A Sure Shot

St Joseph Cemetery No 2.

Established in 1854, the Catholic Church founded St Joseph No 1 to bring in income for the orphanage run by the Sisters of Notre Dame and as a burial place for German families in the community. Like many of the cemeteries in New Orleans, St Joseph comprises defined aisles for plots except for the rear section set aside for the many yellow fever victims. A second cemetery, St Joseph No 2, is located directly behind it, established in 1873. Both are among some of the top places in New Orleans to take pictures and find a ghostly apparition in them!

Odd Fellows Rest
5055 Canal Street
New Orleans, LA 70119
29.981981,-90.110875

For your own safety, do not walk into the cemeteries alone or at night.

Odd Fellows Rest —Spectral Lights

Peering through the locked gate at the Odd Fellows Rest.

Odd Fellows Rest was established in 1849 by the Independent Order of Odd Fellows (a fraternity dedicated to promoting goodwill and helping those in need) on land purchased by the benevolent societies so Protestant blacks could have a proper burial place. It is not open to the public, but you can peer through the gates. Those passing have seen spectral lights inside the walls.

Holt Cemetery
635 City Park Avenue
New Orleans, LA 70119
29.984546,-90.104824
For your own safety, do not walk into the cemeteries alone or at night.

Holt Cemetery—Heavenly Singer

Holt Cemetery with personal touches, both natural and supernatural.

Holt Cemetery began as a graveyard for the indigent. In 1879, a city board of health official formally established the cemetery. The graves here are below ground. It may appear cluttered with a mix of homemade and professionally-produced markers. Do not be fooled by the disarray. Teddy bears and beads are tokens of honor and affection from the families of those who have passed. The personal touches give this cemetery a unique spirit—a sensation of love and devotion leaving visitors feeling like they are among close family and friends. It is why the spirits show up here in ghostly images along with the sound of someone singing.

The Mortuary
4800 Canal Street
New Orleans, LA 70119
29.979292, -90.108272

The Mortuary—Haunted House

Once a residence, then a mortuary—now a haunted attraction.

Mary Slattery had this residence built in 1872. Her family, including six children, lived in it until 1905. After, the family sold the property to Marie Lafontear and William Klein, who owned it until 1923 when it became a mortuary—the PJ McMahon and Sons Undertaking Company. It remained a mortuary until 2004. And then came the ghosts—visitors have witnessed two children on the property along with a former mortician. People have been poked, prodded, and pushed within the building.

Chev A Thilim Cemetery –Gates of Prayer

*Jewish Federation of Greater New Orleans
(next to The Mortuary)*

4824 Canal Street
New Orleans, LA 70124
29.979694, -90.108222

*For your own safety, do not walk into the cemeteries
alone or at night.*

Chev A Thilim Cemetery —Top Hat

This Jewish cemetery was originally established as Tememe Derech in 1858 and renamed Gates of Prayer in 1939. It is called both Beth Israel and Chevra Thilim for the congregations who use it. Those taking the sidewalks past have noticed a ghostly man with a top hat lingering here, walking with hands clasped behind his back.

Masonic Cemetery
400 City Park Avenue
New Orleans, LA 70119
29.983208,-90.106562

*For your own safety, do not walk into the cemeteries
alone or at night.*

Masonic Cemetery—Little Girl in the Tomb

Stairway Tomb.

The Masonic Blue Lodges established the Masonic
Cemetery along City Park Avenue on the Metairie Ridge in
1865 for both family tombs and communal usage through
benevolent societies where members paid dues for the
purchase of a shared plot or vault.

At the stairway tomb, spirits are seen walking the steps toward heaven. But one of my all-time favorite ghost pictures was taken within while I peered into the mausoleum, not realizing that a little ghost girl sitting on the floor within was looking up at me. I wonder who she visits.

Stairway Tomb. While peering into the tomb, I was completely oblivious that a little girl was staring up at me. If you follow the image, you can see her dress and shoes and her arms tucked lazily between belly and lap. *Image: Backroads Boo and Brew*

Metairie Cemetery
Charles Howard Tomb
5100 Pontchartrain Boulevard
New Orleans, LA 70124
29.984264, -90.115464

Metairie Cemetery—The Background and the Loudest Tomb

The Metairie Cemetery had an unusual start—it was once the Metairie Racecourse. At one time, the Metairie Jockey Club owned the racetrack in one of the rare areas of high ground near New Orleans. It was not always easy to gain membership access, and it may have led to its demise—and such, the existence of the cemetery.

In the 1800s, lotteries were a popular way to raise money for civic expenses like building churches and making roads. However, corruption by private lottery organizers was widespread. Charles T. Howard, the Louisiana Lottery Company founder, bribed and coerced legislators and officials to keep the lottery operating and profitable. In doing so, he became not only rich but also a powerful figure.

But Howard was not as influential as he would have liked— the Metairie Jockey Club barred him from becoming a member. Legend has it that when the club denied an infuriated Howard's membership, he declared he would see the racecourse's death and it would be nothing but a cemetery. After the Civil War, the racetrack went bankrupt, and the land was purchased for a cemetery.

You can still see the remnants of the track in the oval shape of the cemetery. Howard was not such a bad guy—he was a huge benefactor of the Orphan's Asylums and Widows' Homes. One last kick in the belly to the old racecourse owners was that his family had him buried in the cemetery after dying in a carriage accident at age 53. So Howard eventually got in whether they liked it or not. His ghost puts up quite a bit of ruckus in his tomb. People hear loud noises and voices within.

The grave of Thomas Howard, *above*, exterior. And within where spirited noises are heard.
Charles Howard Tomb: (29.982208, -90.116320) On Central and Avenue A.

Metairie Cemetery
Francis Masich Tomb
5100 Pontchartrain Boulevard
New Orleans, LA 70124
29.983050, -90.116600

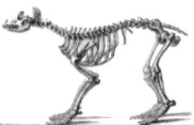

Metairie Cemetery —Weeping Dog

The Weeping Dog of Metairie Cemetery legend begs to tear at the heart.

According to legend, when Francis Masich died in 1893, his faithful dog followed his coffin to the grave and refused to leave, finally passing there. The sad-eyed pup is often decorated and has tears flowing down its face. Or in the case this day, a mask to keep him safe from germs.

Metairie Cemetery
Army of Tennessee Memorial
5100 Pontchartrain Boulevard
New Orleans, LA 70124
29.981492, -90.114332

Metairie Cemetery —Shadows in the Tomb

Army of Tennessee Memorial. *Image: Library of Congress. 1910*

General Albert Sidney Johnston is forever memorialized atop the Army of the Tennessee Memorial riding his horse "Fire-eater" as he did during the Battle of Shiloh. He is not buried inside, but plenty of soldiers are, including General P.T. Beauregard—and some come back to haunt the memorial. Cemetery visitors have seen shadow figures hovering inside the tomb.

Metairie Cemetery
Tomb of David Hennessey
5100 Pontchartrain Boulevard
New Orleans, LA 70124
29.982204, -90.117534

Metairie Cemetery —Still on the Beat

DAVID C. HENNESSY
The New Orleans Chief of Police

HENNESSEY

The grave of Chief Hennessy murdered while walking home from work. He is still on the job—but his beat is now at the cemetery watching the dead. *Hennessey Image: The NY Public Library*.

Thirty-one-year-old Police Chief David Hennessy uncovered a crime organization in New Orleans after two rival groups of Italian immigrants working on the New Orleans docks battled over fruit trade coming in from Central America. While walking home in drizzling rain, he was shot and killed. Hennessy's ghost walks the cemetery, but not just out for a stroll. He is keeping watch over the dead just as he protected the living while alive.

Metairie Cemetery
Arlington/Morales Tomb
5100 Pontchartrain Boulevard
New Orleans, LA 70124
29.983391, -90.115537

Metairie Cemetery —The Wandering Statue

Storyville—The red-light district from 1897 to 1917 where a certain Josie Arlington (born Mary Deubler) became a rich brothel owner. Her bordello has the round, tulip-shaped cupola.

Josie Arlington owned a brothel in the notorious red-light district of Storyville. This district in New Orleans included several isolated neighborhoods set aside by the city where prostitution, although still technically illegal, was allowed. Of all the houses of prostitution, Josie's four-story, sixteen bedroom mansion was certainly the most elegant. Located on the 200 block of Basin Street, The Chateau Lobrano d'Arlington had a tulip-domed cupola. Its interior held lavish furnishings, exotic carpets, and fine furniture.

And her girls were high-end, exotic-looking, and quite educated.

The Storyville community recognized Josie for her beauty, business savvy, and a bit of temper. Indeed, these characteristics contributed greatly to making her a wealthy woman. Such, she did what most of the affluent did in the early 1900s. Josie purchased an impressive, stately home to reside in while she was living. She bought an expensive burial plot in the upscale section of Metairie Cemetery with an extravagantly built $5000.00 tomb for after death. This mausoleum had a pair of stone flames and a Bronze statue of a young woman holding flowers and pushing on copper doors to the tomb.

The tomb of Josie Arlington, later bought by the Morales family.

It seemed like everything was going Josie's way. Then at only fifty-years-old in 1914, and after a sickness, she died.

The undertaker placed her in her impressive tomb, which was visited often by flocks of the curious, much to the dismay of the socially elite who had family entombed close by and felt it reflected poorly on them to be laid to rest near a brothel madam. Little time passed before her heirs spent her fortune, and creditors forced the family to sell not only Josie Arlington's home but her tomb. After, cemetery officials placed Josie secretly somewhere in the cemetery.

Weeks would pass before two stunned grave diggers witnessed the bronze figure on the statue vanish and then walk around the cemetery. Others heard banging coming from within. If that were not enough to bring out the curiosity seekers, street workers installed a flashing red light on a road running alongside the graveyard. The red light illuminated the granite of the tomb and made it appear the mausoleum was on fire. Some people say a strange entity haunts the grave. The bronze figure walks the cemetery, lurking in the shadows, searching for Josie Arlington's corpse to bring her back to her tomb.

St Roch Chapel and Campo Santo (Cemetery)

New Orleans Catholic Cemetery
Owned/Overseen by: Archdiocese of New Orleans

1725 St Roch Avenue
New Orleans, LA 70119
29.975495, -90.051977

St Roch Chapel and Campo Santo — The Background

St Roch Cemetery and Chapel. A place of legends and healing.

Roch, the only son of a rich nobleman, was miraculously born with the mark of a cross on his chest. In his twenties and after his parents' death, he gave his riches to the poor and his government position to his uncle and walked to Rome. Along his journey, Roch found that the plague had stricken countless people. As he stopped to tend to the sick, he miraculously healed many by tracing the sign of the cross on their forehead.

St Roch *Image: The Miriam and Ira D. Wallach Division of Art, Prints and Photographs: Print Collection, The New York Public Library.*

He, too, almost died from the epidemic. Roch went into the woods to not burden others and waited for death but was saved when a dog brought him bread and licked his wounds. In exchange, he gave the dog his blessings. While searching for his dog, the owner found Roch and nursed him back to health. After his death, the Roman Catholic Church officially declared him a saint. St Roch is the patron saint of, among many things— plague, dogs, cholera, bachelors, invalids, and skin rashes.

Reverend Peter Leonard Thevis volunteered to come to New Orleans as assistant pastor to Reverend Scheck of Holy Trinity Church in Faubourg Marigny in 1867. At the same time, a yellow fever epidemic had hit New Orleans. A year later, he would replace Scheck, who died when yellow fever swept through the city. During yet another particularly severe outbreak, Thevis began to send prayers to Saint Roch, the patron saint of protection from epidemics, to care for the people in his church, mainly German parishioners.

Jacob Schoen, the undertaker in charge of all the burials at Holy Trinity at the time, stated that the record books had not a single death among the congregation during the outbreak. When no one miraculously succumbed to the sickness, Reverend Thevis established St Roch Cemetery and built a chapel in gratitude to St Roch. The chapel is reputed as a place of curing the faithful; many have visited to pray for healing. Those who have visited have left such religious offerings in gratitude as glasses, polio braces, prosthetic body parts, and dental plates.

St Roch Cemetery and Chapel
New Orleans Catholic Cemetery
Owned/Overseen by: Archdiocese of New Orleans
1725 St Roch Avenue
New Orleans, LA 70119
29.975495, -90.051977

St Roch Chapel and Campo Santo —Petrified Child

Cross and child. *Image: Genthe photograph collection, Library of Congress. 1920s.*

At the entrance, there is a large cross. Beneath it is a statue of a child lying on a cot. People once believed that this statue was the petrified body of the first child buried in the cemetery—those who touched the broken foot supposed that the figure's porous material was hardened human flesh.

St Roch Cemetery (Campo Santo) and Chapel

New Orleans Catholic Cemetery
Owned/Overseen by: Archdiocese of New Orleans

1725 St Roch Avenue
New Orleans, LA 70119
29.975495, -90.051977

St Roch Chapel and Campo Santo —Saint of—Lovers?

St Roch Cemetery and Chapel. .

Many other traditions and legends have surrounded the little chapel and cemetery beyond miraculous cures. Of course, there is the Good Friday ritual bringing thousands to St Roch to walk through the Stations of the Cross, a 14-step Catholic devotion observing the last days of Jesus as a human. There is a saying, "Saint Roch will give you what you want, but he always takes something else away." Despite the advice, young people would come to the memorial and pray to St Roch for a spouse. If St Roch answered their prayers, they would leave a small trinket in gratitude.

Unmarried boys and men would visit and light candles, aspiring for a fitting wife. A tradition among young women in New Orleans was visiting nine churches and making an offering in each on Good Friday. After, they would stop at St Roch to walk the Stations of the Cross, then light a votive. Should all those tasks be performed with the last step of praying for a husband, she would marry happily within a year. And their mothers and fathers always cautioned them, "Be careful who you walk with through St Roch Cemetery—'tis said, once a man and a maid walk together there, they are sure to fall in love and be married."

St Roch Cemetery. Image: Library of Congress.

But the granting of love wishes was not just among the German Catholics, but also those who practiced Vodou. For those young women wishing for a wealthy husband, a handful of dirt could be taken from the cemetery grounds and sprinkled on the head with certain secret formalities and prayers to bring about the request.

Some believed the customs came from many years ago of a report circulated about a couple who was parted by the wife's death. The husband, wrought with grief, killed himself at her grave. His blood dribbled down the stone and onto the plain clover growing there. It formed a red-brown heart in the center of each of the leaves. Called the Bleeding Heart Shamrock, it was said only to grow there.

In St. Roch's Cemetery, New Orleans, La.

But others thought it might have been a simpler act of love that brought many there in later years. When 53-year-old Catherine Modica died in April of 1912, her husband Salvador would visit her grave every Sunday for the next 11 years, a total of 572 times and each time, bringing her flowers. Every week like clockwork, the sexton knew the 75-year-old man would be there trudging along the road leading to the cemetery. He would watch for him, becoming accustomed to the ritual. Until one Sunday, April 29, 1923. When Salvador did not show, the sexton followed the usual path and found the man dead along the road just outside the cemetery. The devoted husband was still clutching the flowers, and his face was tipped toward the graveyard. He would, at last, be with his love.

Gates of Mercy Cemetery
South Saratoga Street
And Jackson Avenue
New Orleans, LA 70113
29.938292, -90.084189

Lost Golden Children

The corner of Saratoga Street and Jackson Avenue where an old cemetery was once laid. And a ghost walked.

There was once a long-standing cemetery across from Saratoga Street and Jackson Avenue. After many years, it fell to disrepair. Nobody cared for the graves anymore—the grass was overgrown on the plot, the headstones broken, and the fence lay sideways. Once in a while, a neighborhood dog would wander its way inside and dig up an ancient dried legbone or jawbone to gnaw on, dragging its new prized possession home and dropping it on the front porch.

It was much to the displeasure of the family living there. Someone decided there must be a better use of the property than as a home to seventy or eighty cadavers who could not even fix the broken stones seven feet above them. *They* were useless. But the *land* was worth a tidy sum.

In 1957, the city set about digging up what they could find of the moldering corpses to move them elsewhere. But nearly 130 years had passed. What was once hair, flesh, and skeleton had decomposed to a few flakes of moldy skin, an occasional tooth, and a few shards of dried bones—the only identifying pieces remaining of the carcass after being eaten by beetles and worms. But what the workers failed to remove was the ghost that haunted the cemetery.

He certainly did not know it was time to move from his allegedly eternal resting place. Thus, he would still rise from what remained of the little dirt patch of land, then amble his way with slightly keeled shoulders and a noticeable hobbling limp across Jackson Avenue and then along South Saratoga Street. His name was Pierre Lefevre, and he was heading to his home.

Pierre, in life, was quite the miser. He ate little to save money, and he seldom lit a candle in the evening except to read his Bible for one-half hour from 10:00 p.m. to 10:30 p.m. Although the old pinchpenny carefully kept his hair combed, and his beard cleanly cut as neither cost him anything to keep up himself, his clothes were little more than rags. He patched the soles of his shoes with layers of a newspaper he found in the trash.

He had hoarded a huge sum of cash he exchanged for gold coins over many years of hard work. These coins, he would get out each day and look at them, fondle them in his fingers. At night, though, he kept these coins prudently stacked and hid them in a special recess he had made in his chimney.

But he worried so that some harm would come to them; a thief would take his beautiful, beloved coins. He cherished every shiny detail of each, the way they were so round and gold and warm to the touch after he had held them in his palms. Pierre would hug them to his chest, rock them in his arms. Like tiny golden children, they were to him. He loved them so! He would never, never part with them.

Pierre grew old and feeble. Then he got sick. Knowing it was his time to die, the old man stumbled into his backyard. He looked side to side three times to make sure no one was watching him. He slowly dug a hole, and he gently laid his children within one by one. And Pierre buried his little children underneath ten shovels of soil. After, he covered the earth with leaves and brush so no one would discover their hidey-hole. That night he died.

But Pierre Lefevre came back. After a bit, he clambered from his grave as ghosts do. Then he worked his way across Jackson Street and along Saratoga toward his home, stumbling, and grumbling and grunting with each step. The stench of death still clung to his soul. A passerby who saw nothing but took in the reek sniffed, curled his lips, then hurried on. It took some time for Pierre to find his home. When he got there, he could not find his coins. He dropped to his palms and knees and raked his fingers furiously through the stubbled grass again and again. Nothing was there. His children were gone! Someone had discovered his hidey-hole! While he looked, he crooned to them, mumbling bits of old children's songs. When a light flashed on, he crept to the brush and disappeared.

He still returns, night after night, looking for his lost golden children. At times, he brings others from the old defunct graveyard with him, the ones whose souls were left behind. Because when you dig up a grave, you may take the corpse, but the spirit buried there remains.

Just ask those who live nearby now. They will tell you. Even now, Pierre Lefevre rises from his grave, and he still searches for his lost golden children.

Looking toward the old boneyard to the left and the path Pierre Lefevre travels searching for the hidey-hole where he carefully placed his lost golden children.

More Notable Boneyard Haunts

From Potters Fields to Defunct Graveyards

Carrollton Cemetery

1701 Hillary Street

New Orleans, LA 70118

29.947892, -90.121866

Valence Cemetery (City Cemetery-City of Jefferson)

2000 Valence Street

New Orleans, LA 70115

29.930660, -90.106501

Once known for its many society tombs—Pioneer Steam Fire Company, Odd Fellows Rest, and more. Well-dressed, ghostly figures walk the grounds.

Mount Olivet

4000 Norman Mayer Avenue

New Orleans, LA 70122

29.998742, -90.063257

Mt Olivet was established in 1920 as a cemetery for African-Americans unable to be buried in other cemeteries.

Girard Street Cemetery (Defunct)

Lasalle and Dave Dixon Drive/Girod Street where the Superdome Garages 2 and 2A are located.

29.949437, -90.079734

Bad things that happen in the Superdome get blamed on the haunts and curses from this first Protestant cemetery under Garages 2 and 2A. But everybody knows one of the least wise decisions you can make is to dig up somebody's last resting place and think there is not going to be something bad happen to you or your kin in return. Because what comes around, goes around. This cemetery was big and run by the Christ Church since 1822—there were tombs, vaults, and below-ground burial sites and even a mound from an 1832-1833 cholera epidemic. The excuse for bringing it to an end was difficult upkeep and a church that did not want to maintain it. The ground was so swampy that gravediggers had to weigh caskets down to get them to sink in the groundwater. Later, it was considered "the tough side of town" and was constantly looted by graverobbers in the mid-1900s. Now it is gone. Tread lightly if you park in the garage or walk the nearby street; although the city dug up many of the dead beneath, builders find bones now and then nearby. And there are still souls underneath—infuriated, irate, and probably wrathful.

Potter's Field Near Resthaven Memorial Park

10000 Block of Old Gentilly Road

New Orleans, LA 70127

30.015233, -89.964997

This final resting place for the indigent and unclaimed bodies has a reputation for haunts.

St Vincent DePaul Cemetery No 2

1950 Soniat Street

New Orleans, LA 70115

29.931953, -90.109806

Jose "Pepe" Llulla was a well-known duelist who not only owned and farmed part of Grande Terre Island in Barataria Bay (Lafitte's notorious hangout), but also purchased land that would become the St Vincent DePaul Cemeteries. The folks in New Orleans used to joke that he was so good with weapons, he built the cemetery to bury the men he killed in duels. He is buried in Cemetery No 1, and visitors to the old grave lot have seen his ghost walking in St Vincent DePaul Cemetery No 2, usually with a cane.

And . . .Other Things That Go Bump in the Night

Eastern and Central Louisiana and the Bayous Around New Orleans
Rougarou

13 Pennies

The place where legendary Rougarous thrive.

In the early 1600s, some French men and women immigrated from the rural Vendee region of western France to Acadia, now Novia Scotia, Canada. These Acadians prospered in their new homes even as the French and English transferred colony ownership back and forth. The Acadians remained mostly neutral until around 1713, when the British maintained hold of the colony and demanded those who lived there vow their allegiance to Britain. Some complied, but others did not.

During the French and Indian War in 1754, Britain demanded Acadians take oaths of allegiance to the Crown and fight the French. Many refused, and British soldiers removed the families from their land and burned their homes and buildings so they could not return. This event would come to be called Le Grand Dérangement (The Great Upheaval). Many Acadians would die of starvation, disease, and exposure, while others were herded into British ships and exiled.

Three-thousand refugees were able to journey to the 13 American colonies, straggling toward Louisiana, the first arriving in 1756. From 1765 to 1785, these refugees began to settle in Louisiana, then a Spanish colony. Some found their way to the rural deep south of Louisiana west of New Orleans. These Acadian exiles maintained their rich heritage and culture, and their descendants are known as the Louisiana French—*les Cadiens* or Cajuns. Among the many contributions Cajuns have brought to Louisiana are the cattle industry, canning operations, and unique foods. Also passed along is their unique folklore, including the legends of the loup-garou or the Louisiana Rougarou originating from werewolf lore in their native France.

The stories of Rougarou were, most likely, brought to Louisiana through the folk tales passed along by the Acadian from their native France due to alleged werewolf attacks like the beast of Gevaudan (La bête de Gevaudan). Image: Ray, M.. Graveur

It has long been passed down that something lurks among the mossy cypress trees and murky waters of eastern and central Louisiana's swamps and the bayous near New Orleans. For centuries, its bone-chilling howl rides the dusky air of the night. Some say it has a man's body and the head of a wolf, claw-like nails, and ferocious teeth beneath grinning lips. This wolf-man originated from a human cursed for some transgression. In turn, it searches for others of the same wicked character to pass off its malediction and such, free itself—like Catholics who forgo observing Lent for seven consecutive years. Should a human come into contact with a Rougarou and draw the beast's blood, the creature is cured of its burden and will return to human form and reveal its secret to that human. Such, the human will now bear the curse. If the human keeps the secret and does not tell anyone, the curse will leave, but they will carry the affliction for 101 days. Rougarou are always on the lookout for small children—many little girls and boys have heard their mamas and daddies give this warning to be home by dark after the slam of the back door behind them "Or the Rougarou will get you!"

There is protection from the beasts. By placing 13 pennies, marbles, or beans, or any small object on a windowsill, you can keep it at bay. Because the Rougarou is a compulsive creature, it will obsessively try to count them, but Rougarou can only count to 12. It will become so fixated and distracted that it will try to count them all night and forget that it was attempting to enter a home in the first place. Then it will have no choice but to withdraw back to the swamps as the sun rises and morning dawns.

There have been sightings—a black dog chased two men returning from visiting neighbors. In desperation, the pair jumped a fence to evade getting bit. When the dog did not follow, they paused long enough to see a man on the other side of the fence. The dog had vanished.

James Scallen House

Vampire of New Orleans
1041 Royal Street
New Orleans, LA 70116
29.961301, -90.061971

The Strange Tale of Jacques d'Saint Germain

The 1100 block of Royal with 1041 the fourth building on left. Around 1905 when this story—ends. *Perhaps.* Image: Library of Congress

When Jacques d'Saint Germain was born, no one is certain. Some records indicate that it was around 1710. That he died—that is up to with whom you speak. Some documents state it was 1784. Others say he is not dead at all.

Nobody is sure of his real name, exactly where he came from, or what family raised him. Some things are for certain—by various means, in the mid-1700s, Germain worked his way into France's highest society. He was quite eccentric, spoke many languages, played the violin exquisitely, was well-educated in science and alchemy, and was incredibly wealthy. Princes considered him to be a great philosopher. And Jacques could catch an eye and chat for hours, keeping an entire party entranced with whatever subject chosen by himself.

He also claimed to be the son of the prince of Transylvania, Francis II Rákóczi, and he could live forever. Jacques spoke so eloquently and with so little effort about everything from the arts to science that when he would state something outrageous, such as flaunting that he was immortal, many either did not doubt him or thought him insane.

There was even one well-known incident that helped lend credibility to his testimony. Madame de Pompadour was a member of the French court and mistress and advisor to Louis XV. She held elegant parties at her residence, inviting high society members to attend. One event during the mid-1760s included Jacques d'Saint Germain. An elderly woman, Countess von Georgy, was also attending and had seemed shocked when she ran into Jacques, telling him that she recognized his face and was it perhaps his father she knew back in Venice in 1710? Jacques d'Saint Germain had shaken his head, telling her that no, it had been him paying court to her back then. For a moment, she hesitated as if waiting for Jacques to laugh and say he was joking and that, yes, it had been his father. In all honesty, the man she knew those many years before had all the appearances of a man of 45 years of age. Countess von Georgy still had her wits about her and was certain the resemblance was just too uncanny.

He looked just like the man standing in front of her. Yet, he would be 100-years-old if so. Instead, Jacques d'Saint Germain divulged that, yes, he was a very old man. And yes, it was him she had met back then!

He was a great curiosity, even to the Prince of Wales at the time. But even the prince could not extract enough information from the man to set the record straight. Some believe Jacques was lying to conceal his true identity. For what reason, it is uncertain. Others have come up with a different theory. This is where it gets interesting because he is said to have visited New Orleans long after he was dead!

In 1902, a man who called himself Jacques d'Saint Germain became a tenant in a building on the corner of Ursulines and Royal streets. He would have been just another bachelor living in the community if he did not throw elaborate parties, inviting all the community's rich dignitaries. There was not only one, but many events at the building. At first, his invites were not well received. Everyone who was anyone in New Orleans society could pull out a pedigree from a roll-out desk and show their family background far beyond the founding French fathers.

This newcomer was strangely secretive of his past; nobody knew much more than his name. And they were not even sure if that was a hoax. Soon enough, those in his midst were tantalized by his fluency in several languages, his mysteriousness, and his incredible intellect. Even the men whose sweethearts' eyed Jacques with a bit more enthusiasm than was comfortable were mesmerized by his keen ability to make them feel welcome and important.

Jacques seemed to have a single flaw that caused many in the high society circle to tug at their collars awkwardly. He liked to peruse Bourbon Street, rubbing elbows with the common folk, and more often than not, openly bringing a young woman of a questionable standing back to his room.

The Royal Street home where Jacques d'Saint Germain stayed on his legendary trip to New Orleans. *Image: Adrian Chevalier*

That aside, most felt it was beneath them to question someone of such wealth until the night that he vanished. Jacques d'Saint Germain disappeared just as mysteriously as he appeared. It was as if he had never lived in the city at all except for one small detail. A local woman whose reputation might be considered dubious because she frequented the pubs, divulged to police that she had gone back to Jacques d'Saint Germain's residence with him after several drinks one night. While in the upper living quarters, he had begun to kiss her neck. Suddenly, the kisses became violent, and he sunk his teeth into her tender flesh so deeply she began to bleed. Hardly able to resist his strength, she finally slipped beneath his arms and ran toward a window, crashing through it to the ground below. When the police went to the building to investigate, everything belonging to Jacques d'Saint Germain was gone, and no trace of what became known as the New Orleans Vampire was ever found.

Mississippi Riverfront at the Old New Orleans Wharf

A Little Hoodoo on the Wharf

Roustabouts unloading cotton from steamboat circa 1900.
Image: Original album print owned by Phmoreno

Everyone knows that the Mississippi riverfront is full of ghosts of old and dead seamen, murdered slaves, and ornery pirates. But few nowadays have heard the tale of Jakie Walker and the river ghost. But back in the day, almost everybody heard it told, and some whispered that it was his wife who done it all, who had Jakie Walker hoodooed on that particular night he was so drunk. Maybe it was so—

Jakie Walker was a roustabout who had been working on board the steamboats for well over 30 years. His job was to stoke the boilers and move whatever cargo the boat carried to and from the docks. It was back-breaking work, and at the end of an awfully long day, he liked to amble into town and jaw a little and drink a lot with the other roustabouts. Now that would be good and fine if Jakie was a bachelor, but he was not. His wife, a good woman who liked Jakie and also liked his pay, did not so much adore the way he spent an awful lot of that pay on drinking. She also did not like it when he came home late drunk—she was known to snatch up some kitchen tool and chase him about the house.

He had been drinking a lot this night. So Jakie chose to walk off some of the drunk before he went home. After a while, he realized he had walked right back to the wharves where he worked. The watchman had taken him in with a bored expression, recognizing Jakie. "What are you doing out here so late?" the watchman asked with a chuckle, noting the waft of booze on his breath and a wobble to Jakie's steps. "You look—sick." Jakie had grunted, telling the other man about his wife. "I'm sure not going back home just yet. If she sees how soused I am, she'll chase me around the house." The watchman thought this was funny and certainly agreed, laughing, and letting Jakie pass.

Jakie moseyed around the wharf for a few, feeling the warm winds on his cheeks and taking in the good scents of the river. Feeling a little tired, he sat down for a while and watched the water lap about and trying to figure out how he would explain to his wife why he was out so late.

After a while of staring at the river, a strange feeling overcame the roustabout. Something even stranger appeared out in the water, drifting across the calm surface. It came in the shape of a man wearing a black gown with a shadowy train dragging behind.

Jakie could not run; his legs just refused to move. He was stuck where he sat while the misty figure came closer and closer along with a certain amount of heat that felt like charcoal burning Jakie's flesh. The closer the form came, the hotter Jakie got until he thought his eyeballs were going to explode like two eggs tossed in a fire.

"*What*—what you want?" Jakie had been holding his breath, so his words came out stuttering and like a huge burp. He held up one hand as if to ward off the being. He blinked past his wrist, watching the body ebb and flow, a foggy creature not of this earth, but perhaps formed of the river from hands shoved upward from the very depths of hell. "Go away! Just go away!"

"You know who I am, but I'm not telling you," a voice came from the form. It was deep and gurgling, and with every word, a horrible reek of something long dead blasted into the air. "I drowned right here in the river, and I am a ghost of the Mississippi River. And I don't have long because the river's calling me back. But I need you to know something." There was an awful moment of silence as the foggy creature seemed to fade for a moment, then flow back to its form. The mouth, Jakie could barely make out, but it looked like a fish flopped up to the shore and gasping its last dying breath. Then it spoke again, "You are going to die if you don't stop drinking. You have to stop."

Jakie mustered up what courage he had that night, aided by the drink still running through his veins. "How dare you tell me what to do? I am not—"

"I've been sent to take you back with me, but I don't want to do it. You're a good man, Jakie, besides the drinking. Tell me, right now, *are* you going to stop drinking? What is your determination in this matter?" Jakie had wobbled to a standing position, crossed his arms protectively around his chest. He stood there drawing out the moment a long time.

Then he thrust his chin high. He such, then, stated that he loved his drink. And nothing was going to stop him from imbibing in that pleasure each night. "But ghost," he asked a little more softly, "do you know my wife?"

The ghost had let out a stinking sigh and nodded unhappily. "Yes, man, I do know your wife. But I guess I've got to do what I was sent to do—"

And with that, the water on the river began to churn and froth. It started to rise along with great puffs of wind from the darkness beyond. A horrible belch seeped up from the docks' far side, and two waves leaped up and over, two hulking arms reaching out for Jakie. And he knew he was going to die. "So, here's the thing, ghost," he sputtered, suddenly feeling a lot less drunk and a whole lot of sober as the water lapped at his feet. "I think I would like to rethink my determination. I think that if you would like to take away the waves and go back to where you came from, I won't ever drink again. *And that I promise.*"

Suddenly with those words, everything went back to normal. The waves ceased churning, the wind stopped blowing, and the smell of death was gone. And after that, Jakie Walker went home. He knew the smell of booze was still on his breath, and it scared him because his wife was standing at the doorway like she was waiting for him. He pushed out his chest, waiting for her storm to come, for her to snatch up some kitchen tool and chase him about the house. But she did not. Instead, Jakie's wife threw her arms around him with tears in her eyes. "I thought you were dead, Jakie!" she wept into his ear. "I had a horrible dream that you'd been drowned on the river!"

"I am alive, and I am a new man," he said that night. And he was. After Jakie Walker saw that river ghost, he never drank again. And if it was hoodoo or not, his wife never said.

Area near the old wharves and docks. *Image: SydQuackArt.*

If you are looking for the old wharves to take in the story of Jakie Walker, I cannot describe their location better than Kim Welsh in an article for The French Quarterly Magazine (www.frenchquarterly.com)— *Our Riverfront, Past and Present* who explains it like this:

"Sailing ships, flatboats, barges, and steamboats were so closely docked that people could possibly walk the rows of decks for miles without getting their feet wet. Each type of vessel was required to dock at a designated location. Steamboats docked from Jackson Square to beyond Canal Street, while downstream hosted oceangoing ships. In between, Lugger's Landing at the French Market was reserved for small boats carrying oysters and other market goods. Oyster luggers and flat boats sailing from the central portion of the United States delivered goods to the bustling market—"

Walking Tour

Jannette Quackenbush

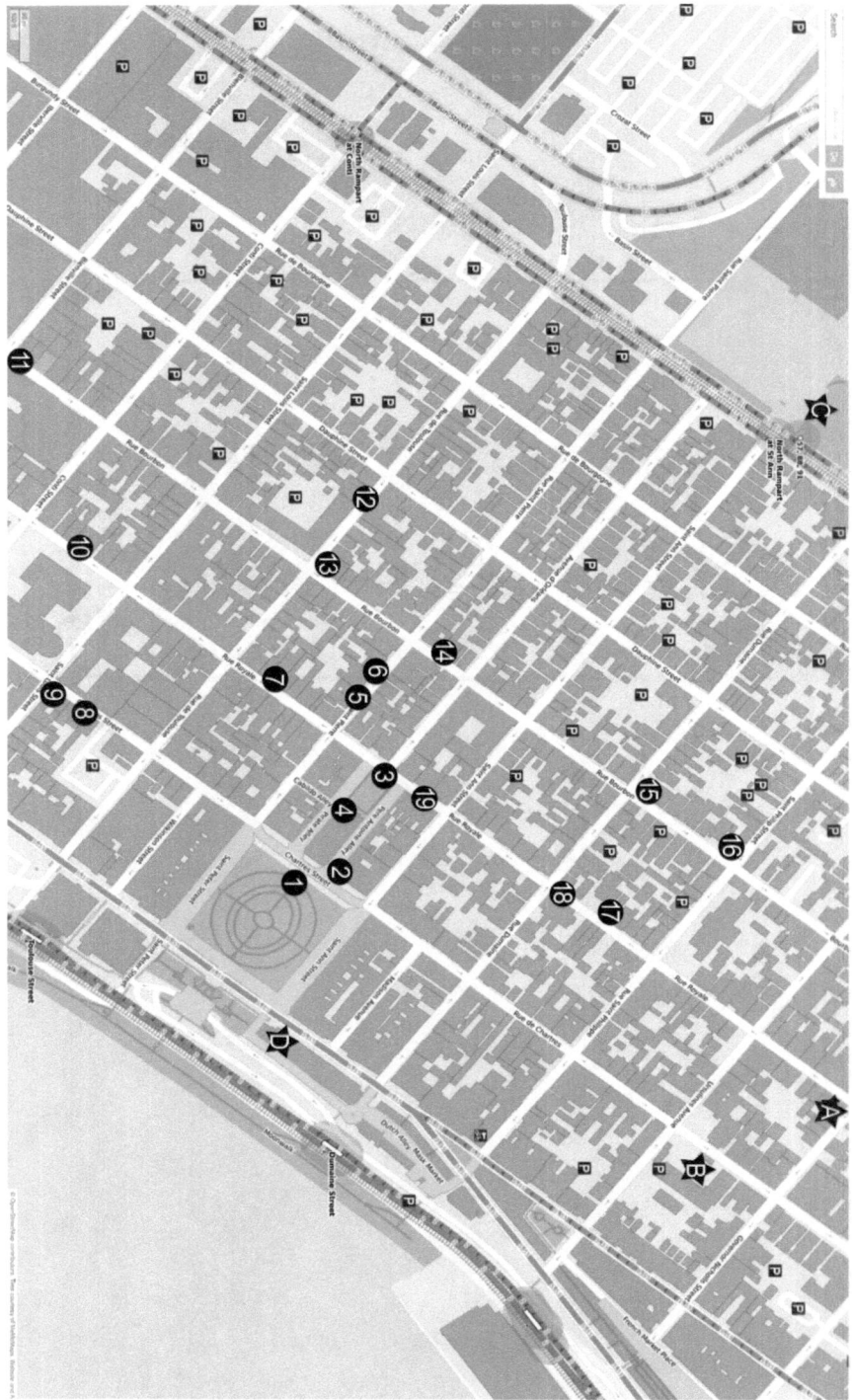

1- Start facing St Louis Cathedral – (746 Chartres Street)

To the left is the Cabildo, the Jail. The alley between is Pirate Alley. To the right of the Cathedral is another alley. It is Père Antoine Alley *Behind you is Jackson Square, where you may run into rebel ghosts of the German Coast Uprising. (page 15)

Take Père Antoine Alley (right alley) first and follow it to the next street (Royal Street).

2-Père Antoine Alley (601 Père Antoine Alley) *The garden to the left is St Anthony's Garden behind St Louis Cathedral, named after the Capuchin monk Père Antoine. His ghost has been seen here in a black robe walking towards Orleans Street where his hut and date palm once stood. (page 39)

3-Take the left along Royal Street as you walk. *This is one of the streets where the Witch of the French Opera passes through in ghostly form. (page 77)

4-Take the next left, which is Pirate Alley. *It is here that the monk, Père Dagobert, sings on certain rainy nights. (page 21) *This is also the path that Jean Lafitte appears once in a while, the halfway point, which is Cabildo Alley. (page 29) *It is also here where Reginald Hicks's spirit shows up at times. (page 33)

Turn into Cabildo Alley, and go straight through to St Peter Street. Make a right on St Peter Street. Cross Royal Street and continue on St Peter.

5-(714 St Peter Street) - Café Beignet Former Old Coffeepot Restaurant-*Where love-crazed dentist Etienne Deschamps murdered young Juliette Deitsch. (page 115)

6-(718 St Peter Street) - Pat O'Briens – *Guests have seen shadow figures at this long-standing Irish pub where a bartender invented Hurricane drinks using rum when whiskey was scarce to come by. (page 118)

Now, head back to Royal Street and make a right on to Royal.

*7-(613 Royal Street) - *A charmed gate, a wishing well, and a deadly duel all have ties to legends at Court of Two Sisters, now a fine dining restaurant. (page 60)*

Follow Royal Street to Toulouse Street. Make a left on Toulouse. Follow Toulouse Street. Make a right on Chartres Street.

*8-(514 Chartres) - New Orleans Pharmacy Museum – *A ghostly girl and boy are among just a couple of the spirits here. (page 46)*

*9-(500 Chartres Street) - Napoléon House – Time for a break to eat and see a ghost! *This restaurant offers fine dining, a ghostly sweeper, and a legend of Napoléon's exile. (page 42)*

*Head along St Louis past the Louisiana Supreme Court Building and Omni Royal Orleans. *While you are passing the Supreme Court building, take a look at the windows for the ghostly lawyer. (page 57)*

Make a left on Royal Street.

*10-(417 Royal Street) - Brennan's Restaurant (Patio Royal) – *Watch for the ghostly man donning 18th-century clothing and peering around the door. (page 59)*

Make a Right on Conti Street.
Make a left on Bourbon Street and go one block.

*11- (240 Bourbon Street) - Jean Lafitte's Old Absinthe House - *People visiting this old pub hear ghostly laughter. (page 73)*

Turn around and head back three blocks along Bourbon Street. Make a left on Toulouse Street.

12-(828 Toulouse) - Olivier House Hotel – A Lady in Black wanders the hotel. (page 122)*

Head back to Bourbon and make a left.

*13- (601 Bourbon Street - Corner of Bourbon and Toulouse) *Site of the Old French Opera where the Witch of the French Opera once worked. (page 77)*

14-*(711 Bourbon Street) – The Tricou House -*Where a ghostly young girl plays pranks. (page 83)*

15-*(901 Bourbon Street) Café Lafitte in Exile - *Tennessee Williams has been seen at the far end of the bar sipping cocktails. (page 85)*

16-*(941 Bourbon Street) Lafitte's Blacksmith Shop Bar –* Perhaps you'll find the ghost of a pirate here. Others have! (page 86)*

Make a right on St Phillip Street.
Make a right on Royal Street.

17- *(919 Royal Street) – Andrew Jackson Hotel – *Once a boarding school for boys, a few have decided to stick around even after death! (page 66)*

18- *(915 Royal Street) -A ghost haunts Cornstalk Fence Hotel—the spirit of a woman who walks around the hotel. She also peers out windows. (page 65)*

19-*(734 Royal Street) – The House of the Octoroon Mistress -*On cold nights, a spectral woman still dances on the roof—naked. (page 62)*

The next side street is Père Antoine Alley, if you make a left, you will be back to where you started!

Notable close by side-trips:
A-LaLaurie Mansion
B- Ursulines Convent and Museum
C- Congo Park
D- Café du Monde In the French Market

Citations

Jackson Square:
-Scott, M., & NOLA.com | The Times-Picayune. (2019, November 6). The 1811 Louisiana slave revolt that was almost lost to history. Retrieved from https://www.nola.com/300/article_680cf224-6f29-5fd7-9a8d-4d39aa55f124.html
-Seven spooky tales haunting the streets of NOLA. (n.d.). Retrieved from https://nolabrewbus.com/blog/ghost-tours-new-orleans/
-Jan. 8, 1811: Louisiana's heroic slave revolt. (1811, January 8). Retrieved from https://www.zinnedproject.org/news/tdih/louisianas-slave-revolt/
-'On to New Orleans, freedom or death': Hundreds to march to reenact 1811 slave revolt. (2019, October 14). Retrieved from https://nola.verylocal.com/on-to-new-orleans-freedom-or-death-more-than-500-to-march-to-reenact-1811-slave-revolt/85644/
-Scott, M., & NOLA.com | The Times-Picayune. (2019, November 6). The 1811 Louisiana slave revolt that was almost lost to history. Retrieved from https://www.nola.com/300/article_680cf224-6f29-5fd7-9a8d-4d39aa55f124.html
-Seven spooky tales haunting the streets of NOLA. (n.d.). Retrieved from https://nolabrewbus.com/blog/ghost-tours-new-orleans/
-Trejo, R. (2016, October 27). A brief history of New Orleans' Jackson Square. Retrieved from https://theculturetrip.com/north-america/usa/louisiana/new-orleans/articles/a-brief-history-of-new-orleans-jackson-square/

Café duMonde:
-https://witchesbrewtours.com/2019/08/14/cafe-du-monde-ghost/
-https://gonola.com/things-to-do-in-new-orleans/history/nola-history-the-french-market

Café Sbisa:
-https://www.opentable.co.uk/

Pirate Alley/Cabildo:
-Have you heard the musical monk of St. Louis cathedral? (2020, June 5). Retrieved from https://nola.verylocal.com/haunted-nola-pere-dagobert-de-longuory-ghost-of-st-louis-cathedral/135076/
-The New Orleans Daily Democrat NEW ORLEANS, -LOUISIANA Sunday, 3/34/1878. (n.d.).
-New Orleans: A love story, Part 1. (n.d.). Retrieved from https://americanhaunts.blogspot.com/2011/12/new-orleans-love-story-part-1.html
-DeLavigne, J. (1946). Ghost stories of old New Orleans. The Singing Capuchin pg 3
-The Ghosts of Pirate's Alley in the French Quarter of New Orleans. (n.d.). Retrieved from https://ghostcitytours.com/new-orleans/haunted-places/pirates-alley/
-Jean and Pierre Laffite. (2019, February 4). Retrieved from https://64parishes.org/entry/jean-and-pierre-laffite
-Jean Lafitte – A "Hero" pirate – Legends of America. (n.d.). https://www.legendsofamerica.com/la-jeanlafitte/
-Schwehm, J. (n.d.). New Orleans weddings pirates alley information. https://www.figstreet.com/guesthouse/firstpiratesalleywedding.html
-Waiting for the redirectiron... (n.d.). Retrieved from https://neworleanshistorical.org/items/show/616?tour=56&index=6
-https://www.werelate.org/wiki/Person:Joseph_Roy_Villere_%281%2
-Pirate Alley, Not Pirate's or Pirates—https://www.nola.com/archive/article_4dde2d84-9782-59fb-aaa9-afd5bea481bd.html
-Lafitte's Blacksmith Shop and the Battle of New Orleans .... https://neworleanshistorical.org/items/show/616?tour=56&index=6
-Interview of traveler staying in New Orleans

Faulkner House Books:
-https://www.thesocians.com/post/faulkner-house-books-new-orleans-hidden-bookstore-where-author-william-pay-visits-from-his-grave
-Interview at bookstore

Former Crescent City Books:
-Dwyer, Jeff. Ghost Hunter's Guide to New Orleans, Revised Edition. Gretna, LA: Pelican, 2016.
-Street guide to the phantoms of the French quarter—Chartres street. (2020, May 2).
-https://www.hnoc.org/vcs/property_info.php?lot=11137

Napoléon House:
-Arkansas Democrat Jul 6, 1907 Napoléon House in New Orleans.
-Famous Napoléon House The Kansas City Star KANSAS CITY, MISSOURI Monday, July 1, 1907.
-The ghosts of the Napoléon house. (n.d.). Retrieved from https://ghostcitytours.com/new-orleans/haunted-places/haunted-restaurants-bars/napoleon-house/
-Napoléon house : About us. (n.d.). Retrieved from https://www.napoleonhouse.com/about/
-NOLA Weekend Fox News Shan Bailey Interview with Executive chef Chris Montero. (n.d.).

Pharmacy Museum:
-This little known Museum in New Orleans is also haunted. (2019, May 23). Retrieved from https://www.onlyinyourstate.com/louisiana/new-orleans/haunted-pharmacy-museum-nola/
-Family Louis Joseph Dufilho, Jr. / Emy Adele Becnel (F141). (n.d.). Retrieved from https://holliergenealogy.info/familychart.php?familyID=F141&tree=Hollier-Dufilho
-The national trust guide to New Orleans.
-Seven spooky tales haunting the streets of NOLA. (n.d.). Retrieved from https://nolabrewbus.com/blog/ghost-tours-new-orleans/

Ursuline:
-Jones, T. L. (n.d.). A shortage of women. Retrieved from https://countryroadsmagazine.com/art-and-culture/history/a-shortage-of-women/
-Milne, A. (2020, April 26). How French 'Casket girls' were forced into the New World to 'Tame' the male settlers. Retrieved from https://allthatsinteresting.com/casket-girls
-Thompson, Maurice Illustrations: Bridgman, L J. (1888). Story of Louisiana.

Beauregard-Keyes House:
-Pensacola News Journal- Tuesday, 12/1/98
-https://www.wwno.org/post/wine-and-blood-beauregard-keyes-house

Louisiana Supreme Court Building:
-The ghosts of the Louisiana Supreme Court building. (2020, May 30). Retrieved from https://ghostcitytours.com/new-orleans/haunted-places/louisiana-supreme-court/
-Klein, V. C. (1998). New Orleans Ghosts.

Brennan's Restaurant:
-Hamilton Daily News January 25, 1927 Ghost Haunted Patio Royal of Vieux Carre; Where Jackson Once Stayed, a Tea Room
-http://www.hauntedneworleanstours.com/buildings/BRENNANS/

The Court of Two Sisters:
-Our History. https://www.courtoftwosisters.com/about-us/our-history
Octoroon Mistress:
-Living among the dead: Julie, the octoroon mistress. (2017, October 27). Retrieved from https://wgno.com/news-with-a-twist/living-among-the-dead-julie-the-octoroon-mistress/

Cornstalk Hotel:
-(2018, November 1). Retrieved from https://wgno.com/news/hometown-horror-stories-the-cornstalk-hotel/

Andrew Jackson Hotel:
-About Andrew Jackson - Historic haunted New Orleans hotel. (n.d.). Retrieved from https://www.andrewjacksonhotel.com/about-us

Madame LaLaurie:
-The Collins C. Diboll vieux carre survey: Property info. (n.d.). Retrieved from https://www.hnoc.org/vcs/property_info.php?lot=22782-30
-Family tree of Marie Françoise Delphine Borja de López Y Angulo. (n.d.). Retrieved from https://gw.geneanet.org/jelumac?lang=en&p=marie+francoise+delphine+borja&n=de+lopez+y+angulo
-Daily States, pg 5 February 28 1892
-History.com Editors. (2009, November 13). A torture chamber is uncovered by arson. Retrieved from https://www.history.com/this-day-in-history/a-torture-chamber-is-uncovered-by-arson
-Marie Delphine MaCarty LaLaurie (1787-1849) -... (n.d.). Retrieved from https://www.findagrave.com/memorial/69748516/marie-delphine-lalaurie
-Martineau, H. (1838). Retrospect of western travel.
-Portals to Hell: Investigating the LaLaurie Mansion - Travel Channel
-Castellanos, Henry. New Orleans as it Was: Episodes of Louisiana Life, p. 52-62 January 1, 1895

Jean Lafitte's Old Absinthe House:
-Bossier Banner Progress August 25, 1955.
-The ghosts of the old absinthe house in New Orleans. (n.d.). Retrieved from https://ghostcitytours.com/new-orleans/haunted-places/absinthe-house/
-Old absinthe house | Historic French quarter bar — Rue bourbon. (n.d.). Retrieved from https://www.ruebourbon.com/old-absinthe-house
-Stanley, Arthur. Old New Orleans: A History of the Vieux Carré, Its Ancient and Historical ...

French Opera House:
-DeLavigne, J. (1946). Ghost stories of old New Orleans The Witch of the French Opera Page 167.
-The witch of the opera house. (2018, May 23). Retrieved from https://nolaghosts.com/witch-opera-house/

Tricou House:
-Phantoms of the French quarter—Bourbon and dauphine streets. (2018, December 19). Retrieved from https://www.southernspiritguide.org/phantoms-of-the-french-quarter-bourbon-and-dauphine-streets/
-Tricou House RESTAURANT AND ENTERTAINMENT COMPLEX Brochure. (n.d.). Retrieved from https://digitallibrary.tulane.edu/islandora/object/tulane%3A17895/datastream/PDF/view

Café Lafitte in Exile:
-https://www.lafittes.com/
-https://stcharlesinn.com/top-10-most-haunted-bars-in-new-orleans/

Lafitte's Blacksmith Shop:
-Asfar, D. (2007). Ghost stories of Louisiana. Ghost House Books.
-Encounter with a Gentleman—New Orleans. (2019, August 15).
Retrieved from https://www.southernspiritguide.org/encounter-with-a-gentleman-new-orleans/
-Is Lafitte's Blacksmith shop the oldest bar in the country? New Orleans
truths vs. tales. (2018, July 11). Retrieved from https://prcno.org/lafittes-blacksmith-shop-oldest-bar-country-new-orleans-truths-vs-tales/
-Lafitte's Blacksmith shop bar, New Orleans, la. (n.d.). Retrieved from
https://www.lafittesblacksmithshop.com/Homepage.html

Sultan's Disappearance and Père Antoine's Date Palm:
-Old New Orleans; a history of the Vieux Carré, its ancient and historical
buildings.
By Stanley Clisby Arthur. New Orleans, Harmanson, 1936. https://
babel.hathitrust.org/cgi/pt?
id=mdp.39015008408570&view=1up&seq=256&q1=date%20palm
-PÈRE ANTOINE'S DATE-PALM. Thomas Bailey Aldrich Boston And New
York Houghton Mifflin Company Copyright, 1873 (http://www.online-literature.com/thomas-bailey-aldrich/3863/)
-Historical sketch book and guide to New Orleans and environs, with
map : illustrated with many original engravings, and containing
exhaustive accounts of the traditions, historical legends, and remarkable
localities of the Creole city by Hearn, Lafcadio, 1850-1904; Pennell,
Joseph, 1857-1926
- Histoire de la Louisiane (1846)
-Gayarré, Charles, C. (1854). History of Louisiana and The History of
Louisiana, successive portions under various titles 1847-1854, assembled
into a final comprehensive edition in 1867 -https://
penelope.uchicago.edu/Thayer/E/Gazetteer/Places/America/
United_States/Louisiana/_Texts/GAYHLA/home.html#note:the_author .
-Hémard, Ned NEW ORLEANS NOSTALGIA Remembering New Orleans
History, Culture and Traditions. (n.d.). Retrieved from https://
www.neworleansbar.org/uploads/files/Fascinating%20Facts%208_2_17
(1).pdf
-https://www.hnoc.org/vcs/property_info.php?lot=18768
-Père Antoine's Date-Palm by Thomas Bailey Aldrich. http://www.online-literature.com/thomas-bailey-aldrich/3863/

The Sausage Man:
-Louisiana Writers' Project. (1969). Gumbo ya-ya: A collection of
Louisiana folk tales.
-New Orleans sausage ghost story : Southern U.S.A culture, history &
travel. (2019, May 22). Retrieved from https://
www.themoonlitroad.com/new-orleans-sausage-ghost-story/
-Amid Roaring Twenties New Orleans, a brutal French quarter murder
shocked the city. (n.d.). Retrieved from https://www.hnoc.org/
publications/first-draft/amid-roaring-twenties-new-orleans-brutal-french-quarter-murder-shocked-city

Place d' Armes:
-The Collins C. Diboll vieux carre survey: Property info. (n.d.). Retrieved
from https://www.hnoc.org/vcs/property_info.php?lot=18521
-https://www.hauntedjourneys.com/haunted-inns/4211-place-d-armes-hotel. (n.d.). Retrieved from https://www.hauntedjourneys.com/haunted-inns/4211-place-d-armes-hotel

Inn on St Ann:
-Creole house - Inn on St. Ann - [2020] FrightFind. (2020, September 11).
Retrieved from https://frightfind.com/creole-house-inn-on-st-ann/

Marie Laveau:
-Boyd, Andrew, A. (2019, July 12). St. Louis cemetery No. 1: Is Marie Laveau where they say she is? www.nola.com/archive/article_25942435-4b6e-5c62-b408-872715db8a21.html
-Eschner, K. (2017, June 23). Voodoo priestess Marie Laveau created New Orleans' Midsummer festival. www.smithsonianmag.com/smart-news/voodoo-priestess-marie-laveau-created-new-orleans-midsummer-festival-180963750/
-Marie Laveau. (2020, January 29). Retrieved from https://www.womenhistoryblog.com/2012/07/marie-laveau.html
-Marie Laveau. (2020, March 19). Retrieved from https://64parishes.org/entry/marie-laveau-2
-Marie Laveau. (n.d.). Retrieved from https://www.britannica.com/biography/Marie-Laveau
-Scott, Mike, M., & NOLA.com | The Times-Picayune. (2019, July 12). Marie Laveau: Separating fact from fiction about New Orleans' voodoo Queen. Retrieved from https://www.nola.com/300/article_b68b1247-169a-5164-a399-9e73bbc732fd.html
- August Darbonne and Kathryn O'Dwyer, editor, "The Church: Marie Laveau at St. Louis Cathedral," New Orleans Historical, accessed November 10, 2020, https://neworleanshistorical.org/items/show/1609.
-Alvarado, Denise. *Introduction*. 2019, https://www.marie-laveaux.com/introduction-1.html.
-www2.latech.edu. http://www2.latech.edu/~bmagee/louisiana_anthology/encyclopedia/student_articles/Marie_Laveau--drake_kywonna.docx
-Introduction - MARIE LAVEAUX. https://www.marie-laveaux.com/introduction-1.html

Bourbon Orleans:
-Noël Voltz. (n.d.). Black Female Agency and Sexual Exploitation: Quadroon Balls and Plaçage Relationships. Retrieved from https://kb.osu.edu/bitstream/handle/1811/32216/Quadroon_Balls1.pdf?sequence=1&isAllowed=y
-https://lib.lsu.edu/sites/all/files/sc/fpoc/history.html
-Interviews at Bourbon Orleans Hotel
-300 in Black: Sisters of the Holy Family - The New Orleans https://theneworleanstribune.com/2017/06/14/300-in-black-sisters-of-the-holy-family/

Le Petit Theatre du Vieux Carré:
-5 tales of haunted theatres to give you a fright. (2019, October 31). Retrieved from https://www.americantheatre.org/2019/10/31/5-tales-of-haunted-theatres-to-give-you-a-fright/
-Le Petit theatre du vieux carre - New Orleans, LA (A stage full of haunts). (n.d.). Retrieved from https://hauntednation.blogspot.com/2016/09/le-petit-theatre-du-vieux-carre-new.html

Deschamp:
-Deschamps Dead. The Times-Picayune May 14, 1892.
-Old Coffepot restaurant - New Orleans, LA (The evil dentist awaits). (n.d.). Retrieved from hatednation.blogspot.com/2016/09/old-coffepot-restaurant-new-orleans-la.html

Pat O'Briens:
-https://ghostcitytours.com/new-orleans/haunted-places/haunted-restaurants-bars/pat-o-briens/

Creole Cookery:
-https://www.hnoc.org/vcs/property_info.php?lot=18436
-https://www.barbarasillery.com/update-new-orleans-ghosts/

The Olivier Hotel:
-Taylor, T. Haunted New Orleans

Antoine's:
-https://www.nola.com/entertainment_life/eat-drink/article_8e8f0e59-a2c1-5ffc-963a-2fd865a72ca9.html
-http://americashauntedroadtrip.com/tag/antoines/

Shell Road:
-Times-Picayune September 16, 1852
-327-301 N Robertson St to basin St. at Bienville St. (n.d.). Retrieved from https://www.google.com/maps/dir/29.9601887,-90.0753607/29.9579449,-90.0719932/@29.9590792,-90.074785,18z/data=!4m2!4m1!3e2
-DeLavigne, J. (1946). Ghost stories of old New Orleans The Specter on the Shell Road page 40.
-Klokan Technologies GmbH (http://www.klokantech.com/). (n.d.). Map of New Orleans, Louisiana. 69 With Shell Road and -Bienville Street Shell Road. davidrumsey.georeferencer.com/maps/f1a3262c-587c-5db8-8a3b-1b247ec28ae5/view
-NOPL: WPA street name index--b. (n.d.). Retrieved from https://nutrias.org/~nopl/facts/streetnames/namesb.htm
-NOPL: WPA street name index--s. (n.d.). Retrieved from https://nutrias.org/~nopl/facts/streetnames/streetss.htm Name Change for Bienville. http://nutrias.org/~nopl/facts/streetnames/streetss.htm Name Change for Shell Road
-RICHARD CAMPANELLA | Contributing writer. (2019, November 2). The story of West End: 'The Coney Island of New Orleans'. nola.com/entertainment_life/article_a0fe597a-fb55-11e9-b8c1-57e08b236c1a.html

Old Parish Prison:
-Louisiana Writers' Project. (1969). Gumbo ya-ya: A collection of Louisiana folk tales. Ghosts pages 289-290
-https://louisianadigitallibrary.org/islandora/object/state-lwp%3A8816
-DeLavigne, J. (1946). Ghost stories of old New Orleans. The Red-Headed Ghost of Parish Prison pg 285

The Basin Ghost:
-The New Orleans Bulletin Friday May 1, 1874
-The New Orleans bulletin. New Orleans La. April 28, 1874
-DeLavigne, J. (1946). Ghost stories of old New Orleans. The Ghost of the Tremé Street Bridge page 220

Haunted Tree—Congo Square:
-The morning news. [volume], August 23, 1891 Under the Voudoo Tree
-Times Democrat (New Orleans), p. 3, col. 4. 8/1/91
-History of "voudoos" (voodoos) in New Orleans, Louisiana August 1, 1891 State Library of Louisiana—Louisiana Works Progress Administration (WPA)
-Voodoo in New Orleans. (2019, July 12). Retrieved from https://whatthesaintsdidnext.com/voodoo-in-new-orleans/
-https://afropunk.com/2018/02/black-history-congo-square-new-orleans-heart-american-music/

House of Sirens:
-Despite a blessing and exorcism, the ghost of a Marigny madame and her dog remain. (2020, July 8). Retrieved from https://nola.verylocal.com/haunted-nola-the-marignys-madame-mini-canal-and-her-loyal-ghost-terrier/155689/

-Peck, R. (2010, October 30). Faubourg Marigny townhouse holds a family, two dogs -- and a ghost. Retrieved from https://www.nola.com/entertainment_life/home_garden/article_abe968e2-8c2c-518d-9d38-d397002ebb89.html

Yankee Soldiers That Will Not Lay:
-DeLavigne, J. (1946). Ghost stories of old New Orleans. The Soldiers Who Could Not Die page 35.
-Tallant, R., & Saxon, L. (1987). GUMBO YA-YA: Folk tales of Louisiana. Pelican Publishing Company.

St Vincents:
-https://www.stvguesthouse.com/
-Staff interviews

Headless Woman:
-DeLavigne, J. (1946). Ghost stories of old New Orleans. The Ghost of the Headless Woman pg 67

Lost Boys:
-DeLavigne, J. (1946). Ghost stories of old New Orleans. Up From the Sea. Page 80

Keg of Rum:
-Lyle Saxon, Edward Dreyer, and Robert Tallant. Gumbo Ya-Ya: A Collection of Louisiana Folk Tales (Boston: Houghton Mifflin, 1945), pp. 152-3.

Fourth Street Ghosts:
-Louisiana Writers' Project. (1969). Gumbo ya-ya: A collection of Louisiana folk tales.

The Devil's Mistress:
-DeLavigne, J. (1946). Ghost stories of old New Orleans.
-Tallant, R., & Saxon, L. (1987). GUMBO YA-YA: Folk tales of Louisiana. Pelican Publishing Company.

Cherokee Street:
-DeLavigne, J. (1946). *Ghost stories of old New Orleans.* Warring Wraiths

Old Carrollton Jail:
-Ghosts of Louisiana 1/18/1939 Progress Administration of Louisiana. (n.d.). Retrieved from https://louisianadigitallibrary.org/islandora/object/state-lwp%3A3639
-The haunted old Carrollton jail in New Orleans. (n.d.). Retrieved from https://ghostcitytours.com/new-orleans/haunted-places/old-carrollton-jail/
-The old Carrollton jail: The ghostly prisoners that can't escape. (2020, June 4). Retrieved from https://nola.verylocal.com/haunted-nola-the-old-carrollton-jail-the-ghostly-prisoners-that-cant-escape/147438
-DeLavigne, J. (1946). Ghost stories of old New Orleans. The Ghosts of Carrollton Jail page 179

Mona Lisa:
-NOLADEEJ https://www.youtube.com/watch?v=ZtL0GsR1jwcThe Ghost of Mona Lisa Drive in Haunted City Park New Orleans
-Democker, Michael. https://nola.verylocal.com/haunted-nola-mona-lisa-the-heartbroken-ghost-of-city-park/104978/

Dueling Oaks:
-https://www.headstuff.org/culture/history/jose-pepe-llulla-the-gravedigging-duellist/
-https://www.findagrave.com/memorial/138395345/jose-pepe-llulla
-https://malkoffgallery.com/Product/ProductDetails/10
-https://neworleanshistorical.org/items/show/110
-http://old-new-orleans.com/NO_Duel_Mississippi_River.html

Suicide Oak:
-http://www.websitesneworleans.com/neworleanscitypark/id25.html

Casa Rosa:
-DeLavigne, J. (1946). Ghost stories of old New Orleans. Taken from the New Orleans Times from January 11, 1874, written by William Dawson.
-Saxon, L. (1969). Gumbo ya-ya: A collection of Louisiana folk tales.

Axeman:
-The Axeman of New Orleans. (2020, July 13). Retrieved from https://nolaghosts.com/the-axeman-of-new-orleans/
-NO Recalls Strange Ax Slayer. (n.d.). The Shreveport Times 12/26/1954.

Ghost in the Photo:
-http://theresashauntedhistoryofthetri-state.blogspot.com/2011/02/ss-watertown.html
-TOP 11 GHOST PHOTOS - Not Proven to Be Fake! - Paranormal https://paranormalhauntings.blog/2018/03/22/top-11-ghost-photos-not-proven-to-be-fake/

Short Tales:
-Tallant, R., & Saxon, L. (1987). GUMBO YA-YA: Folk tales of Louisiana. Pelican Publishing Company.

Myrtles Plantation:
-Daily World Opelousas, Louisiana October 26, 2018, Getting Familiar with the Ghosts
-Enterprise-Journal McComb, Mississippi October 12, 2014
-https://www.ancestry.com/genealogy/records/sara-matilda-bradford-24-dx6sv
-https://www.findagrave.com/memorial/35646402/sarah-turnbull-stirling
-Piscataquis (ME) Observer 23 Feb 1871
-History and hauntings at the myrtles | Louisiana plantation. Retrieved from https://www.myrtlesplantation.com/history-and-hauntings

Destrehan Plantation:
-Destrehan plantation. (2020, October 16). Retrieved from https://hauntedhouses.com/louisiana/destrehan-plantation/
Marie Eleonore "Zelia" Destrehan Henderson... (n.d.). Retrieved from -https://www.findagrave.com/memorial/32288609/marie-eleonore-henderson
-Our history. (n.d.). Retrieved from www.destrehanplantation.org/history/

Singing Children:
-Ghosts of Louisiana 1/18/1939 Progress Administration of Louisiana. (n.d.). Retrieved from https://louisianadigitallibrary.org/islandora/object/state-lwp%3A3639

Frenier:
-(2017, October 14). Retrieved from https://www.mentalfloss.com/article/88132/legend-and-truth-voodoo-priestess-who-haunts-louisiana-swamp
-Julia Brown. (n.d.). Retrieved from https://www.findagrave.com/memorial/197606648/julia-brown
-Julia "Aunt Julie" Bernard Brown (1845-1915) -... (n.d.). Retrieved from https://www.findagrave.com/memorial/140004126/julia-brown
-Merrill, E. (2014). Schlosser/Frenier. In Germans of Louisiana. Pelican Publishing.
-Was 1915 Hurricane Which Wrecked Frenier Foretold? (1972, January 20). La Observateur
-https://www.atlasobscura.com/places/frenier-cemeter
-New Orleans *Times-Picayune* October 2, 1915
-https://www.fox8live.com/story/38483349/heart-of-louisiana-ruddock-and-the-september-29-1915-hurricane/

Specter Canoe:
-Specter Skiff Spread Terror.: PHANTOM CANOE IN THE BAYOUS WAS A ... Cincinnati Enquirer (1872-1922); May 4, 1907

Vodou:
-Know NOLA. (n.d.). Retrieved from https://ww.neworleans.me/know/about/17/Vodoun-Voodoo
-New Orleans voodoo. (n.d.). Retrieved from https://www.neworleans.com/things-to-do/multicultural/traditions/voodoo
-African Symbols-https://uwm.edu/african-diaspora-studies/wp-content/uploads/sites/203/2015/06/Symbols-Adinkra-and-VeVe.pdf
-Henry, Sharon. Voodoo in New Orleans. What the Saints Did Next. https://whatthesaintsdidnext.com/voodoo-in-new-orleans/
-Reckdahl, Katy. (2016, October 13). The true history and faith behind voodoo. Retrieved from https://www.frenchquarter.com/true-history-faith-behind-voodoo/
-https://countryroadsmagazine.com/art-and-culture/people-places/the-truth-about-louisiana-voodoo-vodou/

Mardi Gras:
-The dark side of Mardi Gras | Haunted Mardi Gras. (n.d.). Retrieved from https://ghostcitytours.com/new-orleans/ghost-stories/dark-side-mardi-gras/
-Greenspan, J. (2013, February 12). 9 things you may not know about Mardi Gras. Retrieved from https://www.history.com/news/9-things-you-may-not-know-about-mardi-gras
-Mardi Gras history. (n.d.). Retrieved from https://www.mardigrasneworleans.com/history/
-https://www.nola.com/multimedia/photos/collection_8131cf0e-57db-11ea-ab7d-83cdd69efbdc.html#13

508 & 515 Toulouse Street:
-The Collins C. Diboll vieux carre survey: Property info for 508 and 514 Toulouse St. (n.d.). Retrieved from https://www.hnoc.org/vcs/property_info.php?lot=18436
-The ghosts of Mardi Gras. (n.d.). Retrieved from https://msmokemusic.com/blog/blog/new-orleans-ghost-stories
-Update: New Orleans ghosts. (2018, February 27). Retrieved from https://www.barbarasillery.com/update-new-orleans-ghosts/

Cemeteries:

St Peter Street:
-Archaeology news blog > home - St. Peter street cemetery reburial. (n.d.). Retrieved from https://s2.uno.edu/archaeologynews/Home/tabid/1969/BlogID/35/Default.aspx
-Archaeology news blog > home - What is the St. Peter street cemetery? (n.d.). Retrieved from https://archaeologynews.uno.edu/Home/tabid/1969/EntryId/101/What-is-the-St-Peter-Street-Cemetery.aspx
-Kaplan-Levenson, L. (2016, October 6). The cemetery under the French quarter. Retrieved from https://www.wwno.org/post/cemetery-under-french-quarter
-Scott, M., & NOLA.com | The Times-Picayune. (2019, July 22). Meet the man who put the French quarter on the map (literally). Retrieved from https://www.nola.com/300/article_2c881707-dd01-500f-9a30-10937760aabb.html
-D. Ryan Gray, "Reconstructing the Lives of People Buried at the St. Peter Street Cemetery," *New Orleans Historical*, accessed November 23, 2020, https://neworleanshistorical.org/items/show/1592.

St Louis No 1:
-Find a Grave, database and images (https://www.findagrave.com : accessed 24 November 2020), memorial page for Marie Laveau (10 Sep 1801–15 Jun 1881), Find a Grave Memorial no. 1503, citing Saint Louis Cemetery Number 1, New Orleans, Orleans Parish, Louisiana, USA ; Maintained by Find A Grave .
-Louisiana Writers' Project. (1969). Gumbo ya-ya: A collection of Louisiana folk tales. Cemeteries.
-Tallant, R. (1983). Voodoo in New Orleans pg 130-131. Pelican; Reissue edition (October 1, 1983).
-Alvarado, Denise. *Introduction*. 2019, https://www.marie-laveaux.com/introduction-1.html.
-Tales from the tombs. (2019, May 22). Retrieved from https://www.myneworleans.com/tales-from-the-tombs/
-Spookiest spots in New Orleans, according to ghost tour guides. (2019, October 18). Retrieved from https://www.10best.com/interests/explore/most-haunted-places-new-orleans-ghost-tour-guides/
-https://ghostcitytours.com/new-orleans/haunted-places/haunted-cemeteries/st-louis-cemetery/
-https://www.academia.edu/38988979/The_Tomb_of_Marie_Laveau_in_St_Louis_Cemetery_No_1_a_lecture_sponsored_by_Save_Our_Cemeteries

St Louis II:
- Lucky Bean Tours— public and private walking tours. Self-guided tour of St. Louis cemetery #2. (n.d.). Retrieved from https://www.luckybeantours.com/self-guided-tour-of-st-louis-cemetery-2/
-Louisiana Writers' Project. (1969). Gumbo ya-ya: A collection of Louisiana folk tales. Wishing Vault
-The Salt Lake Tribune July 5, 1931-The Burned Photo That Startled New Orleans with a Voodoo Picture

St Louis III:
-http://www.thepastwhispers.com/Old_New_Orleans
-St. Louis Cemetery #3 - Cemeteries, New Orleans Catholic https://nolacatholiccemeteries.org/st-louis-cemetery-3

Lafayette Cemetery:
-https://www.neworleans.com/listing/lafayette-cemetery-no-1/32160/

Cyprus Grove:
-http://www.greenwoodnola.com/cypress-grove/
-https://www.neworleans.com/listing/cypress-grove-cemetery/33612/

Greenwood Cemetery:
-Save our cemeteries : Cemeteries of New Orleans : Cemeteries : Greenwood cemetery. (n.d.). Retrieved from https:// www.saveourcemeteries.org/cemeteries/cemeteries/greenwood-cemetery.html
-Top ten haunted New Orleans cemeteries haunted New Orleans tours. (n.d.). Retrieved from https://www.hauntedneworleanstours.com/toptenhaunted/toptenhauntedcemeteriesnola/

Charity Hospital Cemetery:
-The New Orleans Bulletin Charity Cemetery Buried Alive Saturday May 29, 1875
-The New Orleans bulletin. [volume] (New Orleans [La https://chroniclingamerica.loc.gov/lccn/sn86079018/1875-05-29/ed-1/seq-1/

St Patrick:
-https://nolacatholiccemeteries.org/st-patrick-cemetery-1
-Branley, Edward. NOLA History: The Irish Cemeteries https://nolacatholiccemeteries.org/st-patrick-cemetery-1
-https://tclf.org/st-patrick-cemetery

St Joseph Cemetery:
-https://nolacatholiccemeteries.org/st-joseph-cemetery-1

Odd Fellows Rest:
-https://www.atlasobscura.com/places/odd-fellows-rest

Holt:
-https://www.nola.com/300/article_a78e8d65-a821-5efb-bbf5-d09e6872b4c5.html

The Mortuary and Chev A Thilim Cemetery –Gates of Prayer
-Interview with a neighbor living near the cemetery that said she saw the figure several times at the cemetery while walking her dog.
-The Cultural Landscape Foundation, https://tclf.org/gates-prayer-cemetery
-http://www.hauntedneworleanstours.com/toptenhaunted/toptenhauntedcemeteriesnola/

Metairie:
Josie Arlington:
-DeLavigne, J. (1946). Ghost stories of old New Orleans.
-Haunted NOLA: Does this Storyville Madam's tomb, statue come to life at night? (2020, June 5). nola.verylocal.com/haunted-nola-the-wandering-statue-of-storyville-madam-josie-arlingtons-metairie-cemetery-tomb/85649/
-Storyville. (2016, Dec 19). 64parishes.org/entry/storyville-2/
-https://neworleanshistorical.org/items/show/1479
Weeping Dog:
https://www.waymarking.com/waymarks/WMC0AN_Weeping_Dog_New_Orleans_LA
Hennessey:
-Schomburg Center for Research in Black Culture, Jean Blackwell Hutson Research and Reference Division, The New York Public Library. (1897). David C. Hennessy the New Orleans chief of police. Retrieved from https://digitalcollections.nypl.org/items/510d47df-bb4d-a3d9-e040-e00a18064a99

St Roch:
-Lyle Saxon, Edward Dreyer, & Robert Tallant. Gumbo Ya-Ya: A Collection of Louisiana Folk Tales (Boston: Houghton Mifflin, 1945), p 333.
-Catholic encyclopedia: St. Roch. (n.d.). Retrieved from https://www.newadvent.org/cathen/13100c.htm
-Ex-votos, shrine of St. Roch, New Orleans. (2020, May 22). Retrieved from https://mavcor.yale.edu/conversations/object-narratives/ex-votos-shrine-st-roch-new-orleans
-Saint Roch patron Saint of dogs. (2011, August 15). .catholiccompany.com/magazine/saint-roch-patron-saint-dogs-5520
-The Daily Monitor Leader. September 11, 1945, Page 7
-Dixon, Mason Perch Amboy. September 17, 1923 This Little World
-The Miriam and Ira D. Wallach Division of Art, Prints and Photographs: Photography Collection, The New York Public Library. "St. Roch's Chapel and Campo Santo, New Orleans, La." The New York Public Library Digital Collections. 1898 - 1931. https://digitalcollections.nypl.org/items/510d47d9-9b6c-a3d9-e040-e00a18064a99
-Richmond Dispatch April 16, 1902 Patron of Lovers—St Roch
-The Catholic Advance, Wichita, Ks March 6, 1926
-The Times March 24, 1938 Two New Orleans Shrines Visited by Sufferers for Generations Who Leave Many Odd Offerings
-Perth Amboy Evening News September 27, 1923
-Our Mountain Home 5/2/1923 Death Ends 11 Yrs of Love Trips to Grave
-https://www.findagrave.com/memorial/110469083/catherine-modica#view-photo=80145677

Lost Golden Children:
-https://www.findagrave.com/cemetery/2472105
-DeLavigne, J. (1946). Ghost stories of old New Orleans The Beautiful Lost Children page 224
-Ghosts of Louisiana 1/18/1939 Progress Administration of Louisiana. (n.d.). Retrieved from https://louisianadigitallibrary.org/islandora/object/state-lwp%3A3639
-http://www.historicmapworks.com/Overlay/?m=1594320&c=US&lat=29.938249&lng=-90.084234

Other Boneyards:
-https://richcampanella.com/wp-content/uploads/2020/02/Picayune_Cityscapes_2014_12_Girod-Street-Cemetery.pdf
-https://www.findagrave.com/memorial/138395345/jose-pepe-llulla

General History:
-History of New Orleans. (n.d.). www.neworleans.com
-History.com (2010, April 5). history.com/topics/us-states/new-orleans

Vampires in New Orleans:
-A closer look at Jacques de St. Germain. (2015, February 17). Retrieved from https://authorlyngibson.wordpress.com/2013/09/27/a-closer-look-at-jacques-de-st-germain/
-The comte de St. Germain: Chapter VIII. Masonic work and Austrian traditions. (n.d.). Retrieved from https://www.getwokebooklist.com/sacredtexts/sro/csg/csg09.htm
-Did count de Saint-Germaine truly discover immortality? (n.d.). Retrieved from https://www.liveabout.com/saint-germain-the-immortal-count-2594421
-Lorio, C. (2019, July 19). One of the French quarter's most photographed homes opens for tours this weekend. Retrieved from https://www.nola.com/entertainment_life/home_garden/article_fc160ab9-012d-56dd-acbd-8727c341f9d2.htmlhttps://www.nola.com/entertainment_life/home_garden/article_fc160ab9-012d-56dd-acbd-8727c341f9d2.html

Rougarou:
-Bailey, Shan. (2019, October 24). Beware of Louisiana's Rougarou! Have you heard of the creepy, cajun swamp legend? Retrieved from https://www.nolaweekend.com/beware-of-louisianas-rougarou-have-you-heard-of-the-creepy-cajun-swamp-legend/
-Bernard, S. K. (2013). Les Cadiens et leurs ancêtres acadiens: L'histoire racontée aux jeunes. Univ. Press of Mississippi.
-Hingle, Emily. (n.d.). The Rougarou is gonna get you: Cajun folklore | Where Y'at. Retrieved from https://whereyat.com/the-rougarou-is-gonna-get-you-cajun-folklore
-LAURA McKNIGHT Staff Writer. (n.d.). Rougarou keeps its claws in local lore. Retrieved from https://www.houmatoday.com/article/DA/20071021/News/608097169/HC
-Louisiana Believes. (n.d.). The Acadians in Louisiana "The Legacy of Cajuns". Retrieved from www.vrml.k12.la.us/8th/8_ss/ss_curr/unit5/cajunquiz1/cajuns.htm
-Rougarou origins (X-post R/CajunHistory). (n.d.). Retrieved from https://www.reddit.com/r/history/comments/1v8215/rougarou_origins_xpost_rcajunhistory/

Riverfront Lore: Hoodoo:
-Saxon, L. (1969). Gumbo ya-ya: A collection of Louisiana folk tales Riverside Lore pages 367-369.
-Our riverfront, Past and Present. (2019, May 1). Retrieved from https://frenchquarterly.com/history/our-riverfront-past-and-present
-https://en.wikipedia.org/wiki/File:Unloading_cotton_from_steamboat_001.jpg. (n.d.).
-River exhibit: Workers. (n.d.). Retrieved from https://archives.nolalibrary.org/~nopl/exhibits/river/roustabs.htm

Little Creepy and Not-so-Creepy Artwork:
Skelton Dog: Christiaan Kramm, 1797-1875
Spider: 1shortdesign
Ornament with Death and an Owl, Stefano della Bella, 1620 - 1664
Bat—Heinrich aldegreve
Beggar with Crutches and a Wooden Leg, Jacques Callot, 1622 - 1623
Monk with Keys: Purchase from the FG Waller Fund
Mari Gras Mask BillytheCat
Death brings a new person to life, Dirck Volckertsz. Coornhert, Maarten van Heemskerck, 1550
Dancing peasant couple, Hieronymus Wierix (attributed to), afteAlbrecht Dürer, 1559
Monk threatens two devils, Jacob Gole (attributed to), after Cornelis Dusart, 1724
Owl with Glasses and Books, Cornelis Bloemaert (II), after Hendrick Bloemaert, c. 1625
Two street artists like Smaraolo cornuto and Ratsa di Boio, Jacques Callot, 1621 - 1622
Venus and Amor and Athena, Marcantonio Raimondi, after Rafaël, 1510 - 1520
-A Young Woman Addressed by Death, Jan van de Sande, 1610 - 1664—Bequest of Mr. D. Franken, Le Vésinet
Man with a Top Hat, Cornelis Springer, 1871
Yankee Soldier—Waud, Alfred R. (Alfred Rudolph), 1828-1891, artist
-Fourteen depictions of devils and women, Charles Ramelet, 1832
Duel between two men with swords, Louis François du Bouchet, c. 1670, Purchase from the FG Waller Fund
Alligator: Gordon Johnson
Coffee Cup Charly Gutmann
"A Coloured Lady of New Orleans"—Schomburg Center for Research in Black Culture, Jean Blackwell Hutson Research and Reference Division, The New York Public Library. "A Coloured lady of New Orleans." The New York Public Library Digital Collections. 1882. https://digitalcollections.nypl.org/items/510d47df-b7bc-a3d9-e040-e00a18064a99
CHICAGO/TURABIAN FOR
-Dancing beggars, Woutherus Mol, after Adriaen Pietersz. van de Venne, 1795-1857 (Bequest of Mr. D. Franken, Le Vésinet)
-Two dancers, both seen on the left, Jacques Callot, 1621
Man and Donkey-print maker: Pieter Gerardus van Os

www.ingramcontent.com/pod-product-compliance
Lightning Source LLC
Chambersburg PA
CBHW051331250626
47155CB00007B/2556